Praise for the novels of
Jessica Barksdale Inclán

When You Go Away

"A truly gifted writer who has a profound understanding of the characters she creates . . . a powerful novel."
—*Contra Costa Times*

"Inclán's third novel impressively showcases her talent for bringing vulnerable characters to the forefront through her luminescent writing . . . by far Inclán's most daring novel and evidence of a rapidly developing talent that nimbly manipulates the tragic aspects of human nature to produce a book that is true to life in its heartbreaking quest for hope."
—*Booklist*

"Inclán is courageous in confronting family tragedy and in trying to put a human face on it."
—*Chico Enterprise-Record* (Chico, CA)

"The poignant story of a mother of three . . . a story that every beleaguered mother will take comfort from. And comfort is good."
—*Voice Ledger*
(Pleasant Valley, NY)

continued . . .

Her Daughter's Eyes

"A debut novel as gutsy [and] appealing . . . as its heroines. But it is the plight of the teenage sisters, in all their clever foolishness, that strikes at the heart."
—*Publishers Weekly*

"A modern-day depiction of familial disintegration with offbeat twists and luminous sparks of hope."—*Booklist*

"Well-written, thoughtful . . . Inclán never condescends and never judges, preferring to let her subtly drawn people speak for themselves . . . The understanding portrayal of her teenaged heroines—stubborn, careless, and fiercely honest—is remarkably astute."
—*Kirkus Reviews*

"An exquisitely poignant look into the heart of a troubled family."
—*New York Times* bestselling author Deborah Smith

"Poignant, sharply introspective, and thought provoking. Every parent of a teenager and indeed, every teenager should read this work with care."
—*New York Times* bestselling author Dorothea Benton Frank

"Haunting, compelling . . . takes the reader on an emotional roller coaster ride."
—*New York Times* bestselling author Kristin Hannah

Other NAL Accent Novels
by Jessica Barksdale Inclán

Her Daughter's Eyes
The Matter of Grace
One Small Thing
Walking with Her Daughter

Jessica Barksdale Inclán

When
You Go
Away

FICTION FOR THE WAY WE LIVE

NAL Accent
Published by New American Library, a division of
Penguin Group (USA) Inc., 375 Hudson Street,
New York, New York 10014, USA
Penguin Group (Canada), 10 Alcorn Avenue, Toronto,
Ontario M4V 3B2, Canada (a division of Pearson Penguin Canada Inc.)
Penguin Books Ltd., 80 Strand, London WC2R 0RL, England
Penguin Ireland, 25 St. Stephen's Green, Dublin 2,
Ireland (a division of Penguin Books Ltd.)
Penguin Group (Australia), 250 Camberwell Road, Camberwell, Victoria 3124,
Australia (a division of Pearson Australia Group Pty. Ltd.)
Penguin Books India Pvt. Ltd., 11 Community Centre, Panchsheel Park,
New Delhi - 110 017, India
Penguin Group (NZ), Cnr Airborne and Rosedale Roads, Albany,
Auckland 1310, New Zealand (a division of Pearson New Zealand Ltd.)
Penguin Books (South Africa) (Pty.) Ltd., 24 Sturdee Avenue,
Rosebank, Johannesburg 2196, South Africa

Penguin Books Ltd., Registered Offices:
80 Strand, London WC2R 0RL, England

Published by NAL Accent, an imprint of New American Library,
a division of Penguin Group (USA) Inc. Previously published in an
NAL Accent trade paperback edition.

First NAL Accent Mass Market Printing, March 2005
10 9 8 7 6 5 4 3 2 1

Copyright © Jessica Barksdale Inclán, 2004
Conversation Guide copyright © Penguin Group (USA) Inc., 2004
Excerpt from *Walking with Her Daughter* copyright © Jessica Barksdale
Inclán, 2005
All rights reserved

FICTION FOR THE WAY WE LIVE

REGISTERED TRADEMARK—MARCA REGISTRADA

For my mother,
Carole Jo Barksdale

She lifted the blankets off her body, forcing her feet to the floor. She couldn't look up. Not even for a moment. The baby would be looking at her. Wanting something. Everything. And she had nothing to give. Not anymore. Maybe she never had. For so long she'd felt empty, her bones hollow tubes, but now the years with the baby hummed in her chest, ready to explode, change everything, hurt everyone.

"Ma! Ma!" The baby flung a spastic arm toward her, but she kept moving, holding her hands to her chest. Don't look. Don't say a word. Keep moving or it will be too late, *she thought.*

There were clues everywhere, all over the apartment, easy to find even though the rooms were full of the boxes she didn't ever want to unpack. If she hung her pictures and filled the linen cupboard, it would mean she would be with the baby forever and ever, this sad collection of square rooms truly her home, the place she lived without her husband who wasn't even her husband anymore. And with the boxes everywhere, she didn't have to see anything, not the other children, not what she'd let happen to all of them.

The hot hum in her chest pulsed and thrummed, and she swallowed, trying to press it back, push it down, closing her eyes and trying to take in at least one deep breath. But she couldn't, her body jittery with nerves and hunger and fear. She forced her eyes open and moved through the apartment, grabbing her purse as she walked, picking things up and cramming them into the worn leather. She needed to take everything that would tell people the story: her letters and bills and address book. No one should know about this; she didn't want to know.

"Ma," the baby cried again, followed by the thump of her body against the wall. "Ma!"

It would just be for a second. A minute. A half hour. The air so clean on her face, she imagined she could actually take it in, breathe as she hadn't been able to do in months. To dislodge this fire inside her, the one that would burn up her life, her children, the baby. All she had to do was keep going, move to her car, fit the key in the lock. Then it was only a matter of her foot on the accelerator, her hand on the steering wheel, and she would have saved them all.

"Ma! Ma!"

She closed the front door against the baby's cry, then put on her sunglasses, the light poison to her eyes, her body skinless and ready to burst like a terrible fruit. As she walked the corridor toward the stairwell, a woman called to her, said, "How are you?"

She put her hands on her ears—one more word might make everything go wrong—and she walked more quickly, her purse heavy and hitting her thigh. Away. For a minute. Everything would be fine then. Better.

"*Mrs. Mackenzie? Are you all right?*"

She would be. In a second, she would have made everything right again. All she had to do was get in the car.

One

Even all alone at the new apartment, Carly knew what to do. She'd discovered the box labeled BROOKE'S ROOM and finally unpacked it, setting up all the supplies she would need. For weeks, her mother had been pulling things out and throwing them back in, the contents of the box a jumble of plastic and metal. Carly arranged the Johnson's baby lotion, hydrogen peroxide, Vaseline, toddler-sized diapers, steel wash bowl, baby wipes, Desitin, thermometer, towels, and Q-tips on the table beside Brooke's bed, as they had been at home— their real home in Monte Veda. Yesterday, she'd found the formula and syringe because she'd had to feed her five-year-old sister on schedule, despite everything. It wasn't the first time she'd fed her, but it had been the first time she'd done it all by herself. Her mother was usually hovering over her, saying, "Yes. Now put the syringe in the peg and depress it. Right. That's very good, honey." Brooke would try to smile, her face sometimes so still it was hard to know what she was feeling. Their brother, Ryan, never tried to feed her, never even watched. He was scared of feeding tubes and syringes.

He didn't know how to do any of this, and Carly was glad he'd gotten a ride to high school with his new friend, Quinn. She was going to stay home today, again.

She pushed Brooke's red hair back from her eyes. "Okay. Let's go," she whispered. Carly pulled down the blanket, then stopped and let her hands fall to her lap. When her family lived in their real house, her mother arranged everything just so each morning, making sure there were enough supplies for the day, sitting gently on Brooke's bed to wake her up, singing the song "Good Morning, Sunshine." Brooke would twist awake, her eyes already open because with her weak muscles she couldn't close them, a tiny crooked smile on her lips, and her mother would begin.

"Hello, Exceptional Individual," she would say, using the phrase in all the letters from the school district. Their mother knew how to make it sound amazing, as if everyone would want to have muscular dystrophy and cerebral palsy just to hear the term *Exceptional Individual* come from their mother's mouth. Their mother used to be able to make everything better. But not recently. Not at all.

Carly closed her eyes and brought forth her mother as she had been a year ago. She tried to move just as she had, even though she was unable to fill the warm space her mother usually took. She wasn't big enough, even if she knew what to do.

But Carly had to do this for Brooke and for her mother. If her mother was feeling normal, the way she had for most of Carly's childhood, she'd want Brooke cleaned and fed and happy, so she started first with Brooke's diaper, gently pulling the tape tabs, peeling away the sodden wet thing that really didn't smell because all Brooke ate was the special formula. Holding on to Brooke's arm, she leaned forward and dropped the diaper onto the overflowing trash can, pressing the soft plastic mound down with her foot. She'd have to dump the trash soon, but she couldn't until Brooke took her afternoon nap.

She put her hand in the bowl, testing the water to make sure it had cooled down. For a moment, she made waves against the steel edge of the bowl and listened to the slight splashing sound. Then she squeezed the wash-cloth until it didn't drip and brought it to her sister's body, sliding it across her skin, up and down. Then she repeated the motion with a baby wipe, lotion, and then Desitin where Brooke had a rash. It definitely looked worse today than yesterday, but she smeared on a big glob of Desitin, hiding the red, raised skin, hoping it would go away. That was the easy part. Then there was the feeding tube—the peg—to check and clean.

When Carly first saw the small valve in Brooke's stomach after the operation, she thought of the blow-up pool toys she used to have, the valve sticking into her skin as she clamped on to the slippery plastic with her thighs. She almost laughed and then swallowed down her stupid thought of opening the valve and watching the then two-year-old Brooke whisk through the bedroom as she deflated.

But it wasn't funny. It was a real hole into her insides. When Carly's mom had changed the tube that came out of it, Carly held her breath and imagined that the tube was a live part of Brooke like a vein or nerve. But her mother had laughed, told her to stop being silly, then tickled Brooke after it was over. Carly had to be care-ful, though. It was important to clean around the peg and rub some lotion on the skin next to it. Red was bad. Red and hard was worse. Red with streaks was the worst of all, but today, Carly noticed, looking at her sleeping sister, everything seemed fine.

After the diaper and the Desitin, it was time to wash Brooke's face and hands and feet and back. Carly quietly pulled up the guardrail and took the bowl to the bathroom, rinsing it out and filling it with warm water, hurrying back into the bedroom. She sat down and dipped the washcloth into the warm water in the wash bowl, wringing it out carefully and stroking Brooke's curved back, her tense feet, her legs and arms that whipped out periodically. Carly didn't really like looking at Brooke. Her skin was the color of plain white bread, all her bones just underneath like a terrible, awful sandwich, and today, there were strange red spots on her hips and thighs. Carly ran her fingers over the red circles, the skin rough but not broken. It wasn't infection. It didn't look like infection.

Carly wiped up and down, mumbling the soothing sounds her mother always did, sort of a "Yes, yes, yes. It's all right. That's good," in a quiet rhythm. She had to move slowly because Brooke was awake now, and she hated too much pressure on her skin. She cried sometimes about a blanket placed over her body or their dog, Maxie, licking her face or a dress that poked under her arms. At least Carly didn't have to worry about Maxie, who now lived with Carly's friend Sam back by the old house. If their father knew, he would be relieved Maxie was gone and so would Brooke's nursing case manager at the clinic. But when people tried to make Mom get rid of Maxie, she would say, "All kids want a pet. And she's like every kid. Like anyone else." Still, Mom had agreed to give away Olive, their black cat, when Brooke got pneumonia that first time.

Brooke had missed Maxie after they moved, and Carly would tell her stories about the Wonder Dog, how she was running up and down Sam's huge yard, barking, wagging her tail. Carly hoped it was true. Sam didn't even have her new number. "We'll call you when we get the phone hooked up," her mother had said, waving to Sam and his mom, Lara, who said, "Don't worry, Carly. It's just till you're settled in a real house. We'll take care of Maxie as long as you need us to." That had been two months ago; the phone still wasn't connected yet, and her mother hadn't even begun to look for a real house. *It's too late to call Sam now*, Carly thought. *Maxie probably doesn't even miss us anymore.*

Carly moved the steel bowl to the floor and scooted up toward Brooke's head because now it was time to take her temperature. It was very important to take her temperature every day because a fever would mean infection, either because of the peg or because of pneumonia. Brooke had gotten an infection twice last year—her fever going up so high her mother had rushed her into a bathtub full of ice. Later, after Brooke came back from the hospital, their mother put antibiotics in through the peg along with the formula. There was some still left in the refrigerator, the bottle quarter-full of pink fluid having been moved to the new apartment along with the ketchup and mustard and salad dressing.

What Carly had worried about since yesterday was the ventilator her mother had been talking about a couple of days ago. Brooke had been fitted with a tracheotomy plug and a collar during her last stay in the hospital, so when she needed the ventilator later, they could start it up right away. Carly hated the sound, the wheezy air, the metal hush that meant Brooke couldn't live on her own. Carly had searched all the boxes in the living room, but she couldn't find anything that resembled the ventilator. If she did finally find it, she mustn't just attach it and turn the switch. There had to be some doctor's visit or at least a therapist to come over and show Carly how to adjust it.

At night, Brooke breathed so quietly at times, Carly was sure she'd died. Now that Carly was sleeping in her mother's bed, she'd creep out and stand over Brooke, listening, finally poking her sister gently on the arm, grateful for a snort and the fling of a limb. She'd pull Brooke up on the hospital bed, using the switch to raise the head, thinking that if Brooke slept sitting up straight, she'd breathe more easily. Only then could Carly go back to sleep.

Carly picked up the thermometer. This was a great thermometer, the important part as smooth as the inside of an eggshell. When she was little, she'd had to hold the pointy stick under her tongue for what had seemed like forever, and Ryan told her stories about getting the old-fashioned glass kind in his butt. Carly didn't believe him because he'd always been like that, kind of gross, talking about boogers and saying "Shit" and "Fuck" even when there were adults around. Now he didn't talk much at all, leaving the house early to catch his ride and coming home long after Carly had fed Brooke, asking her only, "Did you talk to Mom?" But she didn't want to think about Ryan now. He hadn't even asked her if she wanted to go to school. He just ate three pieces of toast and slammed out the door.

After holding the thermometer on her own skin to

warm it up, Carly pressed the thermometer against Brooke's ear, causing Brooke to say, "Ma!" But before her sister could fling a tiny arm at her, Carly had the reading—99.0. That was a fever. She tried it again in the other ear. 98.9. Carly bit her lip. Not normal, but not an official fever. Only three tenths. Or four tenths, depending on which side was real. She put the thermometer down, deciding she would use it again later. Just to be sure.

"Ma!" Brooke said. "Dare i Ma?"

Carly closed her eyes. How should she answer that question? How could she tell Brooke she had no idea where their mother was? "Should I sing?" she said finally.

"Da."

Picking up the syringe, Carly began to sing "Good Morning, Sunshine," knowing that their mother was Brooke's only sunshine. Brooke never made the sounds for Carly that she did for her mother. *How long,* Carly wondered as she sang, *can this go on?*

Before she'd come into the bedroom, she'd mixed up the formula in the kitchen in a Pyrex measuring cup, the one her mother always used, and now she carefully dropped in the medicine. She didn't know what it was for, but her mother had always squeezed out two drops from the brown bottle and two drops from the plastic bottle. As Carly put the can of formula away, she noticed that there wasn't much left, maybe two days' worth. But by then . . . well, things would be better.

Carly sucked formula into the syringe and attached it to the tube connected to the peg for feeding. The tube looked dirty, and she wondered if she had to clean it. Her mother sometimes talked about "flushing" the tube, so Carly decided she'd try later. "Okay. Time for breakfast."

"No!" Brooke began to squirm.

"Does it hurt?" Brooke moved from side to side. "Stop it, Brookey. Let me sing. I'll sing again."

Carly began to sing the song, and Brooke stopped moving, turning her head to look at Carly. It seemed to take forever for the food to go in, and from what her mother had told her, it should never go in too fast. "Keep a steady strain," her mother had said, leaning over Carly's shoulder as she fed Brooke. "That's the way. That's a girl."

Carly stopped singing the words, humming instead, and Brooke turned her face to the wall, reaching out a tiny hand to touch it. *She is so small,* Carly thought, pressing and pressing on the syringe with her thumb.

Brooke had always been small. Back when she had been a tiny baby, before her body had curled and they knew all the ways it would go wrong, Carly would bring her friends into the nursery to show off her new sister. Carly had been seven, almost old enough to baby-sit, she thought, and Brooke was like her living doll. "She's sooo cute," her friends would say, Brooke's eyes wide and blue, her hair like a fire next to the cotton sheets. Her mother would let them take turns holding her in the oak rocker Grandma Mackenzie—their dad's mom—had given her mother when Ryan was born.

But after a few months, Brooke wasn't so cute anymore. She never learned to crawl or walk, sort of pulling and pushing herself on the floor, never rolling over or sitting up for more than a second or two at a time. Her mom and dad went to doctors all the time, and then they came home with awful words that sounded like metal on Carly's tongue: intraventricular bleed, ataxic, spastic. From then on, there were always nurses at the house teaching her mother how to care for Brooke, and the room was full of medicine and supplies, her mother taking down the crib mobile that had been Carly's and pulling out the crib toys because they needed room for the monitors. Carly didn't bring her friends to the nursery after that.

She refilled the syringe and slid it slowly into the peg, knowing that the feeding was almost over for now, until later that afternoon. Her mother fed Brooke three times a day, but before they moved, the doctors told her to feed her four times in smaller amounts because she was getting sick from her feedings. "Like diarrhea?" Carly had asked, even though what came out of Brooke was already like water.

Carly pulled the syringe out and rested it in the empty measuring cup. She lifted and slipped a clean T-shirt over Brooke's head, drawing her thin arms through the holes. Usually, her sister smelled like Christmas, sweet and sugary and soft, but lately the smell had changed, grown stale and older. Like how Carly smelled after playing volleyball during PE. Brooke wasn't a baby anymore, but a person who might want more than lying on the bed and watching TV.

Tugging at the shirt and smoothing it over Brooke's flat belly, Carly realized it was the last clean shirt. She'd have to go down to the laundry room and do a wash, and she hoped there were still quarters in the jar by the front door.

"Okay!"

"Tay!"

"Want to watch cartoons?"

"Tay! Na! Na!"

"Have some patience. Keep a steady strain," Carly said, repeating the phrase her mother used for things that were terrible but had to be done anyway, like math tests and Brooke's diapers and dentist appointments. It never really helped, but Carly always imagined her mother knew how bad it was. She saw what was important.

Carly searched for the remote on the bedside table. Brooke loved to watch *Rugrats* and *Hey Arnold!* on Nickelodeon. Carly flipped through the channels.

"Da!"

The bright-colored kids flashed on the screen. "There you go, Brookey." Carly yanked up the rail on the hospital bed, making sure it was truly closed. Once last week before her mom left, Carly hadn't checked, and she'd come back to find Brooke on the floor, writhing in an effort to pull herself back up, her mother asleep in the bed just five feet away. So now she checked once, twice, sometimes three times, worried that Brooke could break all her bones. Worried that she'd have to call someone for help.

Carly sighed, picked up the measuring cup, the wash bowl, and the washcloth, and walked out of the room, the sounds of the cartoons behind her.

Back when they were still at their old house, Brooke had had visitors every day. Some days, it was the physical therapist Leon Magnoli, who put her on the floor and rolled her around on these big rubber balls he brought, Brooke on top squealing.

For a while, Carly imagined that all kids like Brooke had a Leon, but once when she'd gone with her mother and Brooke to the clinic for Brooke's appointment, the nurse had sighed, running her hands through her hair.

"God, you are so lucky to have a private therapist. We are in a major therapist shortage. I can't even begin to tell you about the backlog. It's a nightmare. I'm dealing with about five hundred kids right now."

"He's the best," her mother said. "I won't trust Brooke with anyone else."

Leon looked like so much fun, Carly had once wished she could play with him. He would rub Brooke's feet, stretch her legs and arms, spin her on the mat. He called her "my little Kumquat." Carly's mother gave him a check when he left, and he always said, "I should pay *you*." Carly noticed that he took it anyway, but she was glad. He always made Brooke laugh.

Then there was Mrs. Morgan, who came to teach Brooke to talk, Brooke saying out vowels—"Aaaa. Eeeeeee. Iiiiiii. Ooooo. Uuuuu"—even though she seemed to make only one long strange sound: "Ahh-heiou." Later, the teacher Susie Glickman came to the house because Brooke was too sick to go to kindergarten even for three hours a day; after all, as their mother said, Brooke was an "Individual with Exceptional Needs." Susie seemed to think Brooke was exceptional, bragging about how fast she was learning to sound out words. "In months, this girl will be reading!" she had said.

There were also the nurses her mother hired to baby-sit so she could walk for an hour on the treadmill at Oakmont Athletic Club or go shopping at Nordstrom with her friends or get a haircut at Anthony's. While Carly often answered the door, leading whoever it was up to Brooke's room, Ryan never talked to anyone because he was so busy. Once Leon asked her mother, "Are you sure you have a son? He looks more like a shadow to me." Back then, Ryan was gone for normal reasons, like baseball or soccer, not like now when he was just gone.

It wasn't until fifth and sixth grade, when her parents were fighting every night and then her dad left, that things changed. From behind her parents' door came yells and harsh whispers and occasionally heavy things falling to the ground. Sometimes, Carly wanted to leave, to walk down the street with her backpack and her friends' phone numbers.

She knew that the divorce had made her mother so sad she'd stopped getting up in the morning unless it was to feed Brooke, and now since the move to the apartment, Carly could feel her own anger at her father flutter like the gas fireplace at Sam's house, ready to flare up at a moment's notice.

In the days and weeks after her dad left, Carly would pick up scribbled notes on the kitchen counter, reading her mother's pretty cursive: *Call Social Security office* and *Check out bills re decreased energy rates*. There were lists of phone numbers and names of places— Department of Rehabilitation, Parent Training and Info Center, Children's Special Health Services.

At first, it seemed that life would go on as it had, but then the answering machine would blink with seven, ten, fourteen messages, calls her mother didn't return. Then her mother couldn't pay for Leon anymore. A therapist at the clinic took over Brooke's care. And when her mother decided Brooke shouldn't go back to the clinic because it was crowded and dirty and far away, no one called to check on Brooke. It was as if she had never existed at all.

Why did a divorce mean all this? Why did everything else have to change just because her parents weren't married anymore? Dad still loved them, didn't he? Or maybe he didn't, because he didn't call that often at first, and then even less, and not once did he ask her or Ryan to visit him. Sometimes she wanted to ask her mother these questions, but her mom cried about how Brooke's teacher, Susie Glickman, had moved to another school district, how nothing was easy anymore. She cried when she had to carry Brooke out to the car because they didn't have a wheelchair yet. And carrying Brooke must have gotten too hard because after a while Mom didn't take her anywhere, and her sister's body grew softer and weaker every day. Letters from the school district piled up on the counter.

By the end of seventh grade, Mom decided that they had to sell the house and move. "We need to get out of here. A fresh start. A place where I can think." Her mother packed and cried, leaving Brooke in her room almost all day long with no visits from anyone, Ryan stayed out later and later with his friends, and Carly watched it all. A FOR SALE sign went up, the real estate agents constantly walked through the house, even during dinner, and her mother ran around with Windex to clean the front door windows every time someone called. "Curb appeal," the agent had said, her mother nodding and biting her lips.

Carly thought if she could just tell her dad what was going on with Brooke, he'd let them stay in their old house. If she could tell him about how she secretly opened letters from the school, the ones that asked why Brooke was not signed up for the new school year. If she could show him the way Brooke's head flopped to the side now. But when she asked her mom if she could call him, her mother leaned her head on her arms and cried for an hour. And once when Carly found his phone number and wrote it on a gum wrapper, she looked up to see her mother weeping on the couch, where she'd been sitting all day. If she called her father, something bad would happen to her mom, something worse than what had already happened, so she folded up the wrapper carefully and put it in her jeans pocket. She forgot about it, and later, she found it twisted and ripped from the washer, her father's number only thin pencil scratchings.

Then they moved. A family from Toronto bought their house, telling her mother they were going to "completely renovate." That meant that Carly's room was probably gone. After they'd been in the Walnut Creek apartment for a month, she asked her mom if they could drive by the house and go visit Maxie. Her mother shook her head.

"What's the point? It's all gone now."

Carly had called her friends Kiana and Ashley a few times from a pay phone, but after a while, she realized they just wanted to talk about the boys at school and what everyone was wearing and the dance on Friday. They didn't care about Carly and her new school, where she knew no one. She couldn't believe that next year she'd have to enroll at a high school where she didn't have one single friend. It had taken her from kindergarten to eighth grade to make friends in Monte Veda, and she bet she'd never have friends like Kiana or Ashley for the rest of her life.

After the calls to her friends, Carly again wished she could phone her dad in Phoenix. She was pretty sure he didn't have their new address, and that meant he couldn't send the checks that bought the formula Brooke had to have. Even if he did leave them and forget to send the money like her mom said he did, she knew he'd want Brooke to eat, to live.

He should have found them. He should have looked. But since the wrapper incident, Carly hadn't had the chance to get the number again, and if her mother found out she'd called, she would cry even more and not get out of bed, where she stayed most of the time now. Since the move, she hadn't bothered to do much more than enroll her and Ryan in school. Carly wondered if her grandmother Mackenzie was worried about them, and if she was, why hadn't *she* searched them out? There had to be ways to find people who disappeared, and if it weren't for the fact that she imagined her mother would fall asleep and forget about Brooke, Carly would have taken BART to Piedmont to find her grandmother, transferring onto a bus at the Rockridge station and staying on until something looked familiar. Or what about Grandpa Carl? Even if her mother was angry with him, so angry she wouldn't even talk to him at holidays, he cared about them. When Carly asked her why she'd suddenly decided he must never step foot in her house again, her mother replied, "He's like all of them. They just leave."

If he were so awful, though, why did her mom name Carly after him?

Anyway, if Carly wanted Grandpa Carl's or her uncle Noel's numbers, she'd have to get them the same sneaky way she'd gotten her father's that one time. Then she'd have to call from a pay phone on her way home from school because it wasn't like she could borrow Kiana's

or Ashley's cell phone anymore. The whole thing was so
much trouble, and she couldn't help but wonder why no
one had come looking for them. Maybe the lawyers had
told everyone to leave them be, had made it clear that
the Mackenzies were supposed to be alone, that she was
supposed to be alone with Brooke, no Dad, no Maxie,
no Mom, barely any Ryan. That's why her mother had
disappeared two days ago after she and Ryan went to
school, not leaving a note, not even feeding Brooke before she left.

Before she went to the laundry room, Carly sorted
the dirty clothes. She'd watched her mother do it often,
and certainly the laundry soap commercials on TV had
taught her about separating whites and darks. Most of
Brooke's clothes were white, so Carly decided to do a
white load first, digging around for her underwear and
T-shirts, and then finding a huge tangled white pile in
Ryan's room. She didn't want to look at his underwear,
something disgusting and knotted about the twists of
cotton. She closed her eyes and grabbed at the clothes,
throwing them in the basket. He owed her for this. He'd
never do her laundry, not brave enough to touch her underwear and bras. He probably only wanted to touch
other girls' underwear or at least bras now that he was
fifteen. Carly imagined that's what he and Quinn talked
about on the way to school. Quinn was a sophomore
with his license. Carly was sure Ryan did drugs or at
least smoked cigarettes, and she wondered if she should
look through Ryan's room. But who would she tell if
she found anything? Who was the person to call about
this? What person could make it all better? And if she
called someone, her mother would be in trouble. She

just had to hold on until her mother came back and fixed everything.

All the machines were full and churning in the laundry room. But the minute she gave up, leaving with her basket, someone would empty a washer, and then someone else would fill it up, so she waited, leaning against the cold metal folding counter. She had the baby monitor in her pocket, and every now and then, she heard Brooke turn, an arm banging against the metal guardrail. Once, Brooke said, "Ma!" and Carly swallowed down hard, feeling sick as she blinked against the soapy air.

Finally, Mrs. Candelero from downstairs came in, leaning against the counter with her, both of them listening to the spinning machines.

"So you home today or what?"

"Like, duh!" she wished she could say, but she wanted the machine more, so she smiled and nodded.

"Your mother's sick, I hear."

Carly looked over at her, trying to control her forehead, feeling it pull into the fear that framed her face. "Um."

"I saw your brother this morning getting into a car with that kid. You know, the one down the hall from me? I asked after your baby sister and mother, and he said she was fine but your mother was sick. 'I saw her yesterday morning,' I tell him, and he all but ignores me and gets in the car."

"You saw her yesterday morning? When?" Carly grabbed the edge of a washer and bit her lip.

"Yeah. She seemed fine then. Maybe sort of in a hurry. She didn't wave or anything."

"What time?" Carly asked, feeling her joints crack as she pressed hard on the machine.

Mrs. Candelero put one hand on her hip and brushed back her hair with another, pausing as she thought. "Morning. I was coming home from my shift at the hospital."

"Oh." Morning. The end of a shift. Brooke had been in her room alone, what? Maybe four hours. Five. Carly closed her eyes and tried to swallow.

"So your sister has what? You don't mind me asking. I'm a nurse."

"MD and CP." Carly was ready for the litany, the explanation, a degenerative disease and a stable, chronic condition. Yes, both. At once. The same time.

But Mrs. Candelero didn't ask a question, simply nodded, finally saying, "That's unusual. But it happens. I've seen it. I've seen just about everything."

One machine stopped, and Mrs. Candelero opened it, pulling out her grown-up son's work coveralls and her nurse uniforms and shoving them in a dryer. Carly stared at the colorful tops and pants, thinking she could ask Mrs. Candelero about Brooke's 99.0 fever and the red patches on her hips and the new one she'd found on her thigh. Mrs. Candelero was a real pain, but her hands looked like they could hold a syringe and find the reason for a fever in seconds.

"Here it is. Grab it before it's gone."

"Yeah."

"It's not going to get any emptier, sweetie." Mrs. Candelero smiled, and Carly put her soap in and then the clothes.

"You need some bleach? You definitely need some bleach for those baby things."

"Oh. Yeah. Thanks." Carly stepped back as Mrs. Candelero poured a half cup into the special container on the side of the rim. Leaning over the open washer, Carly thought of how her house used to smell after the cleaning service had come, the bathroom so clean her mother swore, "We'll eat in there tonight," threatening to set the silverware on the toilet.

"That should do it."

"Thanks, Mrs. Candelero."

"Call me Rosie. Everyone calls me Rosie. I don't know where you got this Mrs. Candelero thingy."

"Okay. That's what our mom tells us—" She stopped, hoping Mrs. Candelero, Rosie, wouldn't pick up the mom conversation again. "Rosie's a nice name."

"It always worked for me. Well, I'll be back. Got to go pay that old fart Ted the rent. Worst day of the month, if you ask me."

As Rosie left the room, Carly nodded as if she'd known this all along, just like everyone. Rent. Would her mother have paid it before she left? What about the other bills? The P.G. and E? The water?

The first few hours after Carly came home from school to find her mother gone and Brooke wet and crying in her room, she'd torn through the house for clues, a note, her purse with a phone number. But everything was gone—her address book, her wallet, her Palm Pilot that she didn't use anymore. She couldn't even find the bills, so she hoped her mother had paid them or at least taken them with her. *That was it*, Carly thought, breathing in sharply. She'd pay them from wherever she'd gone. Or she'd be home soon. Very soon. Soon enough to pay the rent and find out why Brooke had a fever. Soon enough to buy more formula.

Another one of Rosie's machines stopped, the room banging silent, and Carly carefully pulled out the wet clothes, bras, underwear, shirts, Rosie's son's socks and boxers and put them in a dryer. Before she closed the round glass door, she stared at the pile, seeing a life in the clothes she'd never thought about, the personal, private things all glopped together, showing they were a family. Her own loads might be mixed, but they weren't together. Brooke was never a part of anything because she was sick, Ryan tried to forget them every single day, and she? She was alone now that Mom and Dad were gone. It didn't matter whose underwear was next to hers.

Carly closed the dryer door and loaded the washer with the darks, Ryan's shirts and jeans, her pants and tops. Carly slipped the quarters in their slots, one, two, three, four, listening to them clack in place, ignoring the sounds coming from the monitor in her basket, her sister's cries, her whine for "Ma, Ma, Ma."

Carly pressed the quarters in with the heel of her hand, liking the hard feel on her skin, the definite, cold sound of the coins sliding into the machine. Putting her arms on either side of the washer lid, she bent down and pressed her cheek on the top and closed her eyes, wishing the whir could scramble her thoughts so that she would forget about rent and bills and Brooke. Especially Brooke.

Two

The baby was crying. The baby always cried; she hadn't stopped once, not since she was born, not for five long years. Within her body, Peri carried the silence she craved until it grew so big she knew she was going to explode. She could feel it pressing against her ribs like a white balloon, pushing out everything else that was in her—air, voice, tears. For days, she'd forced herself to be still, scared that any movement would crack open what she wanted tucked safe under her ribs. She'd closed her eyes, repeating the old phrase from sixth-grade sleepovers under her breath, "As light as a feather, as stiff as a board." It was a chant they'd used while pretending to levitate each other, the words turning flesh to air. And even though she'd heard herself talk to Ryan and Carly, she hadn't been paying attention to them. Even under the bedcovers, she had heard the cries and felt the way she moved inside her body. She was in the space that was pushing and pushing against bone to get out. It didn't matter if she was feeding the baby or sitting on the edge of the bed staring at her—she was focusing on that part of herself that wanted to explode; she could see glass shattering, body parts, blood, Brooke in the air, flying as she could never walk, Carly covering her eyes, screaming, Ryan in the corner staring at her, his mouth open.

She only meant to leave for a little while. A drive to let the balloon deflate enough so that she could breathe. She got into the used car—a Honda Accord—that she'd bought when she'd sold the Land Rover, and started the engine. She had to get away fast. The balloon now pressed against her throat, a hard pinch like a tracheotomy. If she didn't drive quickly, the explosion would burst from her, and she could hurt someone. So she sped out of the apartment complex parking lot and into the street, turning and stopping, turning and stopping until she was on the freeway heading where? To her house? Yes, her house, where she was supposed to be living. Why wasn't she there? Why was she in those rooms with the boxes and the crying and the mess? The balloon inched into her throat, and she tried to swallow, sweat on her upper lip. Because of Graham. Because he couldn't stand the baby. Because he'd already exploded and destroyed everything, all of them in tiny pieces.

Ryan had disappeared already. Who knew where Carly would go? And the baby? The baby cried and cried and cried. She was sick. Always sick, holes in her throat and in her stomach, her body curled like a pretzel. The baby was going to die but then didn't die, and Peri didn't want the dying to be because of her. That's why she was here, in the car, driving home.

If only her mother were here. Peri needed her mother now, felt her arms, the way they used to hold her. Janice would have fixed it all, made Graham stay, kept the explosion from happening, kept the baby well, better, healthy. Her mother would have held the baby, kept her from crying and crying and crying. Peri swallowed again, the air hot in her lungs.

She parked the car on the street across from her house. But it wasn't her house anymore. It was a different color and there was a new deck, and new tiles on the roof. She wanted to get out of the car and complain, tell them to put it back the old way because she was here now and ready to live there again. Didn't they know she would be back? And then a woman's face was peering in the car window.

"Peri! Oh, Peri! I'm so glad to see you. Why haven't you called?"

From a long distance, the real self inside Peri found words and pulled them out through her mouth. "Oh, Melinda. Hi. It's been such a strain getting the kids situated. I promise I will."

Melinda turned to look at Peri's house that wasn't her house. "Can you believe what they've done? I was saying to Tom just last night that it's the worst color. But they're planning to do a lot of landscaping. Trees out front and all."

This woman was once her neighbor, her friend, but she was not the same, as fake a friend as this house was. Peri looked down, not wanting to stare into the woman's eyes and let her see the crying and blood and shattered glass she was running away from. "I just thought I'd take a quick peek. I've really got to get back."

"How is Brooke? Leon Magnoli actually found our number and called us. He's desperate to see her."

Peri was silent, trying to forget the other life, Leon with his toys, the way the baby could make sounds with him, squeal in happiness. There was the life before that, too, when Graham was there and they were happy, before ... before the doctors told them the horrible names that defined the curve in the baby's spine, the reason for her sad, crooked face.

Putting her hand on the door, Melinda leaned toward her. Peri smelled her Beautiful perfume, saw the short, expensive cut of her hair. "You've lost so much weight, Peri. I mean ... well, you look fabulous."

She missed her flesh, felt her skeleton against the back of the seat, her bones a bowl filled with the air she couldn't breathe.

"Well, I'll call Leon. And I'll call you, too." Peri felt her fingers find the car keys. "My love to Tom. And tell the girls at the swim club hello."

"But, Peri, I need your number! Can't you at least come inside?"

Peri lurched away, gunning the engine, feeling the pressure under her foot. She needed a long drive; she needed to get away from here, too, because she might destroy everything when she blew up, her real house and the fake house and the kids and all the people, everyone.

When she merged onto Highway 99, the air slipped pencil-thin into her lungs. Peri clutched the steering wheel, concentrating on the column of air, watching the road, her eyes watering. She was still dangerous, still ready to explode, so she pressed on the gas. She wasn't far enough away.

By the time she reached Turlock, her hunger was like an angry rat scratching at her belly, and she took the

Monte Vista exit. There had to be a place to eat that was safe, where she wouldn't do any damage.

At the fast food place, the scary clown face in front of her, white and round and smiling, she spoke into the drive-through microphone, scared to let anything but the smallest of sounds out of her lungs. The tinny voice asked her over and over, "What? Ma'am? Could you say that again?"

"A hamburger. A shake."

"What kind?"

"Chocolate."

"What?"

"Chocolate."

"That'll be four twenty-five at the window," and then when the person inside thought the machine was off, Peri heard, "What a whacko."

She paid for her food and pulled into a space in the parking lot, hunching down in her seat and eating the hamburger, the meat greasy and delicious. Licking her fingers, she wished she'd ordered one more, two more, but then she started sipping her shake. The liquid was thick and creamy, but she thought of the baby and her syringe and her powdery formula, the only thing she could eat because otherwise she aspirated food into her lungs. That's what always happened, and the last time at the hospital, the doctors had cut into her throat and slid in a plug so she could breathe with a machine because she was getting worse and worse, her voice softer, her face more still, every muscle clamping down. Every day, Peri filled her baby up with the white fluid, chalky protein and amino acids. There was nothing beautiful about that, nothing tasty, nothing to celebrate, and she felt the chocolate on her tongue, the thick, frozen, viscous drink, and she opened the car door and threw up everything, the hamburger, the pickles, the bun, the shake. *I'm just like the baby*, she thought, wiping her mouth. *I can't eat.*

A woman walking by with a baby—a normal baby, a *normal* baby—in a stroller made a huge half circle around the car, holding her other child, a toddler, close to her and moving quickly, looking at Peri from the corner of her eye, like someone might look at something dangerous, a bomb or a knife. Peri started the car and merged into traffic, heading back toward the highway. Despite throwing up, the rat in her stomach was in a corner cleaning its paws, and she got back on 99, heading south.

That night at the Motel 6 in Azusa, she paced the room, the TV on to *Entertainment Tonight*, that woman with the shiny perfect legs talking and talking. She should call home, talk to Carly and Ryan, but if she picked up the phone, something bad would happen, the poison in her voice strong enough to go through telephone wires. The baby was still crying because she could hear her, even three hundred miles away. Clamping her hands over her ears, she walked faster, and then remembered the Xanax her doctor had prescribed for her two years ago.

"These will help you relax. Don't worry about it," her doctor had said. "You of all people need to relax, Peri. You have too much on your shoulders." But she hadn't taken anything, needing to be awake in case something went wrong, and it always did, especially in the middle of the night. The baby's breaths slowed, jerked, stopped, started. Fevers bloomed like crimson flowers on her neck and face. How could she rest? Then there were the regular feedings and the medicine and the baths, all like clockwork. It was up to her. All of it.

But that didn't matter now. It was smart to calm down; the heat inside her would simmer. Finding her purse, she dug through the junk until she found the brown plastic bottle, opening it and sliding two white pills onto her palm. That would do it. She looked for a syringe to use, but no, the drugs were for her. Her drugs, not the baby's. She didn't have to mash it up and dilute it and suck it into the syringe and press it into her own stomach to appease the hungry rats. It was just her, Peri, and she swallowed the pills without water and lay on the bed, closing her eyes against the sound of her child in her hospital bed so many miles away.

In her dream, her father, Carl, was on the porch of their Berkeley house, finishing a martini and folding up the *San Francisco Chronicle*. He was dressed in his work clothes—a white button-down shirt, a smooth silk tie, his suit jacket hanging on the back of his chair, his real estate agent smile in his pocket. She could almost see the buildings he sold and leased and rented reflected in his silver cuff links. Peri was only seven, and she saw that he wasn't just home from work—he was packed and ready to leave.

"Why are you going?"

"I tried to follow the advice. Can't do it." He looked at her over his martini glass. "That's all I can say."

"What did I do?"

"We can't talk about it here."

Peri crawled to him and pulled on his leg. "I'll be good. Don't leave us. I'll do whatever you say."

But in the dream he ignored her, pushing her off his leg as he stood, and grabbed his packed bag.

"If you can find me, I'll let you know."

She could still feel his pant's fabric in her hands, and she looked up and it wasn't her father—it was Graham. But then whoever it was turned down the path and was gone, and Peri was flat on the floor of the porch because for some reason her legs didn't work. She was sucking in shallow air, imagining his car on the highway, twisting and turning in a puzzle she would never solve.

"Housekeeping."

Peri opened her eyes, her heart pounding. The baby? Had she been fed? Did the kids get to school? Was there any formula left? What was her temperature? She had to take it now. She sat up, rubbing her face.

"Housekeeping."

As she looked around the room, the night before came back to her, the drive, the pills. It was almost ten o'clock. She'd been asleep since eight o'clock the night before. "No. I'm still here. I'll—I'll be checked out soon," she said, pulling the covers from her naked body, seeing as if for the first time how thin her legs were, more like Carly's than how she remembered her own. She stood up, her breath going down into the top of her lungs, the pressure somewhere at her breastbone. Maybe she wasn't so dangerous now. Maybe she should go back home.

She turned on the bathroom light and almost let out a gasp at the sight of her face in the mirror, wanting to flick off the light immediately. But something held her still, made her look. She was as awful on the outside as she was on the inside, all her horrid thoughts taking away flesh and color, leaving huge black circles under her eyes, pushing her cheekbones above the sunken face under them, turning her lips pale and dry. Her collarbones looked like something she and her brother, Noel, might have held between them while making a wish, and each of her ribs was articulated, as clearly visible as if she were the skeleton in a biology classroom. Her breasts were two flat, round tan dots hanging over her bones, and it seemed as if her pubic hair had been erased, thin and washed out, almost like she was a girl again. Nothing was left that said she was a woman. There was not one reminder of the babies she'd borne and fed and held.

She was the monster she felt inside, the terrible person who had destroyed her marriage, her children, their lives, all of them. Peri sank to the floor, the harsh tang of Clorox in her eyes. Everything had disappeared. It was all Graham's fault, all of this, the evil inside her, the baby's ragged breathing, Ryan rushing past her in a swoosh of marijuana smoke, the look on Carly's face in the mornings when she asked, "Are you getting up today?" If Graham hadn't left, none of this would have happened, and he didn't care, he didn't know.

Leaning up on her elbows, the tile hard on her skin, she wiped her eyes. She was going to find him. That's where she had been going all along. She was going to drive to Phoenix and tell him everything, tell that woman he married the whole long story, let her know what her husband had done to the baby. Peri was sure Graham hadn't told her why he wouldn't buy the wheelchair and van. Peri would sit down with this woman and ask her why Graham hadn't sent alimony, enough empty months that she'd finally decided to sell the house so she wouldn't be dependent on him for anything. She would tell her about the hours at home with the baby, her gnarled body, her tiny face, and then she would show that woman how the baby breathed at night, the terrible stillness of how she stayed alive.

Three

Carly sat in the living room, folded the laundry surrounding her, Brooke's clothes in nice neat white squares, hers and Ryan's in looser, more colorful piles. Carly faced the front door as she worked, and when someone walked up the concrete stairs, the noise a *pound, boom, pound* as the steps echoed through the building, her heart thudded with the hope her mother was back. She'd stop folding and watch as shadow feet passed by the door. Each time, though, she caught her breath, thought, *Please, please, please.* But the feet kept on moving to some other door, to some other family. Someone else's mom or dad.

When she was done folding the laundry, Carly made herself stand up and walk back into her mom and Brooke's room, and again she tried to conjure something, Brooke's fever down, gone, her sister's skin back to its normal pasty pale white. Each time she'd checked on her sister during the day, Carly had closed her eyes, hoping for this very thing, but each time instead, Brooke's fever was up, 100.4, 100.9, 101.3, the skin under her diaper boiling. Finally around four, Brooke had dug through her mother's medicine cabinet and found the Infants' Tylenol, reading the bottle and measuring enough from the dropper into the syringe. Brooke hadn't even noticed her pushing the medicine into the peg, and for a couple of hours, Brooke seemed better. With the cool washcloths Carly put on her forehead, Brooke almost seemed normal. But then, her temperature began creeping up, her skin hot and red. Carly searched her sister's body for an explanation. There was none, just those strange round red patches. Her peg was fine, no red streaks, no hardness. Only her breath seemed different, deeper, full of something wet and sticky.

Carly was soothing Brooke when Ryan pushed into the house, throwing his backpack on the floor with a thud. Leaving the washcloth on Brooke's forehead, she went into the kitchen, where Ryan stood looking into the empty refrigerator.

"There isn't a fucking thing to eat around here." He closed the door and leaned against the counter, avoiding her eyes. "Did she call?"

"It's Brooke. She's sick, Ryan. I don't know what to do."

"Like I do?"

"We've—we've got to call someone. We've got to call Grandma Mackenzie. Maybe Dad."

Ryan rolled his eyes. "Yeah. He'll care. He'll come racing up here from Phoenix any second now."

"She's sick. She's really sick. Worse than the time you gave her that chocolate syrup." The sentence stuck hard in her throat. She could have brought up another illness, but she didn't. She needed him to see everything. He'd given Brooke a taste of chocolate syrup when she was two, and she'd thrown up all her formula, breathing in some of the barf and getting really sick. Carly could still remember the way their dad had looked at Ryan, his eyes hard and small, his finger pointing to the middle of Ryan's chest.

Ryan bit his lip and stared at the yellowed linoleum. "What's wrong with her?"

"A fever. I can't get it to go away."

"Shit. Shit!"

"Come and check her."

"I'm supposed to kick it with Quinn. I've gotta go." He started to walk past her, but Carly grabbed his arm hard, feeling how he'd changed, his arm not skinny anymore but more like her dad's, or at least what her dad's used to feel like.

"Please. I—I can't do it. I can't do it anymore."

He clenched his fist, his muscles moving under her fingers, and then he relaxed into the brother she remembered from long ago, the one who used to play foot war with her on the couch. They used to name their feet Graham and Peri, their feet fighting out the marriage, as if one contest could answer the question of why they were all unhappy.

"Fine. Whatever. Okay. Let's go check."

They walked together into the room, the smell of Brooke's hot skin—lotion, formula, peroxide—reaching them before they made it to the door. "Fuck." Ryan pushed ahead. He sat down by her bed and lifted the washcloth. "She's on fire."

"I gave her some Tylenol. In the peg."

"It's not working now. Where's the thermometer?" Carly handed it to him, and he stared at it. "How do you use this thing?"

"Here." Carly grabbed it and moved in front of him, placing it in Brooke's ear. She didn't want to look. She didn't want to see, but then it beeped and she had to, for Brooke. "One hundred and three."

"That's not that bad. Can't it like get higher before . . . ?"

"Before what, Ryan? She, like, totally dies?"

"What's the highest it can go?"

"I don't know. Like 106 or something. But your brain fries."

They were both silent, staring down at Brooke, her skin and hair almost matching. Outside, cars drove in and out of the parking lot, and Carly wondered if one of them might be their mother's. Peri would come home, bringing medicine and doctors and lots of money. "There is that pink shit in the refrigerator," Ryan said. "It's still there. Almost half a bottle or something."

"I don't know. I think we should call 911."

Ryan shook his head. "Mom. She'll be like in total shit."

"I know. But she's not here. She—she left us. And Brooke is bad now. I can't do it anymore."

"I say we give her the medicine. *You* can do it. In the peg."

"No. I've been doing stuff all day. What if the medicine's old? We can't wait anymore. She might stop breathing altogether. She . . . ." Her sister moaned, and Carly stopped talking. Brooke was listening to them, even in the burn of her fever.

"But if we call 911, they'll wonder where Mom is. And she'll be screwed. We can't call Grandma Mackenzie either. Or Grandpa," Ryan said, whispering now.

"I don't even have their numbers. I looked today all over the apartment. Mom took them."

"We could go to Oakland on BART. I bet I could find Grandpa's."

"What?" Carly shook her head. He didn't know anything. "And leave her? Alone? And I don't want to stay by myself anymore."

"Fine. Okay." Ryan sat down on Brooke's bed, pulling the sheet away to expose her legs. "What are those red spots?"

"I don't know. I only noticed them today."

He tucked the sheet around her body and clenched his hands between his thighs. "So . . . what? What should we do?"

"There is someone. You know. Mrs. Candelero. She's a nurse."

"That old lady? Why would we bring her up here? She'll be talking about it for the rest of her life."

Carly grabbed his arm and hissed, "If not her, 911. I'm not going to stay with Brooke like this one more minute. You've just, like, totally bailed on me. I've been with her for two whole days. You go off with Quinn, and I have to feed her, I have to worry. And it's not like it's been normal with Mom for weeks and weeks. So I don't even care what you say. I'm going down to Mrs. Candelero's now."

She said all this, but she didn't move, her hand still tight on his bicep. Ryan didn't pull away, but touched her hand, softly rubbing it. "Okay. Okay. Jeez. I'll stay with Brooke and you go get Mrs. Candelero."

Letting go, she backed away, looking at Brooke, glad that in less than five minutes things would be better. "Her name is Rosie. Don't call her Mrs. Candelero. She doesn't like it."

*   *   *

"If you call, I'm out of here," Ryan said, his hands on his hips, standing over Rosie, who knelt beside the bathtub holding Brooke up in the cold water. "There's going to be cops, and I don't want any part of it."

"Well, you better get your ass gone because I'm calling in about five minutes. Once I get this fever manageable, I'm all over my phone, so pack your bags."

Ryan swore lightly under his breath and then turned to Carly, his face red. "I told you this would happen."

Carly frowned at Ryan, handing Rosie a towel as she lifted Brooke up. "There, sweetie. You feel better? You're not so hot now." Carly helped her pat Brooke dry, while Ryan stood in the doorway.

"What is it? What does she have?" Ryan asked.

"You still here? I thought you'd left already." Rosie lifted Brooke to her chest and carefully stepped through the door and down the hall to the bedroom. "You have that Tylenol?"

Carly handed her the Tylenol and the syringe after Rosie laid Brooke down. "That's all we have left."

"That should do for now. I need that ice pack, Ryan."

"What does she have?"

"Listen, I'm no M.D., as I am reminded every day at work. But I can tell you she has an upper respiratory infection. Maybe pneumonia. She needs to get to the hospital. I've got this fever down, but it's only temporary. You understand?"

Ryan blinked, his mouth open. "Oh."

"So the ice pack?"

Ryan went to the kitchen for ice. Rosie put a clean diaper on Brooke and then covered her with a sheet. "I need my phone, Carly."

"My mom. She'll . . ."

"Yeah. I know. But if she could see what we're looking at, she'd do what I'm doing. I don't doubt it for the world. I've seen your mom. She's tender for you all."

Carly nodded, knowing that was true, even when her mother was still and silent under the covers.

"So, sweetie," Rosie said, "could you get my purse? I have my cell phone in it."

Carly turned and went to the living room, grabbing Rosie's heavy black leather purse. As she carried it back to the bedroom, she heard things jangling and clicking together inside it, and she wanted to stick her hand in and pull something out, remembering the grab-bag presents from her second-grade classroom. Her mother usually carried a sleek tan purse so small all she could fit inside it were her wallet, keys, and sunglasses. But Rosie seemed to have a world inside hers.

"Okay. Let's get the phone." Rosie dug around, lifting out a candle, timer, her wallet, and a spoon. "It's here somewhere. Oh! Okay."

"Tell them it's not her fault," Carly said. "She didn't mean to! She didn't know what she was doing. Tell them—tell them how sick Brooke always is." Tears pushed out her eyes and ran down her face.

Rosie moved her stuff away from her and pulled Carly down on the bed, putting an arm around her. "I'm going to tell the truth. That's what you did when you came to get me, and that's what I'll do when I talk to the paramedics."

Leaning into Rosie's shoulder, Carly nodded, wanting this part to be over even if the next part was worse. At least then, Brooke would be okay. Brooke wouldn't die.

"Ryan, take your sister back to the apartment. I'll stay at the hospital until Brooke's all right, okay? I'll call as soon as I can." Rosie patted his cheek, and Carly noticed he didn't flinch.

Rosie dropped her hand, and Ryan pulled Carly to him, holding her wrist. "All right."

Before the paramedic closed the door, Carly saw Brooke wrapped in a sheet on the gurney, one small hand reaching up. Rosie took it, held it to her cheek, and talked to her. *If anyone should be in that ambulance,* Carly thought, *it should be Mom, not a stranger, even if Rosie is nice.* Carly felt something new inside her flare hot and constant like the pilot light in the apartment's one heater. The ambulance drove off, neither Carly nor Ryan moving until the noise of the big engine disappeared in the night air. The small crowd of people that had gathered stared at them, eyebrows raised, hands at their mouths, and then walked away without saying anything to them. Carly wondered if one of them was the terrible Ted, who was supposed to collect the rent. "Have a good enough look?" Ryan called after them, but not loud enough for anyone to hear. "Assholes." He looked down at Carly. "Come on. Let's wait inside."

"Don't go."

"I'm not going. I'm sitting here, aren't I?" Ryan shook his head and punched at the remote control, flicking through the channels without seeming to look at one single show. He finally paused at *The West Wing,* and both of them stared at the screen, trying to find a way to let the show pull them away from the empty apartment. But all Carly could see was who wasn't there, her mom, Brooke, her father.

"Shit." Ryan threw down the remote. "I can't fucking believe this."

"What's going to happen?"

"Who cares? You don't see anyone here but some lady from downstairs, do you?"

"You like her."

"So?" Ryan moved away from her, crossing his legs.

"But what about the police and stuff?"

"Who knows?"

She thought about all the people who would soon know that their mother had left, the doctors and nurses and lawyers, people who could change things. "What about Mom? What are they going to say about Mom?"

He stood up, running his hands through his red hair. Carly was the only brunette in the family besides her mother, but Carly was even darker. Her mother always told her she had Grandma Janice's coloring, but Carly wondered if people thought she was adopted. Sometimes when they'd all been out as a family, she'd pretended she was adopted, a changeling, pulling slightly aside, walking behind her fire-haired family, imagining who her real parents were, the parents who really loved her. Lately, she hadn't had to pretend. Every night, she wished something would happen or someone would come to take away the sad feeling, the days that felt like bad nights full of horrible dreams.

"Look, Carly," Ryan said. "It's too late to worry now. Brooke's at the hospital. Everyone will know. I don't care at this point. I really don't."

"You're just mad. You care. You were telling Rosie you would leave."

"Yeah, well, I *don't* care. It's not my problem. Mom's no better than Dad now anyway. And I thought he was the complete asshole."

"Don't say that."

"Why? Isn't it true?"

"You left me, too. You left me for two days all alone. You didn't help me take care of Brooke or do the laundry or feed her. You don't even know how. You were off with Quinn, smoking or whatever. . . ." Carly bent forward, her forehead on her knees, the scratch of her jeans on her face, wanting her mother to come in and touch her back, rub her neck, say, "I'm so sorry, baby. It will all be better." But there was nothing except the live wire of Ryan's body, the hum of his anxiety that matched hers, the whine of the refrigerator.

"I . . . I—" he began, but then there was a knock and a voice at the door. He stood up, ready to let in whoever was there. Ready to let their whole lives change.

Four

At 2:30 P.M., Carl Randall was up at the tennis court next to the Montclair fire station, sitting next to his old buddy Ralph Jones, waiting for another two players so they could get a doubles match going. It was Wednesday, the spring afternoon swelling with late heat, the sun reflecting off the metal fence. Carl sat with his elbows on his thighs, spinning his racket on its end.

"Some days it takes a while," Ralph said, leaning against the fence.

"Indeed," Carl said. If someone didn't come in fifteen minutes, though, he was going to go home and work on his sprinkler system. It was getting hot enough to run it every other day, and one head was plugged, causing the water to geyser into the yard of Mrs. Trimble, his old bitch neighbor. "You're causing root rot," she'd yelled over her rhododendrons yesterday. "I can't have that, you know."

He'd spent the morning at Home Depot looking for parts, and he knew he should put them in before switching the system on automatic. He'd end up with Mrs. Trimble on his doorstep clutching her wilted plants, dirt flying everywhere from the mangled, drooping roots.

"Okay! We're on," Ralph said. Bob and Ramon walked through the court, and Carl breathed out, needing this match, needing it every day, like some kind of fix. This habit had started years and years ago, after he and his wife had split up and he found himself free—or empty, he wasn't sure which—after 5:30, so he'd searched around and discovered this pickup match. Carl liked the order of the games, the way people rotated in set after set, spinning to see who played, almost all mannerly, spats over bad calls not lasting more than one or two games. He'd been coming up here for almost thirty years, and once he retired, he was able to start at 2:30, getting in two, sometimes three sets. So he was one of the old guys now, one of the men the younger fellas probably hoped they wouldn't get as a partner. But he was still fit, his legs muscular, his gut not hanging over his pants. And he still had it, too, not needing that Viagra like Ralph did. After that last blasted exam, his doctor said his prostate was as smooth and round as a bean. Not that he'd had the opportunity to use his still-firm anything. He should have remarried when he'd had the chance, but the time was never right, the perfect woman just around the corner. Strange thing was, now life was a straight line, no corners at all.

And damned if the only woman he'd been close to lately was Mrs. Trimble, which was enough to turn him off women for life. But tennis helped him stay ready for whoever might show up. He wanted to play. He needed to.

"Let's go," Carl said, standing up and stretching first his right and then his left shoulder. "I want to beat you all."

*　　*　　*

On his way home, he took a left instead of a right so he wouldn't have to pass Mrs. Trimble's house. She was always out front pruning something, keeping her eye out for his sprinklers, neighborhood dogs, cats looking for soft dirt to scratch in, unusual cars, someone to talk to. He pulled his 1966 Chevy Corvair convertible carefully into his garage, immediately pushing the door button behind him. He could hear the phone ringing as soon as he cut the engine. He'd forgotten to turn on his machine, so he hurried into the house, pausing only when he thought of Mrs. Trimble, but she didn't have his number, so he answered it, trying to hide his breathlessness.

"Yeah."

"Dad, it's me. Are you okay?"

"Fine. Fine. Where are you?"

There was a pause, the sound of shuffled papers. Carl imagined Noel's set face, the way he bit his lower lip when he was thinking.

"Sorry. Can you hold on for a second—I'm still at work."

Carl sat down, putting a hand on his chest, feeling the quick pattern of breath in his lungs. He was relieved to be listening to the muffled sounds of a business conversation. If he didn't have a second to regroup, Carl thought he might turn into an emergency here, his heart pounding as if he'd been playing singles instead of doubles. As his breath slowed a bit, Carl brought the phone closer, the noises of the Kent Raifson Cleary brokerage office in his ear.

When Carl was in commercial real estate, he thrived on the din of machines and voices, the bustle and adrenaline that seemed to fill him, made him wake up for another day, made all the time at home seem as dull as a church service. Noel was exactly the same, waking at 4:30, driving to the office to be able to check the markets back east and in Asia, managing his accounts, clients, deals. "Dad," he'd say, calling from a taxi in Chicago. "We sealed the Toy Town account."

Work seemed to Carl about the same as women— once plentiful, vastly entertaining, and hard to remember. Sure, after he'd retired, it had taken two, three years before he stopped waking up at exactly 5:35; but now, he sometimes had to set the alarm to wake up at nine, the thought of a good project and two fine sets of tennis enough for him.

"Dad." Noel was back, a sigh behind his words.

"What's going on? Are you okay? I thought you were in New York."

"I was."

"How did it go?"

"Fine. Good. We probably have the TexCorp account. They liked our package—but that's not why I called."

Carl felt his pulse glide to normal. "What's wrong?"

"It's not an emergency. But it's the same thing I've been talking about for a month. We have got to get a hold of Graham. I called Peri's neighbor Melinda, and she told me that Peri came by yesterday, looking terrible, but she doesn't have a number either. She said that Peri promised to call her, but she hasn't."

Carl shook his head, rubbing the back of his neck. "I'm the last person Peri wants to have find her, Noel. She's fine. She's a grown woman, who obviously can take care of herself and those kids. You know how well she's done with Brooke. With all the kids."

Noel's voice tightened. "You didn't see her before she moved. And why hasn't she called?"

"She didn't want to see me, Noel. I left a message a while back to ask her about the move. I never heard a word."

"But she hasn't called me either. And she was on the edge. Tired. Completely drained. It's all Graham's fault. I don't even want to talk to the son of a bitch, but he's got to know where they are."

Standing up, Carl moved to the kitchen with the portable phone to pour himself a glass of water from the faucet. As he listened to Noel, he looked out the window at two chickadees on the bird feeder he'd bought at Home Depot, both spraying seed to the ground. *A big waste*, he thought, *and I'll have to worry about rodents later*.

"She's been doing okay," Carl said, but he really didn't know anything. His daughter's divorce had been awful and even worse for Carl because, as she went through the legal proceedings and the emotional upset, Peri seemed to revisit and reexperience his own divorce, his and her mother's. She'd been seven when he and Janice separated, and Carl had tried to see the kids as much as he could, hunkering down with them on weekends, taking them to tennis matches with Bob and dinners at Mel's Diner. But after Graham left, it was as if Peri forgot all of his efforts, looking at Carl as if he were the one who'd left a disabled child. "I can't believe you did this to Mom. I'm glad she can't see this happening all over again," she'd hissed at him the last Thanksgiving they'd spent together as a family. "You are all alike."

He'd wanted to remind Peri that he'd only moved a few miles away, seen her on the weekends, and never stopped supporting her. But he hadn't defended himself, not wanting to add anything else to her misery. Her whole house was saturated with it, as if it had a leaky sprinkler head.

Carl could almost hear Noel shaking his head, the *skiff, skiff* of his work shirt against the receiver. "She's not okay," Noel was saying. "And I blame myself for this. It's all my fault. I should have checked in more often. Especially on Brooke. I've been so busy with work."

"You have to work, son," Carl said. "We all have to work."

"Yeah. But what if something horrible has happened?" Noel's voice deepened, and Carl paced back and forth, remembering how upset Noel used to get as a child. Usually quiet, he would surprise Janice and Carl by suddenly throwing himself on the floor in a classic temper tantrum, flailing his arms and legs, emitting shrieks of sorrow the neighbors could hear.

Standing again by the sink, Carl put his hand on his hip. "Okay. Listen, Noel. I'll go ahead and get on the horn to Phoenix. I can find Graham. You're working. That's important. Don't think otherwise."

"What if you can't find him?"

"If that doesn't pan out, I'll go over to the neighborhood and talk to Melinda. I remember her. The one with the boob job."

Noel laughed. Just a little. "Yeah. That's her."

"She'll know all of Peri's friends. So I'll call you, okay? Let me take care of it for now."

He could hear the decision in Noel's silence. Carl closed his eyes. No matter how he acted, no matter what he'd done for his daughter since the divorce, he'd never be able to make it up. With Peri, he would never be good, not now, not ever. He'd gone to Carly's ballet recitals and school plays and Ryan's soccer matches; he'd sat by Brooke's bed and read her the books Carly picked out for them: *Pig William*, *The Giving Tree*, *Where the Wild Things Are*, *The Trouble with Trumpets*. He'd shown up for every single holiday dinner, even hosting Christmas brunch two years ago. But in the year since Graham left, Carl had been beaten down by the look of disgust in Peri's eyes, the way she ignored what he wanted to give her, them. What she still wanted, he felt, even though Janice had died almost five years ago from stomach cancer, was for Janice and him to get back together—the fantasy of a child of divorce. And in a way, that fantasy was an extension of her hope that Graham would come back, say he was sorry, move them back to Monte Veda and their old life. What could Carl do about that?

"Okay. But we've got to do it soon. Today," Noel said.

"I know. I will," Carl said, thinking this would all turn out fine. Peri could take on any load and carry it farther than anyone else he knew.

"Call me when you know anything."

Carl hung up, adrenaline in his body, a warm spin in his chest. He'd fix the flipping sprinkler head and avert a Trimble crisis. He'd take a shower. He would get on the horn.

"So you're saying there's no listing for a Graham Mackenzie?"

"No, sir."

"I'm not sure how he'd be listed. What about a G. Mackenzie?"

"No, sir. I have a Gloria and a Greg. But no Graham."

"All right, miss. Thank you."

Carl sat back in his chair and pressed the phone against his chest. Zero for two: no listing for Peri in Walnut Creek or Graham in Phoenix. Graham, that slimy SOB, was probably unlisted so Peri's lawyers couldn't find him. Or he put everything in his new wife's name so the IRS couldn't garnish his wages or something. He was hiding—that was for sure. Peri had to know where he was, but if Peri was lost somewhere in suburbia, how could Carl flush out Graham to find her? It was too confusing.

Carl stood up and went to his junk drawer, digging around until he found his small green address book, something he'd had for decades. He flipped to M and found it. Garnet Mackenzie.

He dialed and waited, breathing in when she answered. Her voice was the same, that snooty sound he'd never liked, as if she spoke with her lips pinched in disapproval.

"Oh, Carl. My goodness. How long has it been?"

Not long enough, he thought, not really knowing why he felt this way about Garnet. She'd been decent enough to Peri and good to her grandchildren, never forgetting birthdays, sending them to summer camps at her expense, calling specialists when Brooke was born. But she rubbed him like rough asphalt. Maybe it was the way she carried herself with royal bearing, the widow of a famous Alameda County judge, long dead, his office almost a memorial to his controversial and colorful career. Maybe it was the way she spoke to everyone as if she knew what was right, correcting people's pronunciation of English or any other language she might have studied at Cal as a humanities major.

"It's *chen-tro*, dear," she would say. "Not *sent-ro*."
Maybe it was simply the way that her and her husband's
life together hung brighter when put next to his—his
and Janice's.

"It's been a long time," he said. "Listen, I was wondering if you could give me Graham's number. I need to
talk to him about something."

He could almost hear her biting her cheek. He pic-
tured Garnet, imagined that a maid was dusting her
twelve-foot-long dining room table as Garnet sat in the
parlor, as she called it. Her Piedmont house was bigger
than some hotels he'd stayed in. "Well, I can't do that,
Carl. I can't just give his number out. He's asked me not
to."

"It's important, Garnet. I need to talk to him about
something very important." Carl rubbed his cheek, his
face full of the heat rising from his chest. He wasn't sure
what he was feeling, but as he listened to Garnet's
pause, he thought it might be worry.

"It's not the children, is it? Brooke? I haven't heard
from them since before they moved. I thought they'd
have some kind of forwarding on the telephone, but the
voice simply says the number has been disconnected."

"Well, yes. There might be a problem. I . . ." He
stopped, as guilty as a father who's left his infant for
hours in a hot car. "I haven't heard from Peri since long
before she moved. She never hooked up a phone or it's
unlisted—I don't know. She didn't leave a forwarding
address, that's for sure. Her brother—you remember
Noel—is really concerned. And I just tried to call down
to Phoenix, but they don't have a listing for Graham. He
must know where they are."

In another pause for thought, Carl heard the wet

swish of a mop in the background, back and forth, back and forth. His face pulsed from the impatient words he tucked away from the receiver, knowing that what he'd like to do more than anything was stick Garnet in the middle of his lawn and turn on the sprinklers, Mrs. Trimble's rhodies be damned.

Garnet cleared her throat. "Of course he must know. But you haven't talked to her?"

"Not for a while. I've— Well, we just don't talk as much as we used to."

"I see."

"It's a long story." Carl rubbed his forehead, the beginnings of a killer headache behind his eyes.

"I myself spoke with her, well, five weeks ago. I will say that she wasn't very helpful. I did want to see the children. I am their grandmother."

And you think that brings special rights and privileges? Carl wanted to say. His genetic link was worth about a nickel. But that was Garnet through and through, always raising her own currency. "I really do need to talk with Graham."

"Let me do this. I will call him right now and tell him to call you. He's been very busy, on so many business trips, I know that. But his wife should be there. Please give me your number again, Carl."

He gave her his number, hearing the scratch of her pencil on paper. "It's a real worry, Garnet. We need to find her."

"I know. I've been worried, too," she said, and Carl believed her, trusting that the quaver in her tight voice was true. "We'll be in touch soon, Carl."

He hung up and sighed, standing up and walking to the counter. He rinsed off his lunch plates and stacked them in the dishwasher. It seemed to take a week's worth of eating to fill the whole thing up. Sometimes, he was out of dishes before he even ran the damn thing through. When he was done, he looked back at the phone, imagining that Graham would call him now. But it didn't ring. And it didn't ring some more, even after he'd dusted the living room with Lemon Pledge and folded a pile of laundry.

He couldn't sit in the house, so he put on his jacket and grabbed his keys, remembering this time to turn on the phone machine. He tucked the cell phone Noel had given him for his birthday last year in his pocket and, as an afterthought, slipped in the old green address book and a pen. He had to be prepared for anything. And who knew who would call, what numbers he'd have to write down? he thought. But it wouldn't be Graham. He shouldn't have expected that loser to call back anyway, no matter how convincing Garnet sounded. The guy had left his wife and kids, Brooke needing both her parents, her illness enough of a struggle for an entire village. But then, Carl sighed, he'd done the same thing himself. But this was different. One of these kids was Brooke, and Graham was far away and didn't know that something awful could be happening to his family.

Carl turned off the lights and headed for the Corvair. He had to do something. He couldn't just stand still.

"I really don't know more than that," Melinda said, refilling his coffee. "Peri looked—she looked ill. She was thin, but it was more than her weight loss. It was her eyes. Big circles under them. Before I could get any more from her, she drove away. In that car she'd bought during the *confusion* over the alimony." Melinda raised her eyebrows and put down the coffee carafe, giving Carl an apologetic smile. Her teeth were perfectly white and ordered, like tiny polished dominoes.

"We know the apartment is in Walnut Creek. But did she ever say where it was exactly?" Carl shifted on his seat, looking at his hands around the coffee mug, feeling that same embarrassment over his ignorance he'd felt with Garnet.

"I think she said something once about it being close to the park. You know, Heather Farms. A place she could take Brooke in the afternoons. But I didn't hear much more than that. I asked though, believe me. We all did, all the neighbors. She stopped talking, Carl. It was like—like she shut down."

He nodded. She'd shut down with him long before. And here he was trying to fix it now.

"Wait!" Melinda said. "You could call the movers! I know they put a lot of stuff in storage, but they must have taken a load or two to the apartment."

Carl nodded. "Do you know what company?"

Melinda bit her lip, her eyes focused on the book-shelves. "Oh, wait." She slapped her knee with her palm. "That yellow-and-blue company. Alliance! Alliance Movers."

He pulled his address book from his pocket and wrote the name down. "That's great. I thought about calling P.G. and E, too. Even if they don't have a phone, they must have heat. And I'll call the school district. They'll have the kids on the books, sending records and all. The only problem I'll have is convincing them we have a dire need for the information. They might want me to file a police report before they agree to it. And then . . ."

"And then Peri might . . ."

"Yeah. If anything is wrong, which I doubt."

"Of course there's nothing wrong. She's a great mother. I tell all my friends about her. I know I could never be so patient. Brooke is an angel, but she's so much work." Melinda smiled at him, and he felt the ancient pull of tears under his cheeks. His daughter had been given too much for one lifetime, so much of it his fault. He swallowed. When had he last cried? A bad television show with lost children and dead puppies? When Janice died? His own mother? When he'd retired, the whole office standing around him clapping? He wasn't going to do it now, here, in front of this woman of all people.

"She sure is. I'd better get going. I'm going to get on home. I'm expecting a call from Graham."

Melinda pursed her lips and shook her head. "I've told Tom a hundred times. I don't understand how Graham could have done what he did. Leaving them like that. Leaving poor Brooke. Maybe the marriage wasn't going well, but still. They shouldn't have had to move."

Carl nodded in agreement, grateful that anger was replacing his sadness, and stood up. "I really appreciate your help. Here's my number." He wrote it on his napkin and pushed it toward her. "If you see her again, could you call me?"

"Oh, yes. If I hear anything, I'll call you." Carl was sure she would and sure also that she'd call all of Peri's friends, telling them about how no one knew where she lived, how her family was distraught and anxious. Soon everyone would know. *Poor Peri*, he thought. *Probably nothing is wrong. But in no time, the whole town will think there is.*

*   *   *

He stood outside Melinda's house, the air cool but clear, the stars much brighter on this side of the Caldecott Tunnel. With less light pollution, the Big Dipper spread glitter-white across the sky, the night pooling purple around it. Carl reached for his cell phone and dialed his house, hoping to hear Graham's voice on his message machine. He would hardly be able to bear the sound, but at least they'd know everything was all right. Graham wouldn't ignore a crisis, or at least that's what Carl hoped.

He pushed the right buttons, and there was a message, but it wasn't from Graham. "Hi. Hello. My name is Rosie Candelero. I hope I'm reaching Carl Randall, grandfather of Carly, Ryan, and Brooke Mackenzie. If not, well, I'm plain sorry, but this is an emergency. Well, see, I live in the same complex with your grandkids, and I'm here right now at the apartment. I hate to say this, but I had to call the ambulance. It's not here yet. Your little one, she's not good. She has a high fever. Anyway, what I'm getting at is that you need to get over here. There's something bad going on. I have no idea where your daughter is. Oh, the ambulance is here. The address is 1425 Walnut Avenue, apartment 4D. Carly says you've never been here. My cell number is 925-555-1376. Got to go."

Before the message ended, Carl heard a loud knock in the background and Carly's voice, the woman saying, "Let's do this," and then hanging up. He listened to the message again, wrote down the address and phone number on a map he'd found in his glove box, and then stared out the window, wondering if he'd know how to drive after hearing those words—*I have no idea where your daughter is.*

As he started his car and pulled out onto the street, he realized there had been years when he didn't know where Peri was. There had been the weeks and months of her childhood, when she'd been at summer camp or overnights or parties or dates. Most of her time at college. The first year of her marriage, when she and Graham were in Europe for his work. Then there had been the years of fighting and angry silence in her marriage and the year of the divorce when she considered him persona non grata, her life and the kids' out-of-bounds because he was like Graham, a wife-leaving bastard. For the first time, though, he was frightened. Maybe this time, he'd lost her for good.

Five

"Kids? It's me."

Carly sat up and wiped her face, watching as Ryan let their grandpa in the apartment, barely cracking the door so that their grandfather had to squeeze through, his white hair blown up around his face, his cheeks pale. Once inside, he put his hand on Ryan's shoulder, and then looked around the room, taking in the horrible mess, the half-full moving boxes, the furniture still covered in laundry, the lurch of Pyrex and steel bowls and glasses covering the kitchen counter. "God. What's been going on here?"

Ryan started to tell him, mumbling about Brooke, but then he began to cry, leaning on Grandpa's chest. Carly couldn't believe it. She tried to remember the last time Ryan had cried instead of swallowing down his tears and blinking fast at the hardest moments, even when their father left without saying good-bye. At the sound of her brother's sadness, Carly began to cry, too, but she felt better. Maybe Grandpa was the change that would make things okay. Finally, something good would happen.

* * *

They were at Mel's Diner on Main Street, their bags packed and stowed in Grandpa's Corvair, a car so loud and strange-looking it made Carly laugh to see it. Grandpa had once told her how he bought it when their mother was little and how it was the one thing Grandma Janice didn't want after the divorce. The big engine sounded like an earthquake, but Carly had always loved driving in it, the top down, her hair blowing up behind her.

Ryan had finished his second hamburger and second chocolate shake, and Carly had managed to eat an entire double cheeseburger with bacon plus fries. If she hadn't been so hungry, she would have worried about all the fat she was eating because she knew it caused cellulite (she'd read it in the *Marie Claire* her mother used to subscribe to). It had been weeks since Carly had been really, truly full; she was so sick of the frozen dinners her mother heated up.

"Okay." Grandpa slid back into the booth. "I talked to your friend Rosie. Brooke's doing better already. They have her on medication, and the fever's down."

"What's going to happen?" Ryan asked, wiping his mouth.

"I'm going to meet her and the doctors and some other folks back at the hospital in the morning after I take you two to school. Rosie seems like a real fine lady. And I'm going to call Uncle Noel, Grandmother Mackenzie, and hopefully your dad."

"What about Mom?" Ryan said.

Grandpa shook his head, and Carly realized Ryan had been asking the same question for hours, and nobody—not Rosie, not the paramedics, not Grandpa—could answer the question.

"So we better get home. I need to set you up and get

you all organized for school tomorrow." Grandpa
pulled out his wallet and picked up the bill.

"Do we have to go to school? I want to see Brooke. I
want to know what's going on," Carly said, amazed at
herself. For days, all she'd really wanted was space between her and her sister. She'd been desperate to stop
smelling the sweet, cloying scent of her sister's skin and
pee, not wanting to look at her peg and her trach plug
and the red spots on the backs of her thighs and butt.
She'd wanted to storm out of the bedroom and leave
the apartment, not even bothering to close the door;
she'd wanted to walk all the way back home where she
used to belong, where she'd been happy for so long.
Now she'd gotten the space she wanted, a whole two
hours, but she already missed Brooke, the way she
opened her eyes wider when Carly spoke, the gravelly
strangeness of her five-year-old voice.

Grandpa Carl looked at Carly, his eyes dark like her
own. "No. You don't have to go to school. I'll just call
them. Ryan?"

Ryan looked down at his plate. He probably wanted
to tag after Quinn and smoke cigarettes. They must cut
school all the time anyway, so he wouldn't have to sit
through geometry or Spanish and imagine what was
happening to Brooke. He could hang out at Broadway
Plaza and check out girls in the sunshine and forget
about his sister altogether, just like he'd been doing
since they'd moved. Thinking about all the time Ryan
had left her alone with Brooke made Carly mad, as
angry as she was after the paramedics left, knowing she
was the only one who cared. But then Ryan said, "I
want to go to the hospital, too. I want to know what's
going to happen."

Grandpa Carl nodded and counted out money and put it on top of the bill. "Well, let's get on home. We have to get you all settled."

She tried to catch Ryan's eye, but he scooted out of the booth and followed Grandpa Carl out the door and toward the Corvair. Ryan was almost as tall as Grandpa, which meant he was taller now than their father. Just like Maxie the Wonder Dog, their dad wouldn't even recognize them if he saw them again, walking right past them into his new and better life.

Grandpa's house was dark when they got there, only the sound of sprinklers in the night. "At least I got that fixed," he said. "You don't know the witch who lives next door to me. Don't go in that yard. She probably has an oven like in 'Hansel and Gretel.' "

Carly felt a laugh in her chest but it wouldn't rise up any higher, so she smiled to herself and stepped out of the car, lugging her duffel bag behind her. She wasn't even sure what she had packed other than the clean laundry that had been on the couch. She hoped she'd brought her face soap, but all she could remember was grabbing her toothbrush. It wasn't that she really had any acne yet, but she knew she had to pay attention because she'd turned thirteen in December and that meant hormones and hormones meant zits. That's what Ashley and Kiana had told her, anyway.

When Grandpa Carl opened the door, holding it for Carly and Ryan, Carly half expected Maxie to run up, wagging her tail, thankful to be back in a real house with them. But there wasn't any sound of claws on hardwood or tile or even the small *tick, tick* of cat paws walking toward them. The only movement she could see was the steady red blink of the answering machine. The muscles in her back relaxed at the sight of the phone.

They hadn't been to Grandpa's house for a while, but she remembered the smell, something clean like Formula 409 spray and Lemon Pledge. He'd always been really neat. Once her father had said something like, "I guess that gene is recessive," to her mother, who hadn't thought it was funny. Grandpa read a lot of books, and the living room was full of them. When she'd been little, she'd liked to pull out the ones about castles and sit on his leather recliner, flipping the pages. Sometimes, she knew, he smoked cigars, too, and in his study was a special box for keeping them fresh. He used to have to tell her to stop opening it or what was the point? "I might as well smoke them all now," he'd said.

"So, Ryan, you're going to sleep in the foldout in my study, and Carly, you're in the guest room. Let's get the sheets and make up the beds."

Grandpa Carl pulled a stack of sheets from the hallway closet, handing some to Ryan and walking with her into the guest room with the rest. The room was neat as everything else, a double bed, a nightstand with a brass lamp and alarm clock, and a picture of an old western town hanging over the dresser. Carly looked at her grandpa as he pulled off the bedspread. Who had been a guest here? What was this room for? Maybe he'd hoped that they would come to visit, but they hadn't, their mother not even mentioning it as an option. When Carly stayed at her Grandma Mackenzie's house in Piedmont, she always slept in her father's old bedroom. The old, brownish wallpaper had cowboys on it. When she was really little, she named the different men—the one waving his hat was Buster, the one asleep on his horse, Jed. She could see them even when the lights were out.

There were no family memories in Grandpa Carl's house. When they were at their grandmother's, she would say things like, "Your father used to slide down those steps on a towel, as if he were tobogganing." Grandma would point to the giant oak tree in the back-yard and laugh, shaking her head. "He scared me so much! Climbing almost to the top. And then one day he really did fall and break his arm! Can you imagine?" But their mother had never lived in this house, Grandpa having moved here when she was in college. All the fur-niture, the plants, and the books belonged only to him.

Carly grabbed one end of a sheet and tucked it into a corner and pulled up the blanket. Her grandfather bent over his task, whisking the top of the bed with his palms. Her mother had told her he was in the army before he married Grandma Janice. Maybe that was why he was so neat. But really, she didn't know anything about him except castles and cigars and kitchen cleaners, and as she shook a pillow into a pillowcase, she heard herself ask, "Why does Mom hate you so much?"

Grandpa Carl stood up straight, sliding a hand over his white hair. He looked the same as when he had pushed open the door of their apartment, surprised and pale. Then he sighed and sat down on the bed he'd just smoothed tight. "It's about the divorce."

"Why would she be mad at you over that? It was Dad's idea."

"Not *that* divorce."

"Oh."

Carly looked down at her shoes, the same ones she'd put on that morning, all the way back in the time when she was responsible for everything. She thought about her dad, the way she wanted to see him so badly and the way she wanted to yell at him. At night sometimes when she lay awake listening to her mother's and her sister's breathing, one steady, one erratic and thick, she imagined visiting him in Phoenix, walking up to the woman he'd left Mom for and slapping her. She'd practiced it again and again in her mind until she could feel her hand tingling. *Maybe*, she thought now, *I really want to slap him.* That's how her mom must have felt toward Grandpa Carl all these years.

"Your mom and I never really talked about why I left your grandma Janice. Peri was younger than you when it all happened, and I'm sure she didn't understand. It wasn't like these days when she would have gone to therapy or something."

"We didn't go to therapy," Carly said. The only person who went anywhere for treatment was Brooke. She was the one who needed it the most, and lately, even she hadn't gotten any.

Grandpa Carl shook his head. "I know. But it will be different now. I promise."

"Will it be different for Mom?"

He stood up and walked over to her, pulling her close. As she felt his warmth, tears in her eyes again, she knew why Ryan had cried. The relief of finally feeling a big adult body taking charge, giving them what they had been missing for so long, was too much to contain.

Six

Peri woke up tangled in the sheet, her heart pounding, her hair in front of her eyes. She tried to swallow, clearing her throat of sleep. The baby wasn't here, the crying farther and farther away, but Peri knew she had to keep moving.

Last night, she'd made it to the outskirts of Phoenix, parking the Honda in front of what she thought was a Motel 6, realizing only after she held the key in her hand that the blinking sign read only MOTEL. All night long, Peri had heard the sounds of bodies slapping together, beds pounding against the walls, loud cries of laughter and a few piercing screams. But her head was a twirl of knots, and after the Xanax the extra sound didn't bother her, and she slept without dreaming.

After a shower, she sat on the bed looking at a map of Phoenix and its surrounding suburbs. With Graham's address in one hand, she followed the squares and twists of roads and streets, red and blue like veins in a flat body, until she found where he lived. She grabbed her purse and closed the door behind her. Outside, she blinked, the morning dry and warm, mountains rising out of the flats of the city like dinosaur bones. She'd never been to Phoenix before, but already she hated it, the air empty, too able to carry the sounds of the baby to her, no Bay Area fog to muffle the sounds.

"Hey, baby," a man said from an open window, a can of beer in his hand.

"The baby's at home," Peri said, putting on her sunglasses, and sliding the motel key into her pocket, her jeans three-days worn and soft with dirt.

"Whatever. You know where I am." He smiled, his two front teeth missing.

Peri opened the Honda door, pushing aside the fast food wrappers, and sat down, ignoring the man, who continued to smile at her, raising his can in a toast as she drove away. As she waited at a light, she flattened the map on the passenger's seat, following the grids. Phoenix was easier to follow than San Francisco with its turns and streets that suddenly changed names. But even without the carefully planned blocks and well-placed street signs, it was as if Graham was calling her, his bad deeds leaving a trail she could navigate by. And within a half hour, she was parked in front of a brand-new beige stucco house. She sat with her hands still on the steering wheel and stared. A green lawn spread out from the house like a thick, emerald robe, a brick-and-metal fence surrounded the entire yard, and a closed electric gate guarded the driveway.

Peri felt bile rise in her. The lawn alone could have purchased the baby her wheelchair, and the three-car garage the van she would need soon. Without knowing it, she was crying, and she bit her tongue and hit the steering wheel with the heels of her hands, wanting the feeling to stop, knowing that this was the thing inside her that would explode and hurt people. That mustn't happen. It couldn't. The baby needed her. All she had to do was talk to Graham. She would tell the woman who had picked out this house about the baby and her curved body. They had to give her back what she'd lost, or the feeling would take over and something terrible would happen.

Getting out of the car, Peri smoothed her clothes, tucking in her blouse and adjusting the drooping waist of her pants. She would be calm at first, she promised herself. Calm. That's what she'd do. She'd simply ask for and then take what she needed. Then she would get back into the Honda and drive home. And everything would be better. No one would even have noticed she was gone. She swallowed and pressed on her chest, containing the feeling into a small square under her breastbone. *Stay down*, she thought. *Please.*

At the gate, she pressed on the intercom button, once, twice. As she stood waiting, she looked around the neighborhood. If the air were different, and the mountains disappeared, this could be Monte Veda—the same huge houses, the same expensive cars, everything that she and the kids and the baby had given up so that Graham could what? Come and live here in an Arizona neighborhood so much like his old one, but with one major difference. He couldn't hear the baby and her crying. Peri swallowed again, but the balloon inside her grew. She breathed in lightly and glanced at the houses. There were women inside staring at her. She licked her lips and tucked her hair behind her ears so the women would know she was one of them, a mother of three children, a housewife with 2500 square feet to care for. But she couldn't fool herself—she knew a baby like hers wasn't in any of these houses. The women staring at her could tell that, couldn't they? No matter how she looked, the baby was always there, pulling on her, stopping her from being normal, like all these people on this street. Like everyone else.

Peri pulled on her hair, trying to stop the air that was pushing up and up from inside her, but then there was a woman's voice on the speaker.

"Yes?"

"I need to talk to Graham."

"Who are you?"

She looked up at the house. Like her neighbors, this woman was spying on her, too. "I'm an old friend of Graham's."

"Graham is out of town."

"I need to see him right away."

"He's not here. Give me your name, and I can tell him you came by."

Clenching her fists and jamming them in her pockets, she pressed her knuckles hard against her thighs. The pain forced her to be calm, be good, make this work for the baby. Peri was lying with her fake smile and still body. Just as Graham did when he promised he'd love her forever, as her mother had when she was a child, whispering, "Honey, I'm here. I'll be here for you always." She was lying like her father did each time he smiled at her, trying to make up for everything.

Peri tucked her hair behind her ears, trying to speak slowly. "I want to see him now please. Tell him to come out and talk to me please. He can't hide in there."

"Graham's not here. Now give me your name and then go away. I don't want to call the police."

Turning her head, Peri could see that there really

were women in the windows, one in the house right next to Graham's, her hand at her mouth. *That woman can see the baby*, Peri thought. *That's why she looks so afraid. She's staring at Brooke's poor twisted body, the way her arms flail, the holes in her stomach and throat.* Inside her, the balloon grew and grew, the heat and pressure unbearable. Peri tore off her sunglasses and dropped her purse, unable to force her body into deception any longer. "You know who I am. I'm Graham's real wife. I'm the mother of his children. The one he said he would love forever. You don't know what he did to us. If you came out here, you would see her. Can't you see the baby? Can't you see her now? He doesn't send money. He doesn't call me. She has a hole in her stomach."

"Go away. I'm calling the police right now," the woman yelled, but Peri was climbing up the brick, holding on to the steel fence rails, pulling herself over, landing solidly on her feet, running up the driveway to the front door. She slammed against it, hitting the wood with her palms over and over again. "I know you're in there, Graham. Come out here and see her. Come out and see the baby. Look what you've done to us!"

Pushing herself back, she saw her colored, rippled reflection in the two stained-glass windows in the center of the oak door, and she curled a fist and broke her way into his new life. It was so cool, perfect, and normal, no powdery formula, no holes in soft skin, no sad eyes following her everywhere. Peri closed her eyes, wanting to stay there, hooked up to what she might have had in another life.

The woman inside, the cool and perfect and normal wife, screamed, and Peri reached down the inside of the door for the doorknob, but she couldn't reach it, her fingernails clicking on brass. Her hand felt wet and hot, and she leaned against the door and slid to the welcome mat, her elbow holding her on the broken window, blood pouring down to her shoulder. All the pounding and breaking had forced the balloon out of her, but the only thing that had exploded was this door, and she smiled, wanting to laugh. At least the children were safe. Before the world faded to gritty black, for a clear moment, she heard nothing. No crying. Not the baby. Not one single sound.

Peri swam in a calm white light. There was motion and sound over her, people and machines, but she was separate from it, tucked deep inside her body. Time spun out in a comfortable fuzzy line, and she floated with her eyes closed, listening to the silence from back home. The baby was quiet and the balloon gone. For the first time in months, she could feel her whole chest, and she wondered if she was dead. Or maybe she was happy, smiling. Was she smiling? But it didn't matter because her body curved and sailed like a smile, and she remembered being a child, long before the divorce, sleeping in a sun spot on the couch, stretching into the light.

The woman's shirt had little cats all over it. Peri blinked, her lids heavy, and she swallowed, her throat rough and dry.

"Here's some water." The woman pushed a button that raised her bed and then filled a cup from a blue pitcher on a tray.

Peri tried to reach for it and then felt something holding her arm down. She was about to complain, and then realized the woman was going to hold the cup for her.

Grabbing the straw with her lips, she sucked down the cool water, tasting ice on her tongue.

"What— Why do I have these?" Peri asked, looking down at the restraints. She wanted to wipe the water from her lips.

"You were a bit out of control when they first brought you in yesterday."

"Yesterday?"

The woman nodded, writing something down on her chart. "You've been asleep for about eighteen hours."

"I have?"

"We've been giving you medicine that made you sleepy. But I need to ask you some questions, okay?"

Peri closed her eyes and relaxed against the pillow. The past four days unwound like a terrible movie. The baby. Brooke. Carly. Ryan. The apartment. The formula. She sat up, her arms stuck behind her, the muscles in her chest tight against her heart. "Oh, my God. My children. I—I just left them."

The woman wrote some more on her pad and then looked up at her, her eyes soft. "The police found your purse. We've called your brother. Your father has your kids."

"Brooke?"

The woman seemed to nod, writing down more words.

"Where am I?"

"This is the emergency room at Phoenix General."

"The police?"

"You don't remember how you got here?"

As she sat up, her arms rigid, the drive to Phoenix and then to Graham scratched through her mind: the dirty motel, the street full of big houses, his wife's scream as she cracked into the house. She closed her eyes and saw her own colored reflection, heard the glass shatter, felt the shards rip into her flesh. Opening her eyes, she turned to her right arm and saw the bandages.

"Twenty-five stitches," the woman said. "You're lucky she called the police so quickly. You lost a lot of blood."

Shaking her head back and forth, she longed for her own hands, needing to hide. "So what's wrong with me? Why did I do this?"

"That's what I need to talk about with you, but we don't have to do it all at once. In a bit, we're going to move you upstairs to another ward, and a doctor will talk with you."

Peri knew what the woman was saying. She was going up to the psych ward with all the other people who'd lost their minds. "What about my brother?"

"He's on his way down. He said he'd be here later."

"What's going to happen to me? Will this happen again? Is this what I'm going to be like forever?"

The woman stared at her, not unkindly, but just waiting for all of Peri's questions to come out. "You're feeling better," she said. "Aren't you?"

Again, Peri missed her hands, wanting to touch this cat lady, take her optimism and press it to her chest where it could steep into her like truth.

"Yeah. But now what?"

The woman put down her pad and placed a hand on Peri's arm. "The police have to talk with you. The woman—your ex-husband's wife—may or may not file charges. And then there's what happened with your kids back in California. But you need to work on feeling well. You won't leave until the doctors think you are ready. We're giving you a good medicine that will help you stop feeling bad. And you can deal with what has happened these past few days."

Leaning back against the pillow, Peri tried to nod, but her eyes felt as heavy as doors, and she closed them. She would never forgive herself, even if the police, her family, and her children did. It didn't matter if Graham had deserted them and neglected to send the alimony. It didn't matter if he'd moved out to live with another woman in a big house with a gate. She'd left. She'd left them—even Brooke—all alone. She wanted to cry, but before she could, she was moving back into the fuzzy time, carried by hands away from her actions, taken back and far away.

Seven

After the kids were asleep, Ryan snoring lightly in the study, Carly curled up on the bed in the guest room, Carl closed the hall door and went to the telephone, punching the button on the answering machine, listening first to Noel and then Garnet, both with a wire of panic in their voices. He picked up the phone and walked to the kitchen counter, leaning on it as he dialed Noel.

"Dad? What's going on?"

Carl sighed, the story heavy in his mouth. "It's not good, Noel. Peri left the kids alone. We don't know where she went yet. And Brooke—Brooke's in the hospital." He heard his son suck in air and then swallow.

"Oh, God. Is it serious? Is she going to be okay?"

"I think so. I'm meeting with the doctors at ten tomorrow morning. Carly finally told a neighbor what was happening. A nurse. She saved them."

"Where are Carly and Ryan? With you?" Carl tried to ignore the surprise in Noel's voice.

"They're asleep. Wiped out. I don't even want to think what these past three days have been like for them."

"Did you find Graham?"

"I tried, but before I could get very far, the woman—Rosie—called, and I was off to Walnut Creek. Garnet called, though. I'll give her a ring after I talk with you."

"Is Brooke at Mt. Diablo Hospital?"

"Yeah."

"I'll be there at ten, too. This isn't good for Peri. She might lose the kids over this. And while a judge might give Carly and Ryan to Graham, it might mean Brooke goes into foster care. You do realize that, don't you?"

Carl nodded, the phone rubbing against his cheek. Neither of Brooke's parents seemed a good bet right now. And while he would fight for Carly and Ryan to stay with him, Carl couldn't take care of Brooke the way Peri had before the switch flipped in her head. His life had been about being alone for too long, and he had to admit to himself that he liked it the way it was, tennis, puttering, beers with the guys at the Big C, occasional family moments if he was lucky, a date once in a while if he was even luckier. How did a disabled girl fit into that picture? If he was honest, how did two adolescents?

"Dad?"

"Yeah. It's going to be bad. We have to figure it all out. We can do that tomorrow at the hospital. We have time to figure it out. Keep a steady strain."

"Yeah, I know. You always say that."

Carl nodded, realizing he didn't even really know what it meant, just something his mother always said when he was having a tough time with his sister, Denise, or failing at math. The sound of the phrase calmed him, even now.

"Well . . ." Carl said.

"God . . . Poor Peri. Oh, those poor kids."

"Listen, you might want to search around for a lawyer," Carl said. "I think we're going to need one."

"I will. I have someone in mind. Kieran Preston. And I think I'll call over to the hospital and see how Brooke's doing."

"Good idea. So tomorrow."

"Ten, right?"

"That's right. See you then." Carl hung up and wanted to go to sleep, a terrible fatigue passing through his body like wind. His calves were sore from tennis, and his back twitched from the strange position he'd found himself in during the sprinkler repairs. *Damn that Trimble woman,* he thought. But as he dialed Garnet's number, he wished he could go back to this afternoon when avoiding Mrs. Trimble was his biggest worry.

"Garnet? Carl."

"Oh, Carl. I've been waiting for your call. I tried to get ahold of Graham, but he's out of town—out of the country really—on business. His new—his new wife told me. He won't be home for a few days. But Blair said she would call him to ask about giving you the number. I told her it was an emergency, but she didn't listen. I wish Graham were here," she said all in one worried breath.

"Garnet, I've got some terrible news."

Her silence echoed into his ear, the huge house a rattle of space behind her. "No."

"Peri left. We don't know where she went, but she left the kids."

"Brooke?"

"She left Brooke, too, and now Brooke's in the hospital with an infection of some kind. The doctors think she'll be fine."

"Peri did what?"

He hadn't been there for Peri for a long time, but at Garnet's question, he felt a tightness in his throat, a readiness to speak fighting words. "I guess since the divorce went through, Graham stopped sending alimony. There was something about losing the physical therapist. He left town, I think. I don't really know yet. But she also let some things go. I think the move pushed her over the edge."

"Graham wouldn't have done that to his children," Garnet said with the same defensive sound he felt in his own voice. "Not to Brooke. That poor child. Not to her."

Garnet's voice cracked for an instant, a slim line in a china teacup, and he realized that they were more alike than he thought, both concerned for their grandchildren. But he had to protect Peri. "Listen, Garnet, I'm getting this all from Carly and from a neighbor at the apartment complex. I don't know the whole story—where Peri is, why Graham or Peri did what they did. All I know is that things got so bad, Peri thought she had to hide and then she thought she had to leave. I'm not condoning it. I just don't know what's going on."

"Those poor children. Where are Carly and Ryan?"

"They're here. Asleep."

"They should come and stay here. I have more room than you do. I could even bring Brooke here and get her all the help she needs. I can't tell you how many times I offered to help. Why didn't Peri call me? For heaven's sake, Carl!"

"Garnet, I don't know. She didn't call me, either. Or Noel. Or her old neighbors. But the kids are fine right now. Tomorrow, we'll find out more. But I have to tell you, there's a chance . . ."

"What?"

"That we might lose them. Who knows what the authorities will do."

"Oh, my. That can't happen! Where are you meeting tomorrow?"

Carl imagined Garnet clacking down the hospital hallway in fine leather pumps and matching handbag, pearls at her throat, steel in her eyes, the look that comes from having had what you want all your life. Knowing her, she'd get it, as she'd gotten her husband, house, and children, not that she'd had to work for them.

He didn't speak right away, listening to the sound of her waiting on the other end of the phone. She might expect too much, but she would be good to have in a meeting with officials, her upbringing teaching her all the rules of power. "At Mt. Diablo Hospital. At ten."

"Could you pick me up? Could we go together? I want to see the children, and it would be good to show them that they have family."

Until now, he realized, he'd never had to be alone with Garnet, all other events full of people and ceremony. What would he say? He'd have to dredge something up from his working days, smart and witty banter. But she should be there. He needed her with him as the doctors stared him down, wanting to know how this could have happened. How his daughter could have left her children. "All right. I'll be there about nine thirty."

"Nine twenty would be better. We can't be sure about the tunnel traffic."

"Okay. Nine twenty." Carl said good-bye and hung up, sighing and putting his hands in his pockets. He walked back into the living room and moved toward a bookcase, picking up a framed picture of Peri and the kids, Brooke a wiggly, crooked child in Peri's lap, Carly and Ryan hanging on to her shoulders. *No one tells you squat when you become a parent*, he thought. *No one says, "Your child will go crazy and abandon her children" or "You might have a disabled child who will suck all your energy."* If someone had told him and then Peri these things, neither would have believed the words, life just something that spun out, marriage and children supposed to happen to everyone.

Looking at Peri in this photo, her light brown hair blowing away from her face, smiling up at Graham who had taken it, Carl couldn't imagine her as she might look soon, her arms shackled, her body covered in loose orange jail clothes, her face drawn and pale. Or worse, gaunt and shivering in white hospital garb, her mind frayed beyond recognition. What would he have said thirty-eight years ago if someone had drawn out those pictures? Carl knew that as he had always done, he would have moved forward, not thinking, not imagining the worst because he had always put himself first and that's why this was all happening now.

They sat like four pillars around the conference room table as Dr. Murphy, Dr. Eady, and Fran McDermott, the social worker, spoke. Ryan and Carly were in with Brooke, showing her the toys Garnet had picked up earlier that morning. When he looked at Garnet, Carl's veins contracted and his balls pulled tight under him, as if the notion of manhood was contradictory in her presence. She'd been all right in the car, hugging the children and trying to distract them with chatter about her cat, Eustace, but once they'd all seen Brooke and then the doctors launched into their discussion, her face froze as if the situation could not possibly be happening, not if she were involved. She had the tools to dissect him in a second, flaying him open and exposing all his mistakes. If it weren't for Noel and Rosie, Carl would fall apart under her gaze.

Rosie was a trooper, a great gal, her arms folded, elbows on the table, asking questions. Noel was silent, steady, taking notes.

"So what's the prognosis, Doc?" Rosie asked.

"For the pneumonia, good," said Dr. Murphy. "She's responding well to the antibiotic. We've also been putting her on the ventilator at night. That will have to continue at home. But the pressure sores . . ."

"Excuse me?" Garnet said.

"Bedsores."

"Bedsores!" Garnet stood up part way and then sat back down, pinching her lips together and breathing out loudly through her nose. "What are you saying? She had bedsores?"

All of them but Rosie stared at the doctor, and he flushed—young and not used to such a case—itching his shoulder again, turning to Dr. Eady, who nodded.

"Yes. Not bad. Again, we caught them in time. We are treating them as well."

"What has to happen for someone to get bedsores? What does that mean exactly?" Garnet asked.

Doctor Murphy threw a glance at Fran, and Carl rubbed his eyebrows. He knew what it meant. No one had been caring for Brooke. She'd been kept in one position for too long, with no physical therapy, no swimming, no outings. Maybe no baths or not enough. His own grandmother had died at home, and in her last days, his grandfather had turned her carefully, three times a day, rubbing salve onto her skin, saying, "Round we go." Carl hadn't wanted to go into her room, not liking the smell or the blank look on his grandmother's face.

"What happens is that a patient doesn't have his or her position changed frequently enough. And if there are other . . . issues, the sores can progress. I think that's a big factor here."

"Other issues such as?" Noel asked, his pen still on the pad.

"Age for one, though that isn't a concern with Brooke. Malnutrition is another."

"Are you telling me Brooke is malnourished?" Carl asked. Again, he noticed Rosie looking away. *She saw this last night*, he thought. *She already knows how bad it is.*

"Yes. She's underweight. There is also quite a bit of atrophy, which could be from her illness and lack of therapy as well as lack of nutrition."

"Peri did this?" Garnet asked.

Carl looked at his shoes, imagining for a second he was on the tennis court at the service line, readying himself for a serve.

"Not necessarily," said Dr. Eady. "The feeding tube can be difficult. And if she hadn't been seeing her doctor, getting weighed and so on, the mother might not have known about the weight loss."

"Not known? Not known?" said Garnet. "Brooke is skin and bone!"

"If you see a child every day . . . Well, if the kids were feeding Brooke," Dr. Murphy began.

"You don't know what Peri's been through," Carl said. "How can you pass judgment when your son—"

"We can't know anything until we talk with Peri," Fran said, interrupting.

None of them said a word. Carl let the words in the room knock against his head: *malnutrition, feeding tube, atrophy.* How could this have happened? What had he been thinking? No one, not even Peri, could take on a child like Brooke without help.

When Noel's cell phone rang, Carl flinched, his heart pounding. Noel excused himself and went into the hallway, closing the door behind him. Carl wished he could leave too, stand up, push in his chair and say, "Well, this isn't about me," and get into his Corvair and blast back to Oakland. If he got back home soon, he could finish up with the sprinklers and make it up to the court by 2:30, setting the record straight by teaming with Ralph again and soundly whipping Ramon and Bob. Later, he'd call up Mary, the gal he'd met last month at the Piedmont Bridge Center, and ask her to dinner. Who knew? Maybe he'd get lucky.

"What are we going to do?" Garnet asked, looking first at Fran and then Carl, her eyes so dark he couldn't see her pupils.

Fran cleared her throat. "We have to make some further inquiries, but it's likely Brooke will be taken from the mother's home."

"And the other children?" Carl said.

"The other children as well, though it seems to me since they have family willing to take them, that will be an option. There's always the father, of course."

Carl looked hard at Garnet, who turned away, her lips tight. "But not Brooke?"

"She's special. She has needs. Again, we have so many loose threads here. The father and the mother aren't able to confer on this, so we have to plan slowly without them. My main job though is to try to keep the family together. That's the bottom line."

"My son will not tolerate this kind of discussion. He is a good father. He has no idea what has been happening to his children. Once he finds out, of course he'll want them."

Carl snorted. "I beg to differ, Garnet. Where has Graham been for the last year? From what I know, he's not laid an inch of flesh in California. If he had, none of this would've happened. He knew where they'd moved to—and you wouldn't even give me the number."

"Your daughter did this. Not my son." Garnet pulled her purse toward her, hugging it to her chest as if everything inside it could separate her from Peri and Carl and their terrible habit of running away. "And how can you criticize him?"

"Please, folks . . ." Fran began, when Noel pushed back into the room.

"Dad. They've found her. They've found Peri. She tried to break into Graham's house. I'm going to Phoenix. Now."

Without fighting again, Carl and Garnet managed to agree that Rosie would drive her and the kids back to Piedmont, while Carl stayed to talk with the police officer about Peri. Noel had left minutes after bursting into the conference room, driving home to make a plane reservation and hightail it to the airport. Before the cop showed up, Carl went into Brooke's room and sat by her, the nurse smiling and leaving the room.

"Ba," she said, her eyes wide.

"That's right. It's me. How are you feeling, honey?"

"Ga. Dare i Ma?"

"She went down to Arizona to visit your daddy. She's going to be coming home, soon. Your uncle Noel went to get her."

Brooke smiled, a flick of muscles under her thin skin, and flung her arm out to him. Carl took her wrist in his hand. How soft she was, how warm, a slight fever still burning inside her. She was nothing but bone, and he sucked in his cheek. Malnourished. He pushed down a moan that hovered in his throat.

"Ba!" Brooke said, turning toward him. "Ba, ba, ba!"

And then it came anyway, beyond his control, his eyes filling with tears. *This poor child*, he thought. And as he held her arm, reaching with his other hand to rub her smooth hair, he didn't know if he was thinking about Brooke or Peri.

"So you didn't know where they were living?" The detective leaned against the wall, writing in his notebook.

"No," Carl said. "She had kept us all in the dark in the months before the move. Her family and friends. And, well, our relationship has seen better days. But not even her brother knew. And they are as close as can be, but he travels a lot on business. She promised to call him but never did."

"It was two months since anyone had heard from them?"

"Just about. Noel and I had been calling around. Finally, I went out to their old neighborhood to talk to people she was close to. They didn't know, but then Mrs. Candelero got in touch."

The detective continued to write, and Carl wanted to take the notebook from him. What he'd said condemned his daughter to some punishment. But this man could never know what it had been like for Peri, alone with Brooke and without help, two other children to care for. "Listen. I don't think she was in her right mind. It's like she went into some kind of depression or something. She'd changed since the divorce, and then her ex didn't send alimony regularly and there was some confusion about the therapists. I don't know. You've got to understand that Brooke is severely disabled. I think my daughter just . . . lost it."

Nodding, the detective wrote a bit more and then looked at Carl. "That's what I'm hearing from Phoenix. We do have to investigate this as neglect and endangerment. We have no choice. But her mental state will have a bearing on the charges."

"Charges."

"Yes, sir. When she gets here, we'll take her into custody. I've talked with your son and the social worker, and I don't think it will be traumatic. He'll bring her to us when she's released from the hospital. And then the court will decide if she will be arraigned or sent to a psychiatric facility."

Carl stared at the floor, his chest tingling. For the first time in years, he wished Janice were here to help him cope. One thing about Janice, she'd been a champ in a crisis, whisking the kids to the emergency room after bike accidents and backyard mishaps, calling the principals at school to complain about schoolyard squabbles and teachers' inconsistencies. Maybe they'd found they didn't really like each other after the four-month courtship and wedding ceremony and honeymoon at South Lake Tahoe, but she'd been a good mother, a reliable mother. Peri sure needed her now.

"She was a good mom," Carl found himself saying, realizing that Peri had been just like Janice until the divorce. "She had those kids involved in everything. Brooke had speech and physical therapists and whatnot. A teacher came to the house to help her learn to read. I guess there were money issues. . . ." He stopped, noticing the detective was folding up his notebook and slipping it into his jacket pocket.

"Thanks, Mr. Randall. I'll be in touch." The detective handed Carl his card and held out his hand. "I'm sorry about this."

Carl shrugged. "Me, too."

Parking the Corvair alongside Garnet's Piedmont estate, Carl turned off the motor and sat watching the wind flicker through lime green sycamore leaves. Garnet's husband had died years ago when Graham was in college, but she still seemed to be trapped in the years of her marriage, stuck in time as it had been. That pissed Carl off. Real estate was about change, the deal, what was available, how to make it available. Garnet didn't alter, even though he used to try to shake her up with jokes and stories. After a few years of social events, he'd given up. Who needed it? Who needed her?

In better years, they'd all gathered here for big Thanksgiving, Christmas, and birthday dinners, Garnet and her children and grandchildren, Carl and Peri and even Janice and Noel sitting alongside them at the twelve-foot-long table, passing food prepared by the cook and served by a maid. After dinner, Carly and Ryan had run around the upper floors playing hide-and-seek with their three cousins, children of Graham's sister, Marcia, who lived in New York. As the kids played, the adults settled in one of the living rooms, drinking eggnog or brandy or Peet's decaf, listening to music and talking about jobs and school and the economy. At later parties, Brooke sat on Peri's lap, gurgling and twisting, Garnet ignoring the uncouth sounds.

But all of that had been years ago. Janice had died. The divorce split the two families, everyone taking sides. Peri had begun to shun Carl, leaving only Noel to celebrate with Peri and the kids. What had Peri done this past Christmas? Where had she gone? She'd refused to answer any of his calls and turned down an offer of gifts and money, telling Noel to say, "She said she doesn't need what you can give her now. She needed it years ago. Sorry, Dad." Had Garnet called her to offer anything? Or had Garnet stayed on Graham's side, consoling him, pretending to understand why he wasn't visiting his own children on the holidays?

Carl stepped out of the car, noticing that Rosie's truck, a Chevy 4x4, was parked in the driveway, the apartment parking lot sticker—Walnut Creek Heights—slapped on the bumper. In less than a day, Rosie Candelero had proved herself to be more family than any of them, sticking by the children when she had no need to, hauling Garnet back here to her mausoleum without a fuss. He'd always hoped there were people in the world like that, people who went out of their way for others. Most of the people he knew stuck to their own lives and families, as if that was the extent of their love. He was like that, maybe worse because he'd left Janice, let Peri disown him without fighting back much, explained away Noel's early panic about Peri's disappearance. Sprinklers had come before children. But Rosie Candelero was truly a nurse, and not by profession alone.

The maid let Carl into the house, and as he always had, he looked up, the ceilings in this house amazing with dark wood beams, the deep shine moving down to crown moldings, built-ins, wainscoting, hardwood floors. He used to wonder how many forests had been destroyed to whip this house into shape, but he wasn't an environmentalist. He was simply curious, though he'd never brought the subject up with Garnet. She had this house, her antique furnishings, her half-acre of high-end land, and she didn't like to talk about it. She moved through life as if the house and the money that had bought it had always been there. Carl walked into the living room, knowing that for Garnet, they probably had been.

He heard the children talking somewhere, and was about to go toward their voices, but he stopped as Garnet clicked into the living room, pulling closed the pocket doors that separated it from the hallway. "We have to talk," she said, sweeping an arm in the direction of the couch. Carl sat down awkwardly. His long legs were too big for the delicately upholstered cushions, and he crossed and uncrossed them, finally sitting like he had as a schoolboy at his desk.

"How are the kids? Did they have a lot of questions?" he asked as Garnet sat down on a spindly wooden chair, the back a heart-shaped bow of lacquered wood.

"Not as many as I do, though I've just spoken to Graham. He told me what Peri did."

"We know that. Noel told all of us at the hospital."

Garnet shook her head primly. "She actually jumped the fence and tried to break into his house. His wife, Blair, is still terrified. Carl, you have to face facts. She's gone mad. Stark raving."

He breathed out slowly, the air hovering over his tongue. They'd driven her to this. None of them had paid enough attention, especially Graham. "Maybe, but she's not home yet. We haven't heard what she has to say. Fran even said that."

"What could she say to make any of this understandable? Those poor children."

Carl stared at the wall, finding an ivy vine to follow up the wallpaper. Yes, those poor children.

"Now," Garnet continued, "Graham wants them to stay here. He's hopping the next flight out of Paris and is coming straight here. He's going to take Carly and Ryan back home with him."

"What?"

"That's what he wants to do. I'm going to keep them and then he'll take them home."

"No." Carl slammed his heels against the couch. "No. He doesn't have custody. He can't just take them. He gave them up, Garnet. He signed the blasted papers. He can't change his mind now."

"He's their father. He can do what he wants."

"No, he can't. He absolutely cannot! There are court orders in place here. He didn't want custody, only summer visits, and he didn't even see them once. Peri has full custody of the kids, and she hasn't been charged with anything yet. If she is, then the courts will decide where the kids go."

Garnet brought her hands together, folding them neatly in her lap. "He's still their father."

"Sure he is. And he can tell that to the judge."

"Carl."

He stood up and moved toward the door. "And did he say anything about Brooke? What judge would give two kids up and not the third? What kind of father would only want the pick of the litter?"

Garnet looked down. "Brooke is in the hospital. She needs treatment."

"So what are we going to do? Put her in a home? Until Graham walked out on them to make himself a life without a damaged child, they were doing fine. Brooke's slid back years since then. What judge is going to let him do anything with those kids?"

"That may be, but what judge will give those kids back to Peri? She's lost her mind. She left those children at home alone. You can't imagine she'll be ready to take care of them any time soon." Garnet's voice was at a high pitch, and he could see she was trying to keep her tears in check. This was a woman who would never cry in public. He felt like sneering at her attempt at control, but he knew he wouldn't dare cry in front of her either.

"Your son is totally uninterested in those kids, and that's putting it nicely. There's going to be some wrangling about both of them as parents." He folded his arms across his chest, trying not to notice his heartbeats, one, two, three. So fast.

"But for now, I think I can offer them a better home than you can. They've stayed here so often."

"Forget about it. I'm keeping them for now. Their stuff is at my house. I'm the one who found them. Don't think I'll forget you wouldn't even hand over Graham's number. I'll tell that to a judge, believe you me."

Carl pushed open the doors and left Garnet in the living room still sitting in the chair, her legs crossed at the ankles. He followed the sounds of the children's voices and found them in the eating alcove off the kitchen sitting with Rosie and drinking glasses of lemonade. "Let's go, kids."

"Grandma Mackenzie told us we were staying here. That's what Dad wanted," Carly said.

"She was mistaken. Come on. We're going back to my place. Clear up and say good-bye to your grandmother."

Both Ryan and Carly stood up, taking their glasses to the kitchen.

Rosie looked up at him, her eyebrows raised. "I didn't think they'd end up here."

"No. Not if I can help it. She and Graham are already plotting and no one's heard Peri's side yet. It's bad though."

"What do you mean?" Rosie said, walking with him toward the front door.

"It's just . . . She's not the girl I knew. The Peri I know would never have left Brooke like that. It means— It means she really is crazy."

"Crazy is relative. Like everything else. Trust me," Rosie said, nodding.

"But it's going to get ugly. With Garnet and Graham."

"Look, you do the best that you can with this, Carl. It's not going to be pretty. I've seen such things at the hospital. But if you all keep the kids in mind, it'll go better."

They stopped at the door, waiting for the kids, who were talking with Garnet in the living room. He turned to Rosie. "You've been so great to us. I can't tell you how much I appreciate it. You did more for them in one day than I've done in a year."

Rosie shook her head and placed a hand on his arm. She was warm, and without meaning to, he thought of the rest of her skin. Was it as comforting as her hand?

What a jackass, he thought, trying not to feel her smoothness. *Just what I always do, what I've always done.* He didn't know how many women he'd had while married to Janice, always wanting what wasn't supposed to be his, always wanting more. More women, more money. Sure, he'd been able to retire a bit early. But with whom? And for what? Sprinklers? Tennis? Bridge?

"That Carly pulled at my heartstrings from the first time I saw her," Rosie was saying. "I guess she reminds me of me when I was young. Sort of plucky even when it's terrible weather, you know what I mean?"

"She's an amazing kid," Carl said.

"I loved those years. They were the easy ones. My boy used to listen to me. He actually wanted to be with me when he was that age. Now, well, I'm handy to have around."

"He wouldn't be there unless he loved you." Carl could imagine the warmth of Rosie's home, the wisdom. The food. Not like the stuff he put together for himself.

"Humpf," she said, but she smiled.

"But really, thanks for everything."

"Call me if you need me. I mean it. Anytime." She dug in her purse and held out a card, ROSEMARY CANDELERO, R.N., her hospital address and phone number below it. "It makes me feel like big stuff to have this. I've got hundreds because I never have the chance to use them."

He tucked the card in his pocket just as the kids walked toward them, Garnet following. "Okay, get into the car," Carl said, opening the door, letting Carly, Ryan, and Rosie out. *I beat the maid to it*, he thought, almost smiling.

"Okay, Garnet. We'll talk soon, I'm sure."

"Yes, we will. This isn't over. I hope you understand that, at least."

Carl nodded and walked out, listening to the door close behind them. In front of him, the children were talking to Rosie and hugging her, even Ryan, his gangly teenaged arms wrapping completely around her waist. Carly laughed, made kissy sounds. Ryan let Rosie go and play-punched Carly in the shoulder. As Carl watched his grandchildren, he sighed. Peri couldn't lose them.

For the first time in years, he wanted something bad enough to fight for it.

Eight

On the way back to Grandpa Carl's house, Carly watched him as she sat in the passenger's seat, his hands holding the steering wheel at what her mother would call seven and five rather than ten and two, the safest places. And he didn't seem relaxed as he usually did, the radio playing those old songs he listened to from way back in the sixties and seventies, his head turning to her as he talked for so long she was sure they would crash. Now, he was still and focused. Something she couldn't describe rubbed raw in her stomach, scratchy and hot.

When they got home, the afternoon sun beating on the back of the house, an old lady was leaning forward to stare at them through the bushes—the witch that ate children, Carly remembered. Grandpa unlocked the door and they walked in the house without saying a word. Ryan poked Carly with his elbow, and she looked at him, raising her eyebrows in that silent language they'd developed since the divorce. *I don't know*, she was saying. *I have no idea.*

"So here's what I'm thinking," Grandpa said, turning

around suddenly in the hall. They both stopped their silent conversation, their eyes wide. "Oh, jeez, come into the kitchen and sit down."

They followed him and sat down at the table. He rubbed his chin, his whiskers white under his fingers. "What is it, Grandpa?" Carly asked.

"I'm thinking that—that I should go and live with you at the apartment. We can get it all arranged, and when Brooke gets better, she can come home, too."

Carly looked at Ryan, the scratching in her stomach so loud she imagined he could hear it. Just the thought of the apartment and the stale, stinky smell made the muffin Uncle Noel had bought her at the hospital rise in her throat. When she closed her eyes, she could see Brooke, hear her mumble, "Ma, Ma, Ma," see the unpacked boxes, the laundry, her worry stacked in every corner. Then there were the two months of her mother only a mound under the blankets, the bedroom ripe with the smell of Brooke's pee.

"That place is a shit hole," Ryan blurted out, bringing his hand to his mouth after the words were already out.

But Grandpa only nodded. "Yeah, it is. But we can clean it up. I can sleep on the couch in the living room."

"The rent is due. I know it's a lot," Carly said. "Rosie told me yesterday. Maybe it's too expensive to go back."

"Everyone will know," Ryan said quietly. "They'll know about Mom."

Grandpa sat back in his chair. "Here it is. If we get you back there, you can go to school. You need to go to school. Too much has interrupted your lives. And we can make it better for when Brooke comes back. And your mom."

Carly hadn't allowed herself to think about her mom

more than just the fact that she was gone. She didn't dare because there was too much to comprehend, and a feeling that was red and had a whipping tail came to her when she thought of feeding Brooke and cleaning Brooke and being all alone, even Ryan leaving her. Now she didn't care about her mother because Brooke was okay. And Carly liked sleeping in the big bed in Grandpa's house. "I hate that school. I don't want to go there. I don't want to go to any school but my old school."

"Me, too," Ryan said. "I hate that school. I don't have any friends."

"You have Quinn."

Ryan shrugged. "He's not a friend. He just has a car."

"He's got other stuff."

"Shut it."

"Well, you can't go back to Monte Veda," Grandpa interrupted. "The only option would be to go to school here in Oakland."

This new Oakland life wouldn't be like her old one in Monte Veda, with her best friends and both her parents, and Brooke almost saying "Carly" after her speech therapy. Now neither of her parents was around, her mom probably even arrested. But they would have Grandpa Carl, and Grandma Mackenzie lived right up Park Boulevard. Maybe Ryan would stop smoking and going out because Quinn would be gone, and then it seemed possible that her mom and Brooke could come and live here, too. Carly could share a room with Brooke, and Grandpa could turn his TV room back into a bedroom. She didn't have any friends to miss from Walnut Creek, anyway, so what would be so hard about starting over again?

"Okay," she said slowly. "I'll live here. I'll go to school here."

"Yeah," Ryan said, agreeing. "That's good. That's the best."

Grandpa Carl sighed and shook his head. "Well, this is a piece of work. I'm going to have to get on the horn. I don't know if I can do it like magic. I have to talk to Fran McDermott, the social worker. Maybe the judge. Or we might have to wait until your dad gets back into town."

"When will he be here?" Ryan asked.

"Tomorrow. Tomorrow we can try to work it out."

"But if he's coming, won't he want us to go home with him?" Carly asked, her stomach flaring again, tears behind her eyes. "Will we have to move to Phoenix? Will we have to leave Brooke here alone?"

Grandpa put his arms around her shoulders. "Don't get upset. No one really knows anything. But I'm going to do my best, okay?"

Carly nodded and looked at Ryan, who was staring at the table. He had on the face he wore when he slammed into the apartment, dropping his backpack, staying just long enough to grab whatever food there was and slip some money out of their mother's wallet. It was his I-don't-care face. Why did he have it on now, when people were finally helping them?

"Right. Like anyone's cared all this time," Ryan said, standing up, his chair skidding on the linoleum. "Where were you for the last year? Now everyone's all over us, like we're so fucking important. So do your best, dude, but it won't mean jack."

He walked away and Carly heard the study door slam. She grabbed on to Grandpa, not wanting him to be mad, not wanting him to leave. He patted her hand and sat back in his chair, sighing. "He's right. Everything single thing he said was right on."

Later, when Grandpa was on the phone, Carly tapped on the study door, leaning her forehead against the wood.

"It's me," she said quietly.

"Hold on."

She heard a window open, and then breathed in the cigarette smoke Ryan was trying to push outside as it slid under the door and into the hall. After a minute, the door opened a slit, one of Ryan's blue eyes blinking at her. "What?"

"Are you mad?"

"What do *you* think?"

"It's not his fault."

"Dad's?"

"No. Grandpa's." Carly put her palm on the door to see if there was any give, but he was leaning against it.

"No shit, Sherlock. I can't believe we might end up back in that apartment or with Dad. I don't want to be anywhere."

Carly put her shoulder against the wall, angling the toe of her tennis shoe in the opening of the door. "Let's go for a walk."

"Forget it."

"Come on. Grandpa's on the phone with the social worker or somebody."

Ryan looked behind him, the door opening a bit, the outside noises leaking in. Some kids were skateboarding down the street; a dog followed behind them barking. Cars rounded the corner, and behind the house was the whirring whack of a hedger. *The witch,* Carly thought. *She wants to trap us and throw us in her oven.*

"Fine. But let's go through the window."

Carly almost asked why, but for the first time in maybe a year, Ryan wanted to do something with her. They used to play all the time, board games or Mario Cart or a make-believe game with LEGOs, but that had been before he gave up on them, before their dad left. Ryan let her in the room, closing the door behind them. "If you tell Grandpa I smoke, it's all over."

"It's bad for you."

"Like who really cares? Mom?"

"Grandpa."

"I just don't want anyone on my back, okay?"

She shrugged, but Ryan was already leaping out the window, turning around to watch her. She didn't want to trip and fall on the lawn and look like an idiot, so she bit her lip and concentrated, jumping and landing with only a bit of a wobble next to the bottlebrush tree.

"Hey! You! Kids! What are you doing?"

"Shut up, you old bag," Ryan muttered under his breath, pulling Carly with him to the gate that led to the sidewalk.

"Who are you? Why are you coming out of Mr. Randall's house?"

"We're his grandkids." Carly stopped and looked at the woman, who stood with a hedger in one hand, a length of extension cord in the other. Her face was hidden by her hat's shadow, she smelled like the BugOff! Carly's mom used to pack in her summer camp gear, and her nose and cheeks were covered in zinc oxide.

"Grandchildren! Well. That's a surprise. But is that any way to come out of a house?"

"What's it to you?" Ryan asked loudly. "We're going on a walk, if it's legal."

The witch woman stopped talking, letting her arm with the hedger fall, and Carly gave her the smile she offered teachers when someone else threw erasers or passed notes or hurled spit wads at Johnny Bowman, the retarded kid.

"The retarded kid," she said to herself. Her mom had always hoped Brooke would go to school like the rest of the kids, but if she did she'd be propped in the corner like Johnny, spinning in a wheelchair like a wind-up toy. No one ever talked to Johnny, mean boys making fun of his strangely squashed head and dead eye, and throwing whatever they had on hand at him. How could that be good for Johnny or eventually Brooke? Why would her mother or anyone want that?

"Come on." Ryan pulled her arm, and they started walking fast, faster, and finally running down the street.

They'd found a 7-Eleven and now sat on the steps of the First Holy Trinity Lutheran Church, sipping Slurpees and watching cars drive up the street that led to their grandfather's house. Carly had picked cherry, as she always did, and Ryan had, too, his mouth a circle of red. He still looked the same, she thought, not turning completely into a man yet. Sure, he had some strange, wispy whiskers, his arms were tight with muscles, and his voice cracked into deepness sometimes, especially when he was mad. Which was most of the time lately. And his bones were longer and sharper. But he was still the brother she'd always known, and it felt good to sip the drinks, occasionally brushing his arm, listening to his breath, slow and steady. She was glad they were in Oakland because at home or in Walnut Creek, she wouldn't have been cool enough for him to hang with, the stupid sister who always acted like a kid.

"Ahh," Ryan said, rubbing his forehead. "Cold headache."

"I hate that." Carly was careful, sipping slowly, warming the drink in her mouth with her tongue before swallowing.

He put down his cup and leaned back against the rail. "You know, Dad tried to tell me about it once."

"What?"

"Mom. What was going on with her?"

"With Mom? What do you mean?" Carly looked into the red swirl of her drink, shaking her cup to mix it up.

"He said she'd been depressed since Brooke was born. That she, like, didn't pay attention to anything but Brooke to keep her mind from how sad she was."

"Mom was just fine until he left. Everything was fine until then." Carly shook her head and then sipped down the last of her drink. "I don't remember that."

"Me either. But that's what he said."

"When?"

"Right before he left. He didn't want me to think he was just, you know, leaving." Ryan stood up, walked to a garbage can, tossed his cup in, and then held his hand out for Carly's. She gave it to him and then let her hands fall on her knees.

"I remember all the doctors and Leon and the phone calls. Mom always came to our stuff. Your games and my . . ." Carly paused. She couldn't remember what she had done in that life before the divorce and the move. For a year, her whole life had been Brooke, worry, her mother, or homework. She closed her eyes and pulled at the past, remembering there had been parties with Kiana and Ashley and roller-skating in San Ramon and art classes at the community center. Once there had been Brownies and birthdays at Chuck E. Cheese and the Monte Veda Theater. A whole lifetime ago there had been pottery and gymnastics and drama. "Oh, you know, the art show and all that," she said finally.

"Maybe. But he wasn't happy. He told me. It wasn't really about Brooke as much as it was about Mom. He told me he loved us."

"He never told me that."

"That's what he said," Ryan said, shaking his head. "This is so whack."

"Mom said he didn't send the alimony. If he loved us so much, how could he let all of it happen?"

Ryan rubbed at his mouth with his hand, licking his lips and rubbing some more. He looked down the street, as if some really hot girls were going to appear and find him with a clown mouth. "Do we really know he didn't send the money? I mean, Mom wasn't like totally normal or anything. Maybe she forgot to deposit the checks or told him we didn't need anything."

"Why would she do that? She was the one who had to drive Brooke everywhere. She's the one who had to stay! So Dad wasn't happy. Big damn deal!" The same feeling she'd had in her stomach earlier came back, twisting the red drink around in her body. She knew that if she'd decided to quit the seventh or eighth or whatever grade because she wasn't happy, no one would have let her. They'd have made her stay and listen to Madame Fournier go on and on about truffles and crepes. When she got sick of Ryan and his teasing and hit him in the arm, her mother made them apologize to each other. Once, Kiana had tried to drop her like a disease, but by the afternoon, she was sending Carly notes that read, "I'm soooo sorry. U are my best friend." People couldn't just leave when they weren't happy. Otherwise, no one would stay anywhere.

"I hate Dad," Carly said. "I don't care what he told you. I hate him for leaving. I hate him for what he did to Brooke." Carly leaned against her knees and began to cry, seeing Brooke's body and the scary red spots, the peg in her stomach, the plug at her throat, the way her mother looked surprised each morning as if she hadn't expected to find herself still in the apartment, Carly sleeping next to her, Brooke moaning in the bed on the other side of the room.

Ryan moved closer and put his arm around Carly's shoulder. She tucked her head against his chest, smelling his Old Spice deodorant and feeling the fuzz of his flannel shirt, one that hadn't made it to the laundry room yesterday. Pedestrians walked past them, their voices lowering when they saw Ryan and Carly huddled on the stairs, and all she could think was, *He's touching me and doesn't care who sees, not even if it's girls*. She cried some more, feeling the pain in her stomach lighten and lift and disappear.

Carly was wiping her eyes, laughing at something Ryan said, when the Corvair pulled up, and their grandfather leaned toward the passenger's side window. "There you are."

He opened the door and sat back up. Ryan and Carly stood up and got into the car, and Ryan closed the heavy door, Carly in the backseat this time, looking at her grandfather's eyes in the rearview mirror. He wasn't mad, or he was pretending not to be.

"You two got me in a load of trouble," he said, starting down the street away from his house. Carly bit her lip. Did Fran find out they'd escaped through the window? Did this mean they had to go back to Grandma Mackenzie's or worse, a home or something?

"That witch Mrs. Trimble told me all about the kids pouring out of the house and talking rudely to her. I had to listen to her for about ten minutes before I could get out of there. Next time, go out Carly's window, okay?"

Ryan smiled and said, "I'm sorry. About that and . . . you know."

"Don't worry about it. Maybe later, I'll make you paint the fence. The whole Tom Sawyer routine. But we're okay."

Ryan nodded and looked back at Carly, who sat forward holding on to the front seat. "Where are we going?"

"That's the interesting part. I thought we'd grab some tacos and then head back out to the hospital to see Brooke again. Fran will be there, and she wants to talk with you two about school."

"If we can go to school out here?"

"Yeah. To see if we can get that all started. We really have to wait until your dad gets here. But we can start talking. There's something else."

"What?" Carly asked.

"They want you to talk with a doctor. You know, a psychiatrist."

"Now they think we're whacked out? *We're* the crazy ones?" Ryan said. "They probably think all of this is our fault."

"No, no, no. That's not it at all. They want to know how the divorce and your mother leaving affected you."

"Um, duh!" Ryan said. "Like it takes a doctor to do that?"

"You're right. It's been darn obvious. But it needs to be official. Then the doctors will talk with the social worker and then maybe a judge."

Carly sat back, her words hiding in her throat. She didn't want to talk to another stranger about her parents or Brooke. Telling Rosie had been hard enough. It would take her whole life to forget the way Rosie had nodded, telling her it was okay to keep talking, holding Carly's hand between her own. No matter what Carly said, even when she mentioned the fever and the red spots and then her mother driving away, Rosie didn't flinch or gasp. Because she was a nurse, she'd been able to see what was wrong with Brooke and their whole family, even during the days when Carly walked around like everything was normal.

Carly didn't want another person to think her life was weird or her mother crazy. All morning at the hospital, she'd seen nurses whispering and giving her sad looks, the same looks she herself might have given a litter of abandoned kittens in a woodpile. Poor little girl. Poor little loser.

When she looked up, her grandpa was gazing back at her, his brown eyes crinkled at the corners. "Carly, trust me. Everything will be all right. It might take a while, but everything is going to be fine."

She nodded, wanting to believe him more than anything.

"Ka!" Brooke kicked her legs, turning her face to Carly, who sat down on the chair by the hospital bed. She took her sister's hand and pressed it against her cheek. Brooke's skin was cool now, pale. Without thinking about the nurse standing behind her, she pulled up the sheet to look at the red spots covered with gauzy bandages. Brooke kicked again.

"Dar i Ma?"

"Grandpa already told you, silly. She went to visit Dad. But she'll be back in two day—" Carly bit the last word at the end, wishing she hadn't given Brooke a time frame. She didn't know exactly when their mother was flying in with Uncle Noel, and she certainly didn't know if they'd be able to see Brooke right away. She'd listened to Grandpa Carl on the phone, heard the words *extradited, incarcerated, hospitalized, halfway house*. Carly wasn't sure how they applied to what their mother had done, but none of them meant she was going to move back into the apartment and take care of them.

"Na!"

"No. Not now."

"Ka, Ka. Na! T?"

Carly brought a hand to Brooke's hair. Someone had washed it. Each strand was a gleaming wand of red. "Don't *please* me, Miss Nice. I promise she'll be here soon."

"Pay," Brooke said, holding out her hand.

"You ready to play? Fine." Carly took her hand and held up a finger. "This is the Mommy finger. Oh, and this is the Daddy finger. Where's the Brooke finger?"

"De!" Brooke squealed and held up her other hand, her index finger pointed.

"Oh. I forgot. Brookey is special. She's got a whole hand to herself."

"Mo."

"This is the Carly finger, and this smelly, farty finger is who?"

"Ra!" Brooke's head went back with laughter, and Carly heard feet clack on the tile behind her.

"Carly?"

She turned, and Fran was standing next to the nurse, a notepad in her hand. Behind her, she saw Ryan and Grandpa Carl. "Yeah?"

"Can we talk for a little bit? Ryan and your grandpa will come in with Brooke."

"Okay." She kissed Brooke's hand and put it down on the bed.

"Naaaa," Brooke wailed. "Ka!"

"Shhh. Grandpa and Ryan are here. You heard that. Don't be a bad girl."

"T?"

"Don't *please* me, you. Here they are."

Grandpa Carl patted Carly's shoulder as she left the room. Ryan walked by her, his eyes on the floor. "What?" she asked.

"Don't ask," he said, flicking her a look, his eyes red and watery.

"Tell me what it is," she whispered.

"You'll find out."

Nine

The whispers were like bugs at her ears, and Peri tried to open her eyes, but her lids were too dense and thick to move, so she listened, tasting the air, which had changed, become lighter than before, less chemical, the smells Clorox and cotton and clean tile floors.

"So why is she still asleep?" It was her brother, Noel.

A voice she had not heard before answered. "When she got here, she was psychotic. So she was given Haldol injections."

"Haldol?"

"An antipsychotic."

"Is that what she is now?" Noel asked. "Psychotic?"

"We think it was an episode. A component of her depression, which may be situational or chronic. We don't know that yet."

"Oh. But physically?"

"She lost a lot of blood. She nicked an artery when she broke the glass. We also gave her some pain medication."

"Shit." She heard footsteps, and the creaking of a chair accepting a body. Peri wanted to wave, but she could feel the restraints on her arms and her legs, her body as paralyzed as her voice.

"We'll have to keep her for at least three days before you can take her back. Hospital policy. And the police need to talk with her."

"What do you think?"

There was a silence, the sound of the chair releasing the sitter, and more footsteps, Noel and the new voice walking back into the hallway, whispers she couldn't hear, and she slid once more into sleep.

"How are you doing?"

Testing her lids, which were lighter now, Peri pulled them open, her eyes no longer sore. She looked up into Noel's face. He was smiling, but he looked worried, as he had since a child, permanent creases on his forehead and one between his eyes. "I'm okay."

"Do you know what happened?"

She stared past him at the window, the air behind him so pale, so clear. How could she not know what had happened when so much had? Each of her losses and pains seemed to piggyback on the one before it, her father, Brooke, her mother, her husband. How could she forget when the load had knocked her down?

"Yes. How are they? Are they okay?"

Noel nodded and then shrugged. "Carly and Ryan are at Dad's."

Anger bloomed in her mouth, words forming on her tongue, but she bit them back behind her molars. How could she be mad at her father now after what she herself had done? She was no better than he was. Like father, like daughter, both failures as parents.

"Brooke?"

"She's in the hospital. I don't know all the details because I had to leave to come here, but she's being taken care of."

Peri needed her hands on her face, but the cloth held her down. She couldn't bear to look at Noel, let him see her as she was, a mother who'd left her disabled daughter at home with her thirteen- and fifteen-year-old siblings to care for her. Knowing Ryan these days, it was more than likely that Carly did it all, fed and bathed and comforted Brooke, just as Peri had taught her. Because there was no other way to hide, she closed her eyes, trying to keep in the tears that slid nonetheless down her face, hot and true.

"Why didn't you call me? Why didn't you let us know where you were?" Noel was crying, too, but she still couldn't face him. "Periwinkle, please tell me."

His old name for her was ridiculous here, in the loony bin. She didn't deserve a nickname, she didn't deserve her children. When she was seven and lay in her bed listening to her parents scream at each other, and found all her father's drawers empty, no socks, no underwear, no ties; as the doctors looked at her across the desk, saying palsy and dystrophy, Peri figured she deserved only half a family—or else, why would her father have left? Now, she deserved whatever the police would do to her here in Phoenix and what they would do to her at home. Graham had been right to leave her, to hide in his house as she banged on the front door. She was nothing if not bad, nothing if not a horrible mother. He had known her better than anyone, after all.

Sitting at another doctor's desk, in another uncomfortable chair, Peri tucked her hair behind her ears and licked her lips, not knowing what to say. What could she say? She did it all, didn't she? Running away, deserting her kids, breaking into Graham's house when he wasn't even there. His wife hadn't been lying; Noel had told her that Graham had been out of the country for a week. What else, then, did this doctor want from her that he couldn't read in that report?

She pulled her hospital robe around her and wished she could just go back to her Haldol haze, but they said she didn't need as much now. They said she was better. Her stitched-up arm throbbed.

"So how long before you left your apartment had you been feeling depressed?"

Peri looked up, her eyes filling. Could she give him the true answer, the answer that would make her even worse than before. "Since—since my youngest daughter was born."

"Have you sought counseling before?" He adjusted his glasses and pinched his nose as if holding in a sneeze.

"Yes."

"For what? How you felt about your daughter?"

She rubbed her legs, so glad to have her hands free. What hadn't she seen a counselor for? In college, she had stumbled into the health center after a panic attack before a test, and ended up talking about her father and the divorce. After Brooke was born, she sat in support groups, listening to parents talk about wheelchairs, mainstreaming in public schools, disappointment, fears for the future, anger at God for allowing children to be born so disabled. Peri found herself revealing the tension with Graham, her frustration, the darkness of long, sleepless nights. But after Graham left, there wasn't time for groups, and then there wasn't energy. There was no one to whom she could describe the way Brooke looked at her as she walked into the bedroom, her eyes as wide as they could get, glistening, her arms held up as if Peri could solve all her problems. As if Peri could do anything.

"Yes. My marriage. But I haven't been for a while."

"Medications?"

"Some Xanax now and then. To relax. That's what the doctor said."

The doctor wrote on his pad. He hadn't given her his name, or maybe she didn't remember what it was, the Haldol still gripping her head. She must still be inhabiting that other body that drove her to Phoenix because no one had let her do anything—phone calls, showers, clothes—the nurse saying, "You'll talk to the doctor. Then we can see." Noel had promised he'd call and find out about Brooke, a lawyer, her crime, and she sighed, sinking deeper into the chair. She was glad he was doing it. That someone else was doing everything.

The doctor looked up. "How are you feeling now?"

"Tired. Sort of light-headed. Sad."

"About?"

"All of it." She held his gaze, his eyes blue, blue as Brooke's, and she knew she had to go back home.

"Do you have any of the thoughts you told the nurse about? The sounds? The voices?"

"It was Brooke I heard. No other voices."

"Do you hear her now?"

"No. Not since I broke the window."

"What did you think was going to happen if you stayed at home with your children?"

Peri shook her head, embarrassed and sickened by

her own insanity. "I thought I was a bomb and I was going to explode. I saw— I saw blood and glass and my baby, my youngest, flying through the air."

"And you don't think you're going to explode anymore?"

"I think I already did that, don't you?" She paused, a flutter of fear over her heart. "But will it happen again?"

"With medication and therapy and people knowing now how you are feeling, I don't think so. I think you are going to only get better, Peri."

"You mean my long, wild trips are at an end?"

"I believe so," he said, smiling. "Do you know what's going to happen from this point on?"

"No."

The doctor took off his glasses and leaned forward on his elbows. "Your ex-husband and his wife have decided not to file charges. That's why the police haven't come to talk with you. And I've contacted your doctor at home."

"What doctor?" she asked. For the past year, all the doctors in her life had been Brooke's. She wasn't sure if Carly or Ryan had even gone in for a physical in what? A year? Two? What about the dentist or the eye doctor? Those people used to know the whole family by name, slipping the kids colored erasers, pencils, and sugarless gum on the way out the door. Carly and Ryan had grown unrecognizable, teenagers with no one to care for them.

Picking up his pad and pushing back in his chair, he looked at her. "Your family has found you a doctor. Dr. Kolakowski. I've spoken with her. She'll be meeting with you when you get home. I've even talked with your ex-husband about your insurance. Everything is arranged."

Peri closed her mouth, not wanting to let the doctor see how his words made her lips pull down at the corners. She brought a hand to her cheek, pressing against the blush on her skin. Graham knew. He knew about her screams and his broken front door window. He must have been told about the children, Brooke all alone in her bed, Carly taking care of everything, Ryan floating high through the apartment. She felt as greasy and used as her unbathed skin, the days in the hospital slinking over her. "Oh. What is he going to do about the kids?"

"I don't know about that, Peri. You'll have to wait until you get home."

Peri shook her head. Graham would fly into San Francisco and want his children now that she was out of the way. Because she was crazy and because he could, he would take Ryan and Carly and leave Brooke stranded in her hospital bed. Just like she had.

They'd both abandoned her, not wanting any of the hard work, the feeding tube, the doctor visits, the five years of diapers, the way she could talk with her eyes, saying, "I love you," with a flick of her dark eyelashes.

"I'm going to release you in a couple of days. I'm going to prescribe an antidepressant that will help you. You'll stay on the Haldol for a bit longer. We'll tinker with the dosage. It's not an exact science. But you're going to have to go home and talk to doctors and the authorities in California. It's all arranged. How do you feel about that?"

"What else can I do? I can't just hop in the Honda

now." Her mouth lifted and a strange sound slipped from between her lips.

The doctor with no name laughed with her, nodding. "That will save you. Your sense of humor will save you. Hold on to it. It's going to be a long few months."

Ten

On Friday afternoon as Peri sat on her hospital bed, dressed and ready to go, the woman in the next bed moaned, telling her sister that the bread wasn't ready. Of course, the sister wasn't there, and Peri thought of pretending she was the sister, comforting the woman by saying, "Now, now. The bread is almost done." But it wouldn't matter. No one, except perhaps her mother, could have comforted her just three days ago, promising her she wouldn't explode into terrible pieces. From anyone else, she wouldn't have believed a word, needing all the drugs that now pushed through her veins to make her convictions evaporate. She needed the drugs and sleep, and in a sad way, she'd needed the time away from the children.

The woman cried out again, turning as much as she could in her bed, her arms restrained as Peri's had been. Peri heard the rub of flesh against the cloth, and she closed her eyes. How had this happened? She'd become the butt of her own jokes. She remembered the way she used to say so casually, "This is a madhouse," to another mother in Carly's first-grade class as the children scrambled around the room the minute the teacher went to the office. "I'm going to lose it," she used to say to Ryan when he and his friend Tucker tracked in mud from the creek. "You're driving me *crazy*."

But they hadn't driven her crazy. Brooke hadn't either, really. In a way, Peri could almost see the time—when Brooke was a baby—when she split away from what was real, slowly at first, as if she were in a boat that hadn't launched, relatives still at the dock, waving and calling out their blessings. Eventually, she had been the only one aboard, nothing in sight but black waves.

"You all ready?" Noel walked in, putting one hand on her shoulder, the other clutching a stack of papers. "Do you have everything?"

"No. I mean, just my purse." Peri pointed at her purse. All of the dangerous objects had been removed—nail file, Swiss Army knife, Advil, Xanax, vitamin C, credit cards, money. She'd left the Bay Area with nothing but her purse and the clothes on her back. The nurses had laundered her jeans and underwear, and Noel had bought her a new blouse. Her other shirt had been ripped by the paramedics and sloshed with her own blood. She had the new one on now, a pale pink button-down shirt with half sleeves, exactly her size. He must know how to buy women's clothes after dating all those women. Peri used to remember them, lists of names. After a while, she'd learned to smile and nod, knowing that they'd be gone soon.

She smoothed the blouse with her hands, listening to her brother talk.

"Let's go then," Noel was saying. "We can have dinner and then we'll go to the hotel. But we're getting up early. Our plane leaves at six forty-five. Preston—your lawyer—has it all arranged."

"You mean they're not sending down armed guards to drag me home?"

Noel took her seriously at first, shaking his head, saying, "No. They're expecting . . ." And then he stopped, smiling. "Fine. I'll call them to get you. They'll drive you home in a Hummer or maybe an armored truck."

"When do I get to talk to the kids?" she asked quietly.

"Tomorrow. Or the day after. They'll be able to come visit."

"Oh."

"Come on. Let's not worry about that yet. Let's leave that for when we get home."

Peri stood up and followed him out the door, the woman behind her still mumbling, moaning again about the bread that simply wouldn't rise.

After dinner and a quiet walk around the hotel's block, she and Noel went to bed. Noel was lightly snoring in the double bed next to hers. They hadn't shared a room since after their parents' divorce when their mother moved them to a two-bedroom house in the Rockridge district of Oakland. But even after all these years, his rhythms of sleep were the same, the up-down breath, the shifting of limbs, the occasional sighs.

Peri turned on her side, reaching her hand out without thinking about it, her arm hovering over the bed. Who was she reaching for? Graham? After this long? Or Carly, who had taken his spot in the bed, the apartment too small for any private space? Tucking her arm back against her chest, she knew she'd been looking for Brooke, her poor daughter who tried so hard every day, smiling even when Leon made her stretch her legs or tilt her neck, who didn't cry even after the doctors put the plug in her throat. Peri hadn't cried for any of it either, staying strong and firm at the bedside. But at night she had felt the diseases rise out of Brooke and slip along the floor, twist down the hall and come whisper to her in her dreams. It was her fault, all of it. When the doctors first sat them down, one had said, "It's genetic. *Mothers* carry the faulty gene that causes muscular dystrophy," as if she'd intentionally invaded the process of conception on purpose.

Peri knew she should have gone to the hospital earlier, not laboring at home as long as she did. Graham had paced in the living room and finally carried her in his arms to the car, saying, "I can't take it anymore. Something bad could happen."

"Graham," she'd answered between contractions, which were only three minutes apart, "I've done this twice before. Nothing bad is going to happen."

But something bad had happened. The baby's heartbeat had sunk, slowed, stopped for a minute, was it? Or seconds? First the doctors pulled at the baby with forceps, but then the monitor buzzed flat, and the nurses and doctors rushed in to prepare her for a C-section.

Peri wasn't sure at what second in the labor Brooke's chances for some kind of normal life disappered. Muscular dystrophy was a degenerative disease, but usually gentle with girls, not the devastating illness that finally wore boys to death in their late teens or twenties. With the CP as well, everything changed. Of course, they'd known initially something was wrong, because Brooke's birth had been followed by test after test after test. Even so, Peri had had hope. Brooke seemed like every other baby except for her size. But then she hadn't done what Ryan and Carly had so easily, flipping over on their stomachs, lifting their heads, and at the four-month doctor visit, Peri had listened carefully to the doctor, even taken notes, calling experts immediately.

While she seemed to take on Brooke's illness as she had every other mothering task, for weeks after the diagnosis Peri couldn't bear to look at her own body. She was disgusted with her arms and legs and stomach and breasts, hated her own womb, the terrible incubator that had ruined a child. And now, as Peri lay listening to her brother sleep, the knowledge that Brooke was the way she was because of Peri's genes and body—the way she'd held the child in her womb and her very blood—filled the dark room. She'd passed on nothing that was whole. Without her, Brooke would be living a normal life.

Clutching herself, Peri cried as she hadn't been able to cry before because she was supposed to be the strong one. While Graham, his mother, sister, and her own mother cried and worried over each and every one of Brooke's prognoses, Peri stood firm, calling parent resource centers, joining the local MD and CP parent support groups, chatting on-line with doctors and nurses, hiring Leon, speech and occupational therapists, contracting with the school district for teachers. Maybe she'd have been able to hold on, ignoring the blank fuzz of her brain for anything but Brooke, but then Graham had sat her down, said, "I can't take it anymore. I've found someone else."

Maybe if she'd begged him, gotten on her knees and promised she would change, she wouldn't have ended up bloody on his doorstep. As Graham had spoken to her, ending their marriage, it had been like watching a movie, the sad story of a relationship gone wrong. Peri had viewed it from a great distance, seeing her own dead eyes, the way she lifted her hand and then let it fall to her lap, the way he kept looking at her for a reaction. There hadn't been one because she wasn't even there.

But she was here now, in this hotel room, sleeping next to her younger brother, hundreds of miles from her children, on drugs because she was crazy, hours away from facing the cops who would lock her up so she could be evaluated and arraigned.

If only her mother were here; her mother would have stopped this from happening, and even if it had, she would have sat on the side of Peri's bed, leaned down, and whispered the right words. "You didn't mean it. It's not your fault. I'll take care of everything."

Then she would have whisked the hair out of Peri's eyes, and said, "This is nothing you can't handle. I know you'll figure it out. You're my girl."

But Janice wasn't here. Her mother's spirit wouldn't come to such a horrible place—dry and sad and full of despair. Bringing the pillow to her face to avoid waking Noel, she let the years of holding strong and still turn into liquid, her tears hot and full of the image of her daughter, her red hair a wild rose against the sheets.

"Peri? You awake?"

"Yeah."

"Have you slept at all?"

"A little. I think the antidepressant is keeping me wired." Peri turned to face Noel, the only light in the room coming from outside, a wand of yellow creeping in from behind the thick curtains. After a moment, she could see Noel's face, his eyes that were like their mother's, so blue they were almost white just before turning black around the pupil.

"Well, we went to bed so early. Maybe we should just stay up. We have to get to the airport two hours in advance now."

"Yeah."

"How are you?"

"I'm okay. I mean, don't be worried. I'm not like I was before. I'm just so sad. I can't believe what I did and what it's going to do to the kids. They've been through enough."

Noel was silent, and Peri could almost hear him trying to find the right thing to say. She felt sorry for him because what could possibly be right here? What words wouldn't be a lie?

He rubbed his nose and sat up a bit. "It's going to be hard. I guess there's no getting around that. But I talked to Dad while you were in the shower. The kids are doing okay. They've talked with the social worker and some psychologists or something, and it looks like the judge wants you to have a thorough evaluation, too."

"But what about Graham?" Peri hated how her mouth still held his name, the way she loved the air high against her palate with the *h*.

"From what Dad said, Graham will want custody. I won't lie about that."

"Brooke, too?"

"I don't know—I don't think so. No one's said anything."

Slipping onto her back, she tried to stop the anger that rippled from her chest into the rest of her body, but she couldn't. "Goddamn it! Goddamn him! He couldn't even wait to talk with me." She hit the bed with her fist, grimacing as the stitches throbbed.

Noel didn't say anything. He let her yell and cry, and

after a minute, she sighed, wiping her eyes. "What would Mom think of me?" she asked him.

"If Mom hadn't gotten sick, I can't see this turning out the way it did. When Graham left, she would have moved in with you. Or she would have moved you into her house. She wouldn't have let you slip away like I did. Like Dad did. Like everyone did."

They were silent for a moment, the long moaning wind of the air-conditioning wrapping around them. Her mother had still been well when Brooke was born, her diagnosis coming when Brooke was two months old. But up until then, she came over every single day. She picked Brooke up out of her crib as if she were any other baby, singing the same songs Peri sang to her kids, taking Brooke outside in the Snugli, staying to eat lunch with Peri, listening to her talk about nothing but the baby this and the baby that. Just before all the tests came back on Brooke, Janice had test results of her own, and before Brooke turned one, she was dead. A week before her mother died, Peri brought her home, thinking she would want to be surrounded by those she loved best. But with Janice dying in one room and Brooke struggling to live in another, Peri felt stretched between love, pulled and battered and sore, her heart full of loss. But none of this was Noel's fault.

"Don't think that. I didn't call anyone, Noel. I was in a fog or a dead zone or someplace where I couldn't feel anything except what Brooke felt. And then I couldn't feel anything. I let poor Carly take care of so much. She'll never forgive me."

Noel shifted on his bed, the mattress creaking under him. "You were sick. You've been sick all this while, Peri. It was bad, but everything is going to get worked out."

"Brooke will never get worked out. She's always going to be like that. She's going to get worse." Boys with MD eventually curved into themselves, their muscles turning to fat, the leg muscles too weak to carry them, their hearts and lungs slowly shutting down, no muscles to move them anymore. Maybe none of that would happen to Brooke, but already, she needed help to breathe and eat; she'd never know what it was like to run around a playground with a friend or swim without Peri holding her. She would never date or get married or have children. She would never live on her own. There had been no way Peri could work those facts into her mind, even as she sat in support groups and listened to the experts. She hadn't wanted to believe, but now, on drugs in a hotel in Phoenix, she did.

"Periwinkle. Don't think that way."

"But that's the point. I never have before. And it's true."

Noel sat up and turned on the light, running his hand through his still-blond hair. She blinked, watching the way his fingers made grooves through the curls. "Dad will be glad to see you. He's been out of his— He's been so worried."

"You can't offend me, Noel. I *have* been out of my mind."

"Are you still mad at him?"

She pulled her pillow up and leaned against it, her hands empty in her lap. She wanted a cigarette. She hadn't smoked since before meeting Graham, taught in her senior year in high school by her best friend Michelle, but now she needed that feel of smoke and heat in her lungs, a reminder of how life felt on the outside. "Do you know why he left Mom?" she asked.

"They didn't get along? They married too young? I don't know."

"Dad had an affair with a secretary, and supposedly she got pregnant, even though Mom never heard about any baby. Dad told Mom about it, and that was the final straw. She'd suspected other affairs, but she had proof this time."

"What kind of proof?"

"The woman called the house. That kind of proof."

Noel looked at the clock nervously and cleared his throat again as if his cough could clear the room of the idea. *We're the same*, she thought, *neither of us wanting bad news*.

"How do you know this?" he asked after a moment.

"Mom told me when she was sick. She was on morphine during those last days, and she either talked or slept. She still loved him, too. After all that time."

"So are you mad at Dad for what he did or for what Graham did?"

"Both. I hated him for leaving. I hated how I could always see Mom loved him, even though she didn't tell me till the end. I hated that he thought he could have it all—Mom, the secretary, and us. I hated that Graham wasn't even as good as Dad, not wanting Brooke or me, the damaged parts."

Peri sighed, rubbed her arms, and put them under the blanket. "Dad and I haven't been close since he left Mom. You know that."

"Dad saw us at least," Noel said, his voice at the same time defensive and conciliatory, holding both his father and his sister. It was strange how before the divorce Peri had been her father's favorite, but afterward, he and Noel became friends, buddies. Before Carl retired, they met at least one night a week for drinks and dinner at a financial district restaurant, loosened their ties, exchanged stories about the market and the economy, clients, and women. At least, that's what Peri imagined, Noel not divulging more than she wanted to hear. "Went out with Dad last night," he'd say.

She sank against her pillow. Why did all that had happened so long ago bother her, when Brooke's illness and Graham's and her marriage were still weeping wounds no stitches could mend? But it wasn't just her. The past must bother Noel because aside from his questions about her and her family, his work was all he ever talked about. She never heard much about his short-term girlfriends. And after Brooke was born, her family gave her space and permission to be selfish, focusing on herself and her girl. Now it seemed too late to ask what he wanted. A wife? A family of his own? For so long now, she and the kids had been his family, his only family really. They still were. After all, who was here with her? Her father? Graham?

Staring at the swirls of plaster moonscape above her head, she could not fathom how Ryan and Carly could ever emerge unharmed from their childhood. She didn't worry about that with Brooke—her childhood was written on her crooked body. How could Peri's depression, insane road trip, and inevitable punishment, not to mention the divorce, Brooke's hospitalizations, Brooke's surgeries, Brooke's constant, all-day care not leave scars?

"Dad's trying to change, Peri. He really is."

Turning again to face him, she pulled the covers to her chin, yawning. Seeing him like this, rumpled, his hair sticking up in the back, she almost could imagine it was

1968, and both of them were staying up to listen to the noise of a dinner party in the living room, giggling as adults bumped down the hall, drunk and desperate for the bathroom. Her father's business friends and their hair-sprayed wives would drink martinis around the table until everyone except their mother forgot children were in the house. Once, she and Noel found Mr. Samuels and Mrs. Merrimack kissing in the hallway, their heads clattering against family photos hanging on the wall. She had pulled Noel into her room, both of them breathing hard as if they'd discovered a murder. After that, she made Noel stay in his room with the door closed.

All her life, Peri had tried to forget that worried girl she'd been, make her life better than her mother's, her father's, make her children's lives completely unlike her own. And that's what she still wanted, more than anything.

Of course her father was trying to change, but maybe it wouldn't matter until Peri could truly leave her childhood behind. "Aren't we all trying to change?" she asked, closing her eyes, pulled suddenly into a deep, short sleep.

Eleven

When Graham flew in on Friday, the first thing he must have done was call Carl from his cell phone, his voice echoing in the taxi—or no, limo, the sound too quiet and smooth for a taxi. *Figures*, Carl thought, his heart pounding as he sat down, holding the phone to his ear.

"I'm coming to get them, Carl. I know what you said to my mother, but it's not going to fly with me."

Carl felt angry words like tacks on his tongue, but then his old negotiating self came back to him—the one that had convinced the entire Bestway Superstore board of directors to let him be the one to find them a new headquarters—and he sat back in his chair, wishing he had a cigar to slow his responses down, a word, a drag, a mouthful of delicious smoke, an exhale, another word. "So, Graham, where have you been this past year?"

"What?"

"I said, 'Where have you been this past year?' "

"Don't start with me, Carl."

"I haven't even begun yet. I'm not sure where you get

the idea you can come and take these children anywhere after leaving them. Abandoning them."

"They're my kids."

"Well then where in the hell have you been?" Carl asked, his voice steady, sure, unlike the waver of fear under his skin.

"Look, we can't argue about this now. I am their father."

"That may be a biological fact, sad but true. But I don't think the social worker or psychologists are taking too kindly to your disappearing act. Your I-live-in-wealth-and-splendor-while-my-children-don't routine."

"This isn't about me. This is about Peri and her illness. She's crazy. You should talk to my wife, Blair, about what happened Wednesday morning. Maybe I wasn't there, but at least I'm normal."

Carl felt the blood pulse in his neck. "That's up for debate, I think."

"Look. I'm coming to get them. I'm taking them to my mom's. You can't stop me. I have visitation rights. Let's call this an official visitation, all right? Have them ready."

"Here's a news flash. It's twelve in the afternoon."

"So?"

"Your kids are at school. You know that's what children do?"

Graham was silent, and so was Carl, hearing nothing but the whooshing echo inside the limo, the same buzz that had been inside the conch shell his mother had displayed in the family room. On his way to school each day, Carl had pressed it to his ear, knowing there was only the sound of his own head inside it. Now he wished he could put the phone down as he had the shell.

"After school then. What time do they get out?"

"A friend is picking them up and bringing them back here. Home. The social worker thought it was best they go to school back in Walnut Creek. Of course what would be best for them is to be in the Monte Veda schools, but that's another story, isn't it?"

"What friend?"

Carl wanted to tell Graham about Rosie, mention all that Rosie had done in lieu of a parent, finding the children, calling the authorities, traveling in the ambulance, but he knew that Peri's absence was as keen as Graham's in that story. "Someone who lives near the kids."

"What time, Carl?"

"Come over at three thirty. But I'm going to have to call my lawyer and the social worker. Don't expect you're going to walk off with them."

"I'll expect exactly that. Don't get on your high horse with me. You have nothing on me, Carl. You're the disappearing dad yourself. I'll be there at three thirty. Have them ready."

Graham hung up without another word, and Carl held the phone to his ear, listening to the buzzing sound of his own head.

He walked outside for some air, picking up the clippers he'd bought at Home Depot last week, fancy new clippers with a "rust resistant" coating and a ten-year guarantee. Last week, that had seemed very important. That along with the new string job for his tennis racket with synthetic gut at sixty pounds of tension and his new Wilson DST 02 tennis shoes, both of which he knew would blow Ralph away, scaring him out of his killer backhand. And the sprinklers. He couldn't believe he'd gone ahead and fixed them before getting around to calling about Peri. He'd been more concerned about Mrs. Trimble than Peri, thinking his girl could take care of her life, as she'd always done. Peri had always thought *Carl* needed help, but now, less than a week since he'd fixed the last sprinkler head, he knew that his girl was in big trouble. The worst kind, and now that Graham was in town, things could go to hell in a handbasket, just like that.

Around the side of the house, under the bottlebrush tree, he knelt down and pulled up some oxalis that thrust up year after year despite his best efforts, the bright yellow flowers beautiful but dangerous as they burst from their deep green clovered leaves, shooting seeds everywhere. And then there was the crab and Johnson grass, and it felt good to grab what wasn't wanted and yank it out, taking care of something.

"Mr. Randall? Oh, Mr. Randall?"

Carl closed his eyes, sighing. This was all he needed right now.

"Yes, Mrs. Trimble." He stood up, brushing the dirt off his Levi's and then giving up. He had to change his clothes anyway, needing to look decent for Garnet and Graham. Like someone who could care for a thirteen- and fifteen-year-old.

"How are your grandchildren?"

He looked at her, squinting. The kids? What did she want to complain about now? "They're fine. Teenagers, you know. What can you do?"

She took off her hat and ran a hand over her head. He almost stepped back, amazed by the blond hair that fell just below her chin. He'd assumed she had gray hair. In fact, if he was being honest, he had imagined Mrs. Trimble didn't have any hair at all, going bald in that sad way women sometimes do, patches of shiny scalp below once-a-week hairdos.

"Oh, I have five grandchildren of my own. I know they can be trouble. But I don't get to see them very often."

Carl moved closer, still holding his clippers. "Where do they live?"

"My son works in Saudi Arabia. Oil. It's dangerous, don't I know it. Especially now. And the kids go to school in Europe. Boarding school. They only come home to visit here once every two years."

So that's it, Carl thought. *She's bored and has to take it out on her garden, pestering me about the rhododendrons and their blasted roots.* For the first time, he felt sorry for Mrs. Trimble, who with her blond hair didn't seem like someone he should be calling Missus. Garnet, the judge's wife, was someone he should call Missus. He wished he didn't have to call Garnet anything at all.

"That's too bad they don't come more often."

"Are the kids staying with you for long?" Mrs. Trimble put her hat back on, and his new vision of her disappeared under the brim. She was Mrs. Trimble again, zinc oxide and all.

"I hope so. I really do." He smiled and waved with his clippers, turning back to the house. He had to call somebody, anybody to make things right.

"Do what he wants. Make nice. Be sociable. We want to seem congenial, interested in offering a compromise. Fran said the same thing. He is their father. We don't know what exactly happened. Can I put you on hold?" Preston clicked off without waiting for an answer.

Carl shook his head against the phone, not wanting to make nice to Graham or Garnet. It was as if all the years they were a family together had disappeared and, along with it, Carl's ability to be pleasant. Before, when Garnet bossed Graham or his sister, Marcia, around or made unending suggestions to Peri, Carl had shrugged it off. "A mother," he would say to Noel. "What can you do with those alpha females?" He meant bitch, but because he'd screwed up so damn bad before with his own marriage, he didn't want to make things harder for Peri.

And Garnet was generous with time and money, making sure Peri had access to the experts that would help Brooke. So how could he let her tone of voice ruin a good thing? Once Graham left, though, Carl felt it was the first day of hunting season, all his irritation let loose in such force that Noel finally said, "God, Dad. She wasn't the devil."

And now he wanted to bash both Graham and Garnet with his newly strung racket, beating them with the sixty-pound synthetic gut, and then stomp all over both with his new shoes. Maybe he'd have a go at them with his clippers.

"I'm back," Preston said.

"Oh."

"So what are you going to do, Carl? Remember, this is about Peri and her case."

"If you really think that's the best thing. But how long do they have to stay with them? I mean, how long do they have to stay?"

He heard Preston shuffling papers. "He gets a two-week visit with them a year. It's in the visitation agreement. But it's a bit unclear now that the primary caregiver is incapacitated. Just let them go. He's their father, after all. But I'm on the case, Carl. Don't worry."

"Easy for you to say," Carl said. So many phrases slipped off the tongue easily like "Have a nice day" or "It's not so hard" or "Get over it" or "Cheer up." He said them all the time, not imagining that someone might go home and try to actually use his words as advice.

Preston snorted. "Yes, it is. But I mean it."

Hanging up, Carl looked out the window as Rosie pulled up in her truck, Ryan and Carly jumping out of the passenger's side door. It had only been a couple days, but he swore the kids looked better. Carly had lost the pale blue tinge along her jaw that had initially frightened him until he realized it was the fan of veins just under her skin. What she needed was more food and sleep, and here it was only a half dozen meals since he'd gone over to the apartment and she looked almost pink. Ryan still looked like an idiot in his baggy pants, the hem-in folds on top of his hulking skateboard shoes ("Everyone wears them," he'd assured Carl), but he was smiling at something Rosie was saying to him. Was there any way Carl could pretend nothing had happened? For one second, two, three, his grandchildren were home, the world only this scene in front of him, none of the others he knew were playing out all around them. Carly's skin, Ryan's laugh. That was it.

"We're back," Rosie said, pushing open the door as Carl walked to it. Her eyes were full of light, brighter than that day at the hospital, and Carl breathed out, feeling lighter himself.

"I can see that. How about a cup of coffee? I've got sandwiches for the kids."

"I just want meat," Carly said. "I read about this carbohydrate addict's diet in *Seventeen*. No bread. No starch."

"For crying out loud," Rosie said, putting her heavy purse on the kitchen table as Carl pulled out the plate of sandwiches. "Pretty soon you'll be reduced to cucumbers."

"How's Brooke today?" Ryan asked, his backpack thumping on the ground.

"Good. The doctor says her infection is almost gone. Your grandma Garnet was out there this morning."

Despite her addict's diet, Carly sat down at the table and grabbed a turkey sandwich, biting off a corner that included the white sourdough. "So are we going to the hospital later?" she asked, pushing the lump of meat and bread into her cheek.

"Well . . ." Carl turned to the Mr. Coffee he'd bought at Kmart two years ago when his percolator finally died a sizzling electrical death. He measured out six cups of water and scooped grounds into the cup.

Carly picked up a curl of crust and popped it in her mouth. "Brooke's fever was down yesterday," she said. "She was much better."

"That's good, right?" Ryan asked, and Carl could see he wasn't just talking about Brooke. He meant good for his mom.

"Of course. It's very good." Carl took two cups out of the cupboard, looking inside them quickly. He swallowed, realizing he was a little nervous with Rosie here, as if suddenly he was the kind of man whose cups were home to cockroaches.

"I have some time," Rosie said. "I'd like to see her again. She's a trooper, that one."

"Grandpa?" Ryan asked, taking a ham and cheese, chewing as he stared at him with eyes that were just like Graham's. "So are we going to go?"

Carl pressed the on button on the coffeemaker, water starting to roil in the machine.

"Grandpa?" Ryan said again.

Carl searched in his body for the light feeling Rosie had given him just minutes ago, but all he could find was a dull dark spot that felt as heavy as Ryan's shoes. "Okay, here's the latest. Your dad's in town. Now. He's coming by in about fifteen minutes. I guess you're going to stay the weekend with him. Maybe—maybe longer."

The kids both looked down at the table, still chewing, and Rosie stood up, grabbed her purse, and then patted each child on the shoulder as she walked by. "I'll take a rain check on that coffee. There're things for you to do then. So I'm hightailing it. You guys keep up the good work at school. If I can, I'll get you a couple times next week. All right?"

Neither said anything, nodding into their food. Carl shook his head and followed Rosie to the door, walking outside to stand on the porch, just out of the kids' view. "I don't have a choice here," he told Rosie. "He does have rights. My lawyer says to play nice, and we'll have the lion by the tail when it's over."

"I don't know what to say. He's their father. That's true. But I swear, Carl, if I have to testify, I will. I saw that apartment first. I know what those kids were going through."

Carl almost laughed. Of course! What Rosie had seen that night in the apartment might be the answer to his legal prayers. But then he closed his eyes for a second, letting the laugh still in his chest. What happened in the apartment wasn't all Graham's fault. It wasn't. He understood that, at least, despite the defensiveness that crawled with prickly fingers across his chest. "That night says just as much about Peri as it does Graham. Maybe more."

Rosie put a hand on his arm. "She is plain sick. Mental illness is the brain suffering. Just like a kidney or a liver. It's an organ, no better, no worse. This husband doesn't have an excuse. He was a perfectly healthy man who left his kids and didn't send them what he was supposed to. Don't forget that. Not ever."

The underside of his jaw felt thick and tight, and all he could do was nod, feeling her hand on him, pressing hard. She was the only one he'd been able to talk to about any of this. Maybe he could have gone up to the tennis court with the terrible story, but Carl knew he'd have made a joke about being a father again, teased Bob or Ralph, asking them to baby-sit on a Saturday night. And no matter what happened, Carl could count on this woman, this virtual stranger, to do for him what no one he knew could.

"Thanks. Thanks a lot."

Rosie let go and smiled. "No problem. Give me a call when you need me. I'll try to sneak a visit to Brooke."

Carl waved as she drove off, knowing she wouldn't have to sneak into Brooke's room. Graham wouldn't be paying attention, wouldn't want anything to do with his damaged child or care who saw her.

Before Carl went back into the house he blew his nose and coughed, turning inside only when he saw Mrs. Trimble round the corner with her dog, an old dachshund.

Ryan was finishing off the second half of his sandwich

and had brought out a carton of milk and two glasses to the table, a milk mustache spreading under his nose. Carly stared at him, a crumb of bread at the corner of her mouth. Carl brought his thumb and forefinger to her lip and pinched it off, the small swipe of her soft skin reminding him of Peri, of how she would watch him as he read the newspaper or watched TV. He'd turn around, and there Peri would be, her light eyes full of a question Carl supposed he'd been unable to answer. He'd never known what she really wanted from him except to be near him. And when he hadn't been there anymore, the question had been answered by his absence. *Yes*, he might as well have said aloud. *I really will leave.*

He walked to the counter and flicked off the coffee machine, not wanting to put anything in his aching stomach.

"So, like, when is he coming?" Ryan asked, his earlier smile gone.

"Now. Soon. When you're done eating, you should pack up what you need. Which is everything, I guess. I could go back to the apartment and pick up whatever else you want."

"I don't want to go." Carly sat back in her chair, her gaze still on him.

"Well . . ."

"I don't want to either. He's an asshole," Ryan said. "He, like, totally bailed. I don't think he gives a shit about anything. Why is he even here now?"

Carl felt a glimmer, a way to work his grandchildren's desires into the end he wanted. With a few well-chosen words, he could make them hate Graham. His itch to seal the deal flared, but he clenched his jaw again, his muscles sore. Carl didn't want to be the kind of man to say something like, "Your father is a full-on son of a bitch. How could he have left you and moved to another state? And did he ever visit? Did he worry about Brooke? Did you even meet his new wife? I think you should tell him you want to stay here, with me. I think you should tell your grandmother what a terrible job her son did as a parent. Do it! It's the right thing! I'll get the phone." He could easily be that kind of man, the cruel truth of his words rolling in his mouth like warm butter. He was capable of those few sentences, of making this fight so much easier for Peri and himself. But if working in sales had taught him anything, it was to hold back, wait for the right moment, tell the correct person the information that would change everything. And Carly and Ryan, frightened and nervous, needed him to be wise in the only way he knew how to be.

"Your father is staying with your grandma, and he wants to see you. He called me as soon as he got into town. I think— I think you need to give him this chance." He pushed air into the words, hoping to give them a buoyancy he didn't feel.

"Yeah, right." Ryan pushed away from the table and went to the study, slamming the door again in his own form of teenaged communication. Carl figured this slam meant *I'm pissed, but I'll pack up. Asshole.*

Carly sat still, rubbing her thumbs together. "Kiddo," Carl said, putting his hand on her head. Her hair had the same thin silkiness of Peri's, the feel of his granddaughter's skull bringing him back to the days when Peri would sit by him at the kitchen counter at the old house, sneaking pretzels. Janice would be jabbering in the background, pulling a casserole out of the oven, Noel in the living room reading, but Peri was with him. Always. Even when he'd left home, he could still feel his daughter's head just under his hand. How had he let that go? "It'll be a visit. That's all. I'll come get you as soon as I can."

He felt her nod, her hair slick between his fingers. And then Garnet's Mercedes sedan pulled up, idled for a second, and stopped. Carly was looking down at the table and didn't see her father yet, but Carl watched, saw Garnet's mouth moving, her hands emphasizing a point, probably the same wisdom that Preston had: *Be nice. Be good. Then the world will be yours.*

Graham seemed to agree with his mother, leaning into her, almost exactly as Carly had leaned into Carl seconds ago. Garnet patted his shoulder, and they pulled apart, opened car doors, and stepped out onto the sidewalk, Graham smoothing the creases from his pants. Carl bent down to Carly and saw that she had been looking out the window, too, her eyes peering from between her bangs. This one didn't miss a trick.

"Here goes." They were so close he could almost feel her girlness, the afternoon smell of a child, long ago morning soap, school and lunch and desks, the grit of asphalt playing surfaces, loneliness.

"Grandpa," she said, turning swiftly and hugging him around his neck so hard he had the urge to pull back. But he couldn't, not again, not from this one, and he leaned in even as Graham and Garnet walked to the front door and rang the bell, looking in the window at them both.

Ryan slunk out of his room, carrying his backpack stuffed with clothes, his eyes on the floor, his free hand balled in his pocket. Carly was still clutching Carl, but they were standing now, Graham, Garnet, the kids, and he making a half-circle in the living room.

"Would you like to sit down?" Carl asked. Graham shook his head, but then Garnet brought a hand out to stop him.

"That would be nice. They all need some time to get reacquainted." She smiled, her lips in a perfect red bow. Garnet was like the women he used to walk past in Union Square during lunch, cashmere sweater sets and wool pants, leather shoes, pearls, hair dyed to youthful colors and styled back, pushed away from surgically rejuvenated faces. As he strode around them and their Neiman Marcus and Macy's bags, he'd wonder what they looked like at night, without the fancy makeup and fine clothing. What protected them then?

Carl tried to smile back and then gently pulled Carly to a chair and cocked his head toward the other chair, urging Ryan to do this one thing. Ryan sighed and sat, his backpack still hanging on his shoulder.

"This has been tough, kids," Graham began, sitting with his elbows on his knees. "I'm really sorry I didn't . . ."

"What?" Ryan said.

Graham looked at his son and sucked in a cheek, just as Garnet often did. "Well, for not being here. But I want that to change now."

Carl looked at his former son-in-law and remembered back to the time when he'd trusted him. At Graham and Peri's wedding, Carl had believed the vows they had written and recited, the smiles on their faces, the classy way they'd carefully fed each other cake, not smearing a bit of frosting. When Ryan and then Carly were born, Graham filmed every bloody minute, holding all three of his children seconds after each birth, making sure all the grandparents saw the videos. For years, Graham had been the one to give Carl the school photos—Carly and Ryan with fresh haircuts and missing teeth—that he put on his refrigerator. Graham had also been the one to call about soccer matches and dance recitals, glad to have Carl to whisper to during the *Cinderella* ballet, nudging him and hissing, "I can't tell which ones are the *ugly* sisters."

How could that father have turned into this one, sitting here like a bad dog with its tail between its legs, begging for his children's love? Was it just Brooke? Or Peri? Or was it the full plate of responsibilities that drove him off? Why had he stopped sending money? Or had he? Maybe in her illness, Peri had stopped knowing how to take care of anything, the bank as foreign and upsetting to her as her own child's body. Carl shook his head. He'd never understand family the way he was supposed to, how one stayed and lived through it despite everything.

"I want to stay with Grandpa," Carly said suddenly. Carl could feel her fingernails in his forearm.

"Oh, Carly," Garnet said quickly, as if her voice could erase Carly's words. "You love staying at my house. You'll have your regular room. Ryan, too."

"What about Brooke?" Carly asked. "She needs to live with us. I help take care of her."

"What about Brooke?" Carl asked. "What is your plan for her?"

"You know there isn't a plan yet," Graham said, the soft pleading look on his face hardening into anger. "Let's not get into that here."

Play nice, Carl thought. *Don't make waves*.

"So shall we go?" Garnet stood up, clutching her purse. "Maritza is making a lasagna. I know you'll love it."

Carl's tongue flicked with comebacks about how much Maritza must love cooking for the mistress of the house, but he heard Preston's voice in his ear again and imagined Peri strapped in her hospital bed and pumped full of drugs, regarding him with anxious eyes. This second of reticence was for his daughter, and he swallowed back his sarcasm.

"Okay, kids. Time to go. You'll have a good time," he said, and he squeezed Carly's arm, trying to tell her he'd be with her, even in Garnet's echoing house, even in her dreams.

"Grandpa," Carly pleaded.

"Come on, now. It's just your dad."

Graham threw him a suspicious but grateful glance and stood up, taking both children by the arm. Carl could see Ryan bend away, but Graham held on, walked to the front door, and out with the children he'd left a year ago.

"Thank you, Carl. They'll be fine," Garnet said, her eyes soft, too, asking him for things he didn't want to give her.

He folded his arms and nodded. "That they will. I'll guarantee it."

Garnet pinched her lips and walked out to the porch and toward her car. Carl closed the door, unable to watch, not even from the spy hole. He couldn't bear any of it, but most of all he feared the smooth grace of Carly's head, the way she held it high even as Graham took her by the arm. Carl closed his eyes, feeling a child on either side of him, Carly and the ghost of the girl named Peri who sat next to him at the kitchen counter, laughing.

Twelve

That night, if she'd been able to turn off the light with her mind, Carly would have done it, just so she didn't have to look at her father, see what she knew were tears in his eyes. She didn't believe his tears were honest, though, and that's why it would be way better to lie there in bed and listen to him in the darkness, whispering to herself, *It's not true. None of it's true.* Instead, she stared at his eyebrows. They were the palest brown, and curved over his eyes like Ryan's did, smooth moons of hair. If Ryan would let her, she would love to rub her fingers on them like she used to do to her dad. But now there was no one.

"Carly? Are you listening to me?"

"Yes."

"Well? Do you know what it would mean if I got custody of you?"

"We'd live down in Arizona where it's hot and I don't know anyone?"

Her father wiped his eyes and sat back in his chair, looking up at the ceiling and the crystal light fixture Grandma Mackenzie always warned her about, saying,

"It's an antique. Don't ever throw anything in this room." How had her father gotten through his entire childhood without breaking it with a baseball or bat or something? For a second she wanted to ask, but she wasn't sure she knew how to talk to her father without hating him.

"Carly."

"What?"

"That's not all it would mean. It would mean that you wouldn't be living with your mother. You might see her only a couple of times a year."

"Uh-huh." She pulled into her blankets, covering her face, familiar in her own smells. A while ago, before they moved, she used to check herself in that place every night for her period. Ashley got it one day when they were at the zoo on a field trip, and Carly was sure any day she would have it and turn into a woman. At least, that's what her mother had told her it meant back when she was ten and they had "the talk." But Carly had forgotten to check lately, and she couldn't do it now with her father on the other side of the blanket. If she got her period, she would really be a woman. She could tell her dad that she didn't want to go with him anywhere or live with him because he didn't want her. Because he didn't want Brooke. He hadn't even gone to the hospital when she mentioned it after dinner. She hated him. She really did.

"Are you paying attention to me?"

"Yeah."

"Come out from under the blankets, please."

Carly pulled her head out and shook back her hair. "What?"

"Do you want to live with me?"

For a second, Carly heard her mother say, "Be nice." She had been so polite to people lately, saying "Thank you" or "Excuse me," the way Grandma Mackenzie especially always wanted. She wasn't like Ryan, who swore and stomped around. But as she looked at her father, she knew he hadn't seen what she had, hadn't taken care of Brooke in so long, didn't know about the hole in her throat. She sat up and hugged her knees. "No. I don't want to live with you. I want to live with Mom and Ryan and Brooke. And you can't make me go down there. Ever."

She tucked her head tight against her body, flinching when she felt his hand on her shoulder. "It won't be so bad," he said, but he was a liar. That's all he'd ever done—lied.

"You said that before when you left the first time. And it was really bad."

Her father didn't say anything, so she looked up over her knees, the smooth thin flannel of her pajamas rubbing against her forehead and nose.

"It was that bad." He wasn't asking a question, but she had to answer him. He couldn't walk around here one more minute without knowing about Brooke and the red spots and her mother under the covers and Ryan in and out and in and out, the dank smell of pot in the air, and only her, only Carly, paying any attention at all.

"Don't you get it?" she said, looking up. "Don't you even see? I had to take care of her. I didn't even know your phone number. I didn't even know what street you lived on!"

"Calm down. Don't yell."

"Why? Why shouldn't I yell? Would you pay attention this time?"

He leaned toward her, his hand out. Even after all he'd done, Carly remembered how it felt to be next to him. How it would feel to let go and move close to him.

"What's going on in here?" Her grandmother pushed open the door, her hair pulled back for sleeping, her lips still red.

"Mom, it's okay. We're just talking." Her father moved back into his chair and then stood up. "I was telling Carly about what will happen."

"Oh. Now isn't that wonderful?" her grandmother said brightly, her teeth white against her lips. "I can't wait to begin having vacations in Arizona. And then who knows? You all may move up here soon."

"Mom."

Her grandmother smoothed imaginary hair off her face and pursed her lips. Carly could see a glint of gray roots at her temples. "In any case, I think it's just the thing. Don't you, Carly?"

"No. I don't," she said, feeling herself empty out and flatten against the mattress as her words hit her grandmother's stare.

"Carly!"

"I don't. I don't at all. I'm not going." She didn't dare look up, but she stared at her grandmother's nightgown, pale gray, shiny, falling in folds at her fluffy slippers. Her mother never looked like that at bedtime. Mostly, she just fell on the bed still wearing the clothes she'd put on in the morning or even the night before, her T-shirt or sweatshirt covered with Brooke's formula and medicines, swishes of red and pink like first-grade fingerpaint.

"Come on, Mom," her father said, moving toward the door. "Don't say no now, Carly. You never know what's going to happen."

He closed the door, and she lay back against the pillow, blinking against the dark until the cowboys on the wallpaper came to life, some whipping their horses with hats, others twirling lassoes, one sleeping with his hat pulled down over his face. That was the one she'd named Jed long ago, the only one on this wall she understood, even though Buster riding after the cow was cuter. Jed knew how to hide, and no one bothered him.

Under the bed, Eustace the cat yawned and scratched on the bottom of the box spring. If she thought about her life, one, two years ago, no one could have convinced her that she'd be sleeping in this bed while her mother was crazy-sick somewhere in Arizona. At least, that's what Fran had said, telling both her and Ryan that their mother had tried to break into their dad's house with her fists. Fran had looked her straight in the eye and said things like *depression* and some kind of *psycho* reaction. She'd also heard her grandpa talking on the phone, repeating phrases like *felony child endangerment*. But before that, no one could have made her even think that her mother, the one who did everything, would have left them alone. So her father was right. You never really knew what was going to happen.

As she felt her body sink into sleep, she realized that his last words were the only ones he'd said the entire afternoon since he'd picked them up at Grandpa's that she believed.

Thirteen

When they stepped off the plane in Oakland on Saturday morning, Peri expected to see armed police officers or men in white scrubs holding a straitjacket, the white wagon from Saturday morning cartoons waiting by the curbside. With the new airport regulations, no one was there waiting for them at the gate, and it wasn't until they passed the security checkpoint that Noel walked up to a plain, neat woman in a red suit.

"Fran. Right? This is Peri," he said, smiling his business smile. "Peri, this is Fran McDermott."

Fran stuck out her hand, and for an instant, Peri wasn't sure what she was supposed to do. She gaped, staring at her own hands like the crazy woman she was, and she flushed red, her whole body steaming in embarrassment.

"Hi," Peri said, pushing her hand out, knowing Fran would see how warm she was.

Fran's handshake was firm, and she pretended not to notice Peri's nervousness. "Hi, Peri. Has Noel explained what's going to happen now?"

Nodding, Peri knew that the cartoon quality of her first vision—the paddy wagon, the men in white suits, the straitjacket, the handcuffs—was just that. This would be an orderly transfer. Fran would give her up to the authorities in Martinez. Peri would be taken in, questioned, fingerprinted, put in a cell, grilled by detectives, psychologists, and probably this woman Fran. Even though she'd acknowledged her guilt and the Phoenix doctor had sent her file to the court, she would be charged and arraigned. She already had a lawyer, someone Noel had hired, a sleek San Francisco man with all the answers. Someone like Graham.

"Okay. Let's get to my car," Fran said as if she were a tour guide instead of a social worker taking an insane woman to jail. *Jail*, Peri thought. *Then what?*

"What about the kids?" Peri said quickly. "Do I get to see them before I go? Do I get to see Brooke?"

Fran turned to her, and Peri ducked her head again, knowing this woman could rightly spit on her if she wanted. How could she, a mother who'd left the very children she now wanted to see, ask for anything? "Later," Fran said. "Not for a day or two at least. And of course, they'll come to you and be supervised the entire time."

"Of course," Peri said. She deserved nothing more, maybe not even that.

Peri had a roommate, a woman who swore under her breath as she moved around the cell. Her name was Sophia, and she jangled as she talked, her hands and jaw like musical instruments that needed constant strumming. "Got any cigarettes?"

"I don't smoke."

"You will," Sophia said, walking into the great room, where other women sat at tables reading or playing cards. Peri watched her move from group to group, never sitting down, touching her hair and shoulders, finally getting a cigarette from a woman who was reading the *Contra Costa Times*. The woman put her pack down on the table, and slid it toward Peri's roommate, then looked up at Peri, and shrugged.

"Mackenzie. Visitor."

Peri almost flinched at the guard's announcement, and stared at the cigarette woman, who cocked her head toward the door. Peri smoothed her hair with nervous hands, stood up, and walked into the great room, nodding slightly at the woman, but she'd already pulled the paper up and hidden her face. A guard stood in front of the open door, looking at the other women as Peri approached.

"Mackenzie?"

"Yeah."

"Follow me." Outside of the room, she was invisible to other eyes. Guards and staff walked past her, knowing what she had done. Here she was, the woman who left her kids and went crazy. Peri kept moving, but all she wanted was to be back in her cell and her bed, needing to hide under the blanket as she had for months, the world a fuzzy noise beyond her.

The guard didn't stop, and Peri stared at the woman's thick rubber-soled bootheels, up and down, up and down, until she was in a room where her father sat at a table. She glanced at the guard, assuming there'd been a mistake. Peri had expected the traditional scene from movies, visitors sitting on one side of a Plexiglas screen, prisoners on the other, all conversation held through black phones. But this? This was almost normal, even though the guard stood right outside the door watching them.

Her father stood up gingerly, as if he had a tennis injury, but as she walked closer to the table, she saw that he was nervous, his hands shaking slightly, his face pale. "Peri? How are you, honey?" He held a hand out and then let it fall to his thigh before she'd had a chance to decide what to do about his offering, the hand she'd ignored for a long time.

"I'm okay. I've talked with Fran and a doctor and my lawyer."

"Ah. That Preston fellow."

"Right." Peri was still stunned by the amount he'd talked, his ideas and papers flowing the entire half hour. She'd wanted to like him—really, she wanted to feel he would save her—but she found herself nodding, staring at his perfectly white teeth, his cleft chin, the blunt ends of his long fingers. He'd answered his own rhetorical questions, patted her on the shoulder, and left, promising her, "This won't be as bad as you think."

"So are you feeling— Do you feel better?"

"Did Noel tell you what the doctors said?"

Her father nodded, and she saw the new pink bald spot on the top of his head, freckled from countless sunny hours of tennis. How old was he now? Sixty-five? Maybe less. For all the years since the divorce, she'd only kept track of her mother's birthdays, and once she died, Peri had forgotten that, too, grateful there was one less thing to remember.

"I'm okay. I just went crazy," she told him plainly, as if she were reporting any old news.

"You're sick, Peri. Not crazy." He nodded as he

talked, pulling out a chair for her, then reseating himself, his clasped hands resting on the table.

She looked down at her own hands, thin, the skin dry. "Whatever it is, I think I've been like this for a long time. But it wasn't until . . ."

"The divorce. Graham."

"Yes." She sighed, rubbing her forehead. "I couldn't hold it together. Every time I thought I had one thing fixed, I'd find something else was wrong."

Her father reached a hand across the table. "Oh, honey, I know there's been some bad blood between us, but you had to know you could call me. You could have gotten me on the phone anytime, and I'd have been there in a second."

His hand was warm, as it always had been. When she was a little girl, she loved it when he picked her up by her wrists and put her on his shoe tops, dancing from the hall into the kitchen, where her mother was making dinner. She used to watch him do the crossword puzzle, asking her mother, "What's a lustrous fabric?" or "What's another word for ripen? Three letters." She'd share his bowl of pretzel sticks and take tiny sips from his martini, begging for the olive with its red pimento middle. Her mother and Noel faded into the background, and it was just her father, his smile, his hands rubbing her hair, handing her a pretzel.

"I know. I should have done a lot of things," Peri said.

"You're better." He nodded again, hopeful.

"I am. I'm on tons of drugs, at least for a while. Dad?"

"What?"

"It wasn't me. It wasn't me at all."

"Honey," he said, moving closer, holding her arm, then shoulder, pulling her head to his shoulder. "I know it wasn't you. It wasn't you at all. You're a good mother. You love those kids. You were at the end of your rope, that's all."

"I left them. I thought I was going to explode. I left them at home. I left Brooke in her bed and she got sick," she wailed, pushing her face against him. "I did it all wrong."

He scooted his chair even closer, and she felt his breath, full of something he wasn't saying. "Don't. Don't say that about yourself. You did your best. You thought you were going to hurt them, so you left. That's brave. Very brave. Now . . . we just have to— We have to wait."

"What do you mean?"

"Shhh . . . shhh . . ." he whispered, holding her tight, patting her with his hands, the same hands from all those years ago. "You didn't mean it. You're better now. You'll get even better. We all make mistakes. Shhh . . ."

"Oh, Dad. I'm so sorry. I'm so sorry," she said, not knowing what she was apologizing for. "But it doesn't matter. They'll take them from me. I don't deserve them. I don't deserve anything. I never have."

"Don't say that. No, no. Don't say that at all. It's not over. I'm taking care of it, my brave girl," he said, and Peri closed her eyes, wanting to believe the promise of his words, choosing to ignore the fear in his voice.

Fourteen

Saturday afternoon, Carly climbed the oak tree in her grandmother's backyard, pulling up on the very branch her father supposedly fell off when he was little, breaking his arm. Maybe she would fall, too, and then all the attention could be on her. And then maybe they'd take her to the hospital, and she could see Brooke. Otherwise, no one would offer to take her today, and Brooke would be lonely all by herself. Maybe Grandpa Carl or Uncle Noel had gone. Her mother couldn't because she was in jail now. Carly wouldn't be able to see her until tomorrow, and that was only a half hour visit in some room with Grandmother Mackenzie there and guards.

Ryan had disappeared, barely finishing his Corn Chex and not even looking at their father, who'd left the house shortly after Ryan did to talk with lawyers. Carly leaned down on the thick branch, hugging it with her thighs, letting the bark dig into her cheek. Closing her eyes, she breathed in the smell of the tree, the dirt and rain and moss that grew like fuzz on the undersides of the branches. When she was at Grandpa Carl's, at least people had paid attention to her. Fran had asked her a lot of questions and so had the doctor who'd wanted to know all about her family. Grandpa and Rosie had made sure to visit Brooke. Now it was like her dad had taken over the show, forgetting that she was the one who had made the hard decisions. She'd taken care of Brooke. She'd gone to get Rosie.

Carly sat up and pushed back, finding the trunk with her feet, gripping with her Keds as she climbed down the tree. Rosie would know how to get her out of this mess. She'd find out about Brooke and her mother. And after the last two months of not knowing where anyone was, Carly had made sure to write Rosie's, Grandpa Carl's, and Uncle Noel's phone numbers down in her notepad. She'd never be lost again.

"What's going on there?" Rosie asked on the phone.

Carly looked around Grandfather Mackenzie's old study, the phone an ancient black thing from the sixties. It even had holes where you put in your fingers and dialed the numbers, just like a baby toy. Somewhere in the house, her grandmother was talking with Maritza about dinner, her impatient heels clacking on the wood floors as she ordered everyone around.

"Ryan took off," Carly said. "I don't know where he went. No one cares. My dad is, like, talking to lawyers. He thinks I'm going to go down and live with him in Arizona."

Rosie sighed and dropped something, a spoon on the counter or a fork in a sink. Carly could almost smell the kitchen she'd been in once, a dark red meat sauce bubbling on the range. "When do you get to see your mom?"

"Not until tomorrow. For, like, a half hour. Then we have to talk with Fran again. That is if we can find Ryan. And no one is talking about Brooke."

"Listen, she's okay. I'll sneak in today to check on her. I know your uncle Noel and grandpa Carl are working really hard on all this. You shouldn't be worrying about it."

"But I'm the one who cared in the first place."

"That's true. But now the so-called adults are taking over. It's what always happens. No one cares and then too many people care, and probably the wrong ones at that. But let me tell you this—no one is going to let anything else bad happen to Brooke."

"Can you come get me? Can I come stay with you?" Carly said, forcing out the ridiculous words. More than anything, she wanted a warm smell and a warm person, and if she were with Rosie, she'd be closer to her apartment and what was left of her mother.

"Listen, if it were up to me, I'd come get you in a heartbeat. No lie there, sweetie. But I'm only an older woman with no real connection to you. Not that I don't care, don't get me wrong. I really do."

Carly nodded, realizing it was true. Maybe they hadn't known Rosie more than a week, but she did care about them. She liked them, even Grandpa Carl. Carly could tell. Rosie had even been nice to Grandma Mackenzie. "I know. But I hate it here. I hate my dad. I don't hate my grandmother, but she's acting totally weird now. Like she knows more than anyone else."

"Too many people with too much to lose, Carly. In a way, your grandma lost your dad when he moved to Arizona. And with him not home and your mom getting sick, she lost you three kids, too. She's fighting for you the same way your grandpa is."

Carly had never imagined her grandmother needing anything other than order and quiet. "You think so?"

"Sure do. Everyone is digging their trenches. But it can't go on forever."

When she was little, forever seemed exactly that; time went on and on and on. Summers used to stretch out in long hot waves of time. But when she suddenly had to wake up to an alarm during the fall of her seventh grade year, time was cut in pieces, measurable chunks in periods, semesters, months. Forever became a dream. Now she wanted someone to tell her, "This will all be settled in exactly two months and one day," or something like that. No one—not even Rosie—seemed to know anything. "Okay."

"Don't give up. I'll call your grandpa and find out the latest. Try to give me a ring tomorrow. I have to work during the day, but I'll be home in the evening. And then you can tell me what it was like to see your mom. Just remember that it's going to be weird. She's in a jail. Don't let the setting scare you. She's still your mom."

"I know," she said, but she wasn't sure if she really meant it. A mom didn't leave. A mom didn't leave a child like Brooke. "Bye, Rosie. Thanks."

"Bye, sweetie."

As she hung up, she looked out the window at the tree, and there was Ryan, sitting on the same branch she'd clung to earlier, smoking a cigarette, not caring who saw. But no one except Carly did see, and she watched him until he'd finished and smashed the butt on the branch, flicking it toward the house and then lighting another one.

* * *

After a ton of phone calls that Carly pretended not to listen to, and a huge miracle, Grandpa Carl ended up picking both Ryan and her up on Sunday afternoon. Grandma Mackenzie had combed her hair like she was six again, but because Carly knew her grandpa was coming, she let her, even tolerating the purple barrette her grandma clipped in her hair.

Ryan combed his own hair, parting it the way he used to a couple of years before, and they both sat in the living room by the picture window, waiting, their father pacing in the entryway.

"I don't like this, Mom. I don't see why we can't take them. I don't think they should see her the way she is. You know—strung out."

"Graham, we've already gone over this. And not here." She pulled him into the kitchen, and Carly listened not to the words but to the inflections, waiting to see who would get mad first and if the anger would change anything. She tried not to breathe, hoping the moments would pass, and then as if in her imagination, the Corvair rumbled and hummed up the hill. Grandpa tapped out a honk, once, twice, and before Grandma Mackenzie or her father could do any more than say good-bye, they were out the front door.

Grandpa had put the top down, and Carly sat in the backseat. After a couple of windy miles, her Grandma-ed hair flipped up and out of the barrette, the smooth spring air pushing at her face. Grandpa Carl had the radio on the same oldies channel, and when she closed her eyes, it was three, four, five years ago, and he was taking her to Tilden Park to ride the little trains or to the merry-go-round. Ryan was with them, talking about soccer, and Brooke was home in Monte Veda, Leon giving her a workout on the big rubber ball. Her mother and father were drinking coffee at the kitchen table, and nothing at all was wrong anywhere.

They were silent the whole way to the jail—all of them pretending to listen to the Hotel California song. When they finally arrived, Carly's body was full of swirling wind and air, her head buzzing as she slid out of the back and closed the door. The parking lot was almost deserted, and downtown Martinez was quiet except for a few cars and people on bicycles swooshing by. Right now, she guessed that no one thought she was a girl going to see her mother in jail. Maybe they thought she was a girl going shopping with her grandfather and brother, a typical Sunday thing to do. Or maybe it all showed, the terrible things that had happened in the past year like writing on her back, the words spelled out in glitter pen on her shirt: *I'm a girl whose mother went crazy. I'm a girl whose parents don't care.*

"Come on, guys. Here we go," Grandpa Carl said, and he did know the way because he'd come here yesterday. He knew what to expect because he'd seen Mom already. When they first got in the car, he had told them both, "She's better. She really is. She'll be more like the mom you remember."

Carly and Ryan followed behind Grandpa, letting him lead the way past security devices and guards. Carly closed her eyes as a woman guard whisked a wand over her body, thinking of the cartoons and comedies she'd watched where an enormous file or gun was hidden in a cake. Did they really think she would do that? Did they really think she would try to get her mother in more trouble after all of this? Carly wanted to catch the woman's eyes to tell her it was better her mother was in jail than wandering the streets or driving to another state in the Honda, but the guard was all business, and soon Carly was waiting for another guard to finish with Grandpa Carl.

After doors opened and shut behind them once, twice, they were in a room with a door on the other side and windows in a row. There were empty tables and chairs pulled away from them, evidence that another visiting family had just left.

Carly pressed her hands flat against the new jeans Grandma Mackenzie had bought her at Macy's. She wondered what it would be like to have two "different" people in her family—Brooke and now her mom. She'd gotten used to having Brooke, knowing that some girls wouldn't want to be her friend, as if what Brooke had was contagious. Her friends would be grossed out by the way Brooke's body twisted and by the strange way she had to be fed, so Carly didn't talk about her, and no one ever asked to see Brooke. Once, even before the divorce, she'd found her mother crying, the telephone in her hands. When her mother had seen Carly, she'd stood up, wiped her eyes, and hung up the phone, saying only, "When it comes down to it, Carly, some people aren't really friends." Carly expected the looks strangers gave them as they took Brooke places, especially after her father left and her mother had to carry her into appointments. She saw the "Poor family" and the "What's wrong with the kid?" in their eyes. Worse was "How disgusting!" and "They should keep her inside," when her mother took Brooke to the swimming pool or the movies.

But now her mother was strange in her own way,

locked up in this concrete building, guards at every door and window, everyone stern and focused, knowing that they kept the good people safe from the bad. Carly knew the newspapers had gotten hold of the story because Grandma Mackenzie had grabbed the Metro section before Carly could look at it, saying, "Maritza, take this to the recycling."

Carly sighed, and then looked up. What happened next was like a movie, her eyes the camera, her body somewhere behind it. Her mother walked down the hall beyond the row of windows, step by step coming closer to the door. In front of her was a woman guard, who wouldn't know that this was the very first time Carly or Ryan had seen their mother since she'd run away. If she did, maybe the guard would be whispering to her mother, telling her the right things to say and do, which would make Carly feel better, like there was a plan to all of this. *What do you say to your mom after she abandoned you?* Carly wondered. How could she ever say she understood?

The heavy door opened and closed with a whish of air, the sound of the lock a metal echo that seemed to rattle the empty tables and chairs. The guard stood just outside the door, looking in but probably not really seeing anything, probably thinking about her real life.

Carly's heart was pounding, but she couldn't do it, couldn't look at her mother. Ryan wasn't looking either, his skateboard shoes sliding back and forth over the dust on the linoleum. There was movement she felt with her shoulders and legs, and her grandpa was standing, his arms around her mother. Carly felt her mother's sadness, the same heavy air that had hung in the bedroom for two months. But still she couldn't look up, and she reached out for Ryan, who seemed to have been searching for her at the same time, and they held hands while their mother cried into Grandpa's shoulder.

Then there was a pause, the space before something had to happen, like just after something bad happened, awaiting the punishment that would follow—a slap on the playground and the time it took for so-and-so to get the teacher or the yard duty. Anything could happen then. She and Ryan could get up, beg the guard to open the door, and walk into the parking lot, a place where their mother couldn't go. Nothing had been said yet. Nothing was changed. But any second her mother would say something and it was sure to make everything worse, and they all should go now, now, now.

"Carly? Ryan?" her mother said, and Carly sucked in a breath. It was too late. She moved her head up toward her mother, who was standing in front of her and then kneeling down. She had to force her eyes to look at her mother's face. And it hurt, all the muscles in her cheeks and forehead not wanting this, this look at a new, terrible mother.

Her mother smelled different, wrong, like the soap in the girls' bathroom at school, pink and grainy, the paper towels brown and rough. Her skin was blotchy, red and white, her pupils huge, floating in a shimmer of tears, her hair flat and stringy against her head. Her body was hidden in ugly orange clothes, and she held one arm close to her body.

Grandpa Carl was wrong. This wasn't the mom she remembered. This wasn't her mom at all. This was some Peri Mackenzie put together by someone else, a Frankenstein mom someone was trying to pass off as hers. This was the woman who had done all those crazy things in Arizona and who had left Brooke. Her real mom was somewhere else, maybe in the jail still or, even better, far, far away on vacation in Maui, a place they all loved.

Then this fake mom turned her head slightly and smiled wide, none of her teeth showing, stars of lines at her eyes, and Carly shook her head. It was mom. This was her mom's smile, the smile that even Brooke could mimic. They all used to sit around her bed and say, "How does Mom smile?" and Brooke would tilt her head and break into as big a quiet smile as she could, not one tooth showing.

"Mom?" Carly asked, making sure.

"Yes."

Carly glanced at Ryan, who was looking up now, too. He knew it was Mom, the one who had left them for real. So much was going on in her body, Carly wasn't sure what to do. Her fingers tingled, and her thigh muscles burned. Inside, her stomach was full of bubbles and even lower, something was churning away. She had to go to the bathroom. She squeezed herself shut, but whatever it was wasn't going to wait.

"I have to go. I have to go now," she said, turning to Grandpa Carl.

"We just got here."

"The bathroom."

"Oh," he said, standing up, looking at the guard behind them, who had already opened the door.

Carly stood up, clutching her stomach, and ran toward the guard, who motioned to another guard down the hall. Hearing her grandpa behind her, she ran, all her feelings pressing against her guts like spikes, scraping down her body, desperate to get out. She wouldn't make it, she knew, not in time, but the guard held the door open, and she rushed in, ripping the button off her new jeans as she pushed them down and sat on the toilet. It came fast, but it took forever, so much locked inside her. Would she ever be able to stand up again, weak and jittery after the waves pulsing out of her body?

She must have fallen asleep for a minute, her forehead on her knees, sweat in her eyes. She sat up and flushed the toilet, not sure if she was done; then she heard the door open a crack.

"Carly?" Her grandpa sounded scared, as if she'd fallen in and disappeared.

"Don't come in!" she said, breathing in to test the air. This was so embarrassing. Things like this never happened when you were safe at home, but always at a Burger King or a park or at a skating party. Now all the guards would remember her as the girl who sat on the toilet for an hour.

"Are you okay?"

"I think so."

"Is it— Is it a female thing?"

Carly hadn't even checked, not paying attention for weeks and weeks, but this had definitely not been that end. She wasn't a woman yet. That's why she had to run like a baby down the hall. "No. It's my stomach. I feel better. I'll be out in a minute, okay? Close the door."

Her grandpa almost said something and then didn't, the door clicking softly against its frame. She wiped herself and flushed the toilet again. This time, she didn't tuck in her shirt but pulled it over her waist to hide the missing button. Grandma Mackenzie would be irritated with her if she didn't look for it in the corners of the white bathroom, but all she wanted to do was wash her hands and get out of this building forever.

When she walked out, the guard smiled at her. Grandpa nodded at the guard and then put his arm around her shoulders. "Are you all right?"

"Can we go now? Can we just go?"

"Don't you want to talk with your mother?"

If the woman in there was some sort of fake mom, an impostor, well, Carly could go in and say anything she wanted to. But it was her real mother, the one who had sung her "Good Morning, Sunshine" and read her *I'll Love You Forever* and *The Giving Tree* at bedtimes.

How could she tell her grandfather that for the past few months, she'd pretended that another woman had taken her real mom's place, and that it was so much easier to hate that woman? But how could she hate her mom? And how could she tell him that she did? She hated her mom and her dad. She didn't ever want to see them again. All she wanted was to go to Rosie Candelero's apartment and sit in her kitchen, eating a bowl of something warm, something that filled her up. Grandpa and Ryan and Brooke could come with her. But no one else. Not ever.

"No. I want to go home." She meant Monte Veda and her own room, her shelf of books and CDs, her friends, Maxie the Wonder Dog playing in the backyard with an old tennis ball, her father laughing, Leon making Brooke giggle. But it was all gone, like a delicious dream. "I mean, I want to go back to your house."

"Carly, you know you have to go back with your dad. It's not my call. You know I'd have you in a second."

"I don't care. I'm not going back there, and I'm not

going to talk to that—that person. I'm leaving." She turned left down the hall toward the entrance.

"Wait. Let me tell your mother what's going on."

Carly stopped and looked back at her grandfather. "Don't call her that. Don't say that again. She's not my mother anymore."

Fifteen

After the visit with her father and children, Peri let herself be led back to her cell, ignoring the looks of the other women as she floated by. Her body was numb with what had happened (or hadn't happened really) and the drugs she'd taken earlier. All she wanted was sleep. That's what had worked before—pulling the blankets over her head and drifting into the place between wakefulness and dream, where noises from the real world entered her head and were twisted into imagination. A place where Peri didn't have to do anything.

But once she lay down on her cot, she realized that plan wouldn't work here. The blanket was scratchy, rough, worn, the fluorescent light on, the din from the outer room rocketing into her cell and pulsing around the small rectangle. Peri heard every card slapped down on the Formica-topped tables, every female voice talking about lovers and children and the "shit they were in." And Sophia—her legs dangling from the cot above her, her scabby ankles and hairy shins swinging back and forth, back and forth like a pendulum in a body-care nightmare—blew smoke up toward the light, the blue-gray plumes sinking and sliding over Peri.

For maybe one, two minutes, she closed her eyes, but all she saw was Carly running toward the door, her arm around her stomach, her father's shrug and quick retreat. Then there was Ryan looking at her with Graham's eyes, waiting for her to say something that would fix everything. But she hadn't had anything wise to say. For a long time, all she could do was put her hand on his arm, feeling how his boy bones had changed into a man's. When had that happened? When had the hair pushed out of his chin? When had his voice grated into an uneven version of Graham's? He couldn't have transformed so completely in the week she had been gone, so she simply had not noticed. Or cared. While she was tending to Brooke and herself, a slave to her and her child's pain, everyone else had gone away. She had probably missed more than Ryan's puberty—what about Carly? Had her breasts grown into the bras she'd bought her? Had her period come? And what about herself? Unlike her children, she hadn't changed at all, simply gone backward, inward, away from everything that mattered.

"So what went down in there?" Sophia asked. For a second, her eyes still closed, Peri imagined her cellmate was asking about inside her body. Once she realized Sophia was talking about the meeting, her answer was the same.

"Not much."

Sophia jumped to the floor and sat on the toilet, crossing her legs and grabbing her elbow with one hand, her cigarette elegant in the other. In any other place, in any other clothing, Sophia—with her long blond hair

and full lips—might have looked sophisticated. Peri
blinked once, twice, and then rolled on her side, prop-
ping her head with her hand. There was a time when
someone smoking next to her made her sneer and mention sotto voce the California law prohibiting it in a
public place. She would have raised her eyebrows and
whispered in Graham's ear something about ignorance,
and he would have agreed, as he had with most everything she'd said until . . . until Brooke.

"Whadaja do?"

"Excuse me?" Peri asked, confused.

"To get here. In this place." Sophia whirled her cigarette around the room and then took another drag.

Peri flipped on her back and stared at the cot slats
above her. What didn't she do? "I—I went crazy and left
my kids at home and drove to Phoenix where I broke
into my ex's house and almost killed myself doing so."

Sophia nodded, as if this was something she was used
to hearing or even something she had done. "What kind
of crazy?"

"I thought I was going to explode and kill people.
Like I was filled with terrible chemicals or gas or something, and I would bust open and throw my kids around.
The doctors said it was a psychotic episode. I'm on an
antipsychotic drug right now." The truth felt good on
her tongue, a flavor she hadn't tasted lately.

"That shit is horrible. They gave it to me once and I
had this reaction. I couldn't stop staring at the ceiling
and my toes and fingers, like, curled. My sister thought
I was flipping out or something."

Peri turned back to Sophia, watched her smoke and
flick ashes on the floor. "Why are you here?" she asked.

Sophia stared at her a moment, their conversation

frozen in the cell air, and as she exhaled the dark cloud of her story, Peri heard something rattle in her cellmate's chest, a bad cold, flu, TB. "I was smoking crack and didn't notice I was having a baby."

Revulsion curled in her chest, and she wanted to get up and walk out to the tables in the great room, asking to be dealt in. No wonder Sophia stayed mainly in here or fluttered around the edges of the group, bumming cigarettes. But then the truth that had just felt so good pushed its hard steel line into her brain. She was the same as Sophia. She forgot to notice her own children, children who had been alive for years. She had left a five-year-old with MD and CP in her bed. For almost two months, she hadn't taken Brooke out of her bed. No appointments. No occupational therapy. No physical therapy. No music. No mother, really. She'd stopped touching her, stopped turning her as often as she should have. And when she couldn't ignore the letters and calls from the school and the clinic anymore, Peri had moved so no one would bother them. My God. What had she been trying to do? Had she wanted Brooke to die so she herself could go back to her old life? Did she imagine that without Brooke, everything would be fine? She was no different than this drug-addicted woman sitting on the toilet in front of her. She couldn't whisper into someone's ear about the wastefulness of a drugged-out life, turning to her loving husband with a superior look in her eyes. There were no blankets big enough to hide her anymore.

"So we did kind of the same thing," she said finally, sitting up, hunching a bit between the cots.

Sophia smiled. "We did?"

"Well, yeah. I left— I abandoned my children."

"You said that already."

"Right. But one of them was . . . is bed-ridden. She has cerebral palsy and muscular dystrophy. I just left her there in her bed."

"Man. At least I didn't even know I was pregnant."

Peri made a sound that almost sounded like a laugh and shook her head. "At least."

"But you were crazy. That's different. You didn't make yourself become crazy. I took those drugs on purpose. I needed them. Your brain just got fucked up. But, man, you're never going to get those kids back."

Sophia stood up and threw her cigarette in the toilet. "You better think of what to say on Monday during that arraignment. Me, well, I said all the wrong things, and I'm still here on no bail. I'm a danger to the community and all my unborn children. Like I'm going to find me a big ol' dick the minute I get out there and get knocked up. I'm going to find me a big ol' rock of crack. . . . Well, that's probably true. But you watch it. You try to make them believe what you have to say."

Sophia stepped out of the cell and did her figure-eight loop around the tables, touching a hand of cards, slipping a cigarette out of a player's pack. Peri lay back down on the cot and closed her eyes. Behind her lids, Sophia writhed on the filthy floor of a crack house, a baby between her legs, the bright blue of the crack pipe the only light in the room. As Peri slowly fell asleep, the baby turned into Brooke, and Brooke twisted on the floor, surrounded by beer cans and syringes, moaning, "Ma! Ma! Da a u Ma?"

"What about Graham?" Noel asked Kieran Preston as they sat in the meeting room in the jail. "What about what he did? Or didn't do?" It was Monday afternoon, an hour before Peri was to be taken to the cell below the courtroom to await her arraignment. She was glad Noel had driven in from the city to be with her for this. She'd never understood anything legal. Once, she thought she'd be a teacher, and she majored in liberal studies, learning how to play a musical scale and spell out words phonetically and understand the chemistry of wine. The law was, then and now, something only for TV and the newspaper, where writers reduced it to its essential parts.

"Listen," Preston said. "We have three things going on here, but today's arraignment has nothing to do with Graham yet. Trust me, he will factor in during the custody battle."

Peri looked up. Preston opened his briefcase and pulled out a few papers, nodding as Noel asked him a question. Peri saw that Preston didn't even realize he'd said the word *battle*. He knew they were going to have to fight hard. And she would lose the kids. She knew it.

"Right, right . . . So let's deal with what is before us. First is the felony charge of child endangerment. That's what today is about. I'm working on getting the charge reduced to a lesser one, but today I have to get you out on bail. It's possible that the judge might want you to go to a facility for observation."

"What?" Noel asked. "She's already been in a hospital. Observed for days. And then she's been here. What more can he want?"

Preston leaned back in the metal chair, smoothing his hair away from his forehead. In another lifetime, she would have appreciated his tan skin and blue eyes. She'd always been a sucker for eyes that color, light and translucent and full of ocean. Like Graham's. Like Graham's eyes.

"We're pleading not guilty, Noel. By reason of insanity. It's documented. The judge has the option of wanting her at a facility. But I'm going to press for living with your father and seeing a psychiatrist, daily if necessary. I think it will fly. All the documentation from Phoenix supports it. Depression with a psychotic episode. Temporary. Fine on the drugs. Remorseful. No future threat. All that."

"But what about Graham?" Noel asked. "He's going to get the kids."

"Now wait. Hold on. The felony charge is the first item. We've also got the complaint and the petition filed by Graham's lawyers for custody removal from the home. That's number two. A court officer has made a request for removal. The kids actually are removed already, and that's why they are with Peri's ex-husband right now. The problem we have is that one and two are all mixed up. To remove kids permanently from a home on child endangerment charges, the court has to prove one of a few grounds. The truth is . . ." Preston trailed off and sighed. Peri knew that meant she had already proven those grounds, destroying everything as she slid into fear. What hadn't she done in the time since Graham had said good-bye?

"The truth is that the court can prove a number of them: abandonment, desertion, imminent danger, mental illness. It's not going to be easy for us to fight back from that. It's not impossible, but it's going to be dicey."

"So I've lost them?" Peri asked, knowing the answer already. She'd seen it in Carly's eyes yesterday. Even if she could get them back, her daughter had left her behind.

"Not yet." Preston cleared his throat. "So let's move to number three, the custody battle."

There's that word again, she thought.

"They're related. They're all connected," Noel interrupted.

"Yes, of course. But the juvenile court oversees this case."

"Now we can finally talk about Graham," Noel said. "I e-mailed you the timeline of his actions."

"I received that."

"So?"

"He's a deadbeat dad, no question."

"And?"

"He's petitioned for custody. The court appointed a guardian ad litem, whose role is to advocate for the children. There's also an investigation going on to see what's in the best interest of the children."

Peri sat up. "He doesn't want Brooke. He doesn't want what's in her best interest. He'll put her in a home because he can't stand looking at her."

"Could you?" Preston asked. "Isn't that why you left?"

"Preston! Seriously!" Noel said loudly.

"Noel, I know this is hard. But we've got to get real here. That's what the prosecutor will ask. That's what the judge will want to know."

Peri looked at her hands, thin and white and ringless. *These hands could belong to anyone*, she thought, *but they belong to me, a mother who left*.

"She was sick. Mental illness is just that. An illness." Noel slammed his hand on the table and pushed back in his chair, crossing his legs. "And doesn't anyone want to know how California Children's Services could have allowed this to happen? What about Brooke's nursing case manager?"

Preston shook his head. "Look, dragging an underfunded state agency into this right now isn't going to help us. Plain and simple, parents have the final responsibility for their children."

"But should they be responsible?" Noel asked. "Totally? Always?"

"Not always. We could take that tack," Preston said softly, nodding. "Right now the court is looking to put the children in the home that will be in their best interests. Think of those words: best interest. And they won't want to separate them. We've got that in our favor. Right now, Peri, you don't have a home that can support them. Graham does, and he can swear up and down he's going to keep Brooke with him and later move her into a facility. I can argue that, even with Graham, Brooke is a child in need of protection or services. But let's stop speculating. The arraignment is today. With luck, you are going to be out of jail by this evening. You'll stay with your dad, go to the doctor, get well. The investigation will go on, and I'll keep at it. After today, nothing is going to happen fast, that's for sure."

"Will I see them again?" Peri asked. "Can I see them? Can I visit Brooke?"

Preston's eyes were steady and kind. He was a man like any other, not a slick person with all the answers, simply a man who understood complaints and petitions and statutes, and had answered her brother's phone call. Said yes. Taken the case.

"We'll have a custody hearing soon to establish visitation. It will probably be supervised, but yes, you will see them again. We'll get you to the hospital to see

Brooke. But you have to be patient. The court was very lenient with you. They could have had you arrested and then extradited. You walked yourself in here without a police officer."

"I know."

"So your depression and the situation with your family took months, years, to happen. It's not going to be patched up in a matter of weeks. Now that the court is in charge, it's going to take time to fix. You need to go home and get better. See the doctor. Take your meds. Visit your kids."

She nodded and folded her arms, listening to Preston and Noel talk more about doctor and detective reports, supervised visits, judicial actions. All she could do was hold this moment to her like a blanket, clutch it as it slipped away. There wasn't any use looking at tomorrow or the next day or month or year, since everything that happened to her and her children would be decided by other people. *Oh, I was so stupid*, she thought. *I made some horrible decisions, even though I thought they were good ones at the time.*

Preston was right. She hadn't wanted to see Brooke anymore. She deserved nothing, not even to get out of this jail and go home to live with her father. She deserved what Brooke had, a twisted body, bedsores, pneumonia. If some judge could order that, then the world would be set to biblical rights, an eye for an eye, a tooth for a tooth.

"Peri!" Preston said.

"What?"

"Time to go. Remember. Be patient."

The guard led her away from Noel and Preston, her county clothes hanging on her like guilt. She would

never be able to forget Preston's words, not one, even if
she tried.

She sat in her father's Corvair, clutching a white
paper bag full of medicine. She wished she had a hair
elastic, but then her hair was already such a mess, no
amount of wind was going to matter. And the air felt
good on her body, pushing away Sophia's cigarette
smoke that still smothered her like a body sock. Even in
the jeans she'd worn to Phoenix and the blouse Noel
had bought for her there, she felt almost new. Almost
free. As if when the judge had set the bail at thirty thousand and hit the gavel, she'd been released.

"So," her dad said, his voice carried up and out of the
car. He had one hand on the steering wheel, the other
resting in his lap. With his Ray-Bans and his baseball
cap, her father could be driving her to high school, college orientation, both of them transported back fifteen,
twenty years, except for the fact that she was here next
to him, all grown up, arraigned on felony child endangerment charges, penal code 273a. In her cell, there had
been words to describe her condition—*psychotic*, *depressed*, *abuser*—but not until today in the courtroom
did she know there was a number for her mistakes. If
there was a number for what she'd done, it was real, on-
paper real, punishable. Peri could still see the look in
the judge's eye as he read the charge aloud.

"So," her dad said again, "how do you feel?"

Peri breathed in and was about to answer him, but
then they were in the Caldecott Tunnel, the car noise a
drum against her ears. She looked into her lap where
she held the drugs tight. These were her sanity now. She
couldn't let these get away, or she might jump in a

car, drive down to Phoenix, break another window or worse.

Her father pulled into his driveway but didn't open the garage door. He shut off the engine and got out of the car, hurrying over to her side to let her out. She tried to smile, but her body felt full of jitters. All she wanted was to go inside and fall asleep, let the sleepy side effects of the drugs take over and get her out of here, for now.

"You haven't been here in a long time. I thought I'd show you the work I've done in the yard."

"Okay," Peri said, holding the bag, letting her father take her arm as they walked the lawn. The sun was too bright, the flowers too loud, but she nodded through his discussion of the foul oxalis weeds and evil crabgrass, managed to "Ohh" over the Boston ivy climbing the south wall of the house, the snowball shrub on the white picket fence. Now he had a white picket fence? Wasn't this what she had given her Barbies in her imaginary play, a white picket fence and a lawn for croquet games and picnics? Did he really think everything could be perfect and controlled—a weed, a lawn, a fence? He'd never worked at controlling or managing her or Noel once he left. Or even when he'd been there. Yards were so much easier to handle than children, and as she looked around, she could see her father's care in every plant and stepping stone and fence slat, all his love poured here. Peri bit her lip, trying not to feel the ache of sobs under her ribs.

When she was a child, he'd been like a special, late-night movie that she was lucky to catch, and then the show was shut down forever. How come he developed into a homebody now, when it was too late? Too late.

"Oh, Mr. Randall?"

Her father sighed and then turned to the corner of the yard where a blond woman in a white gardening apron stood, holding a basket full of daisies. "Yes, Mrs. Trimble?"

"This wouldn't be your daughter, would it?"

Mrs. Trimble smiled at her. Peri's body loosened, and she pulled away from her father, answering for herself. "Yes. Hi. I'm Peri Mackenzie."

"I'm Louise Trimble. I brought these for you." She raised the basket, and Peri walked over to her, clutching her crumpled bag of medicine to her chest.

"I've met your children, you know. Very confident children."

Peri held out her hands and took up the daisies, yellow with long green stems and white eyes. "Lovely."

"My yard has gone wild with this heat. So unusual for this time of year. But look at the bounty!" Louise smiled and patted Peri's arm. "You're lucky to have such a wonderful father."

Peri looked back at her dad, who was kicking at an imaginary dandelion in the lawn. "Oh."

"He took care of those kids of yours. I heard a lot of laughter."

"Oh. Well. Thanks for the flowers."

Louise smiled, and Peri looked into her eyes, light brown and full of green, the perfect eyes for a gardener. "Good luck to you," Louise said, lifting a gloved hand and disappearing into the deep green of rhododendron bushes. Peri turned to her father, who shrugged.

"Don't ask me."

She started to smile, but then remembered that this was what he'd always been good at—charming women,

all women, secretaries, schoolmates' mothers, col-
leagues. She could still feel the flush of embarrassment
when she'd watched him talk to her very best friend
Tina's mother at sixth-grade open house. One hand on
her sleeve, his earnest nod, his lips turning up in a smile.
Tina had said, "Look. Your dad is talking to my mom!"
And Peri had known what this meant to Tina and her
divorced mom. Her father's moving in toward Tina's
mom as if with interest, his jaunty hand on his suited
hip, was a promise that both Tina and her mother would
now expect to be fulfilled. She didn't blame them for it
either. She wanted the same thing. But he wouldn't
keep the promise. He'd forget Tina's mother's name on
the ride home and turn to Peri, asking "Who?"

Mrs. Trimble's eager greeting proved that nothing
had changed at all.

Her dad had made up the bed in the same room Carly
had slept in, and Peri wished he hadn't changed the
sheets, wanting to bend down and smell her girl, breathe
in what Carly had denied her during their visit. She ran
her hand over the bedspread, and then stood up and
walked down the hall to the study where Ryan had
slept. But no, the hideaway bed had been converted
back to a sofa, pillows fluffed, blankets folded and put
away in the closet. If she wanted her children, she had
to behave. She had to get well. Or sneak out of the
house and hike to Garnet's late at night, peer into windows, slip through open doors. But that was the exact
behavior that had gotten her here, back with her father,
lost to her own life.

In the kitchen, her father was just hanging up the
phone. "Guess what? I've been able to arrange a visit

with Brooke. Day after tomorrow. Of course, Fran will be with you in the room, but you'll get to see Brooke. And Fran is going to work on setting up another visit with Ryan and Carly. It will probably have to be at her office, though. Or on some neutral ground."

Peri sat down, jittery again. "Thanks."

"And tomorrow you start your visits with the doctor. The psychiatrist. Once a day, really."

"Okay."

He sat down at the table with her, and put a hand on her arm. "Keep that steady strain. Or as a buddy of mine up at the tennis courts says, 'One day at a time.' He's usually talking about winning tennis games, but it's a good point. Let's just do one day at a time."

Peri pulled her arm back and stared at him. "What do you think I've been doing for five years?"

"What?"

"With Brooke. One day at a time. That's all I could see, and then I couldn't even see the day. A minute was too much to look at."

"Oh, Peri. I'm so sorry."

"Are you? Why didn't you try to find me earlier? Why did you have to wait until Noel called? He told me how it all happened."

Her father stood up and walked to the refrigerator, opening the door, yellow light illuminating his wrinkles. *There*, she thought. *He looks his age.* He took out a carton of orange juice and poured them each a glass, bringing them back to the table.

"I think about that all the time now. I don't know. I guess I was scared. You were so angry with me. After Graham left, it was like you brought out all that old stuff and laid it on the table."

"You're still the same." Peri shook her head, her hair in front of her eyes.

"What do you mean?"

"It's not old stuff."

Carl raised his eyebrows and gripped his glass. "It was thirty-one years ago, Peri."

"You're still scared to talk about it. You never talked about it."

Her father held his glass, spinning the juice in circle waves. He nodded but didn't say anything.

"Why weren't you around more?" she asked, looking at him now.

"I told you. You were so angry with me."

"No. No. I mean before. I mean when you left Mom."

"Oh, Peri. Like I said, that's water long under the bridge."

"Not to me. Not to me it isn't. It's right now. All of this. It's all the same thing."

Her father glanced up, the color drained from his face. "You're not blaming me for—for this, are you?"

"For the first part. For what you did to Mom. But I'm just like you. I learned how to leave." She folded her arms on the table and brought her head down, her cheek resting on her hand. *Close your eyes*, she thought. *Close them and it will all disappear*. But she didn't close them, listening instead to her father running his hands through his hair, tapping his feet on the floor, sliding the glass back and forth on the table.

"Maybe you did," he said finally.

Peri leaned her head against her palm, watching him. "Why did you go? What did she do that was so wrong? What did we do?"

"You did nothing. Your mother didn't really either.

We were just married too fast, too young, too early. I didn't know— I didn't know the difference between love and, well, lust. The next thing I knew we were married and then you came along, and I had a job and then another kid. There was my life, all charted out forever. Your mom could see I felt that way, and she fought back, and I decided I didn't need any of it. So I sacrificed you and Noel for myself. I did. I did." He placed his hands on the tabletop, fingers spread wide. "I've regretted leaving you two since, but I haven't regretted leaving that life. And I can't apologize because I wouldn't mean it, Peri. I didn't want that life."

"You didn't want us."

He swallowed. "Maybe so. Maybe so. But I do now. I want you now. I want the kids."

Outside, four small birds chattered and fought over rungs on a birdfeeder, and Peri watched them peck each other and then rearrange themselves. There was some perfect order they were trying to find, and they battled for it, a bird squawking periodically over something lost. A car drove by too fast, and they flickered away, the feeder rocking back and forth, empty.

She'd always known that what her father said was true, but the air felt smoother now that he'd admitted it. The hate she'd built up since Graham had left settled, stopped rising, still visible and deep, but calm. "I know you want us, the kids and me. I'm glad. Thanks."

He almost jerked at her words but then leaned forward and touched her softly, moving a warm hand down her arm and grabbing her hand. "If I can make it up, I will. But for us, it's like with this trial. One day at a time, like Ramon says. Stupid, but the way it is. Just like it was with Brooke."

Peri nodded and her father stood up and took a casserole dish out of the fridge. "Looky here. I've made us dinner. Believe it or not, it's your mother's old Frito and chili bean casserole."

Peri stared at him, smiled, and then laughed, the sound punching her solar plexus. The hum of anxiety in her chest thinned and disappeared, turning to relief and space, this one minute clear and wide open.

Sixteen

On the way to visit Brooke at the hospital Wednesday morning, Peri didn't say a word. Carl kept his eyes on the road, his thighs tense, sighing deeply as the moments passed and Peri made no sound. What would he do if she were having a relapse into her depression or whatever it had been? Carl didn't have much experience with tending to kids, much less a depressed adult, and he wished he'd made an appointment for himself with Dr. Kolakowski to ask how. When Peri and Noel were little, Janice took care of all their ailments, colds and flu and whatnot. There had to be a protocol of some sort for depression, a way of talking to a person who was falling into that dark pit. As he drove, he sneaked peeks at Peri, expecting his daughter to laugh weirdly or pull at her hair, but she was only silent, her arms crossed over her body, her eyes on the freeway ahead of them.

In the hospital parking lot, he shut off the engine and turned his body toward her, his jeans sliding easily on the smooth leather, and hooked his arm over the seat back. "Peri, are you ready for this? You don't have to do it right now."

She closed her eyes. "I have to do it now. I should have done it before. I should have always done it. I can't leave her alone one more day in that place."

"She's doing great. Rosie's been there to see her as often as possible. Garnet even called to tell me how well she's doing."

"Has Graham seen her?" Peri's eyes widened.

Carl shook his head. "No. No he hasn't."

"Who's Rosie again?"

"Rosie? Your neighbor— Oh, well, she's the one I told you about. The woman who found the kids. Who called the ambulance?"

Peri shook her head and sighed, running one hand through her hair, which was still damp from her shower. "Oh yeah. The one who saved my kids. From me. She must be something."

"She's a nurse. She really likes the kids, too."

Peri almost smiled. "Yeah. Likes the *kids*."

Carl looked at her tentatively, expecting her to rehash the conversation they'd had a couple of days ago about why he left Janice. Peri thought he was some sort of woman magnet, and maybe he was in a superficial way, a first date kind of way, all sorts of gals jostling around him. But after a while, the crowd would thin and then disappear altogether. He was alone, wasn't he? He was trying to rustle up a date at the bridge center, for Christ's sake. Carl didn't have what it took to keep anyone. The only woman who stayed with him was Mrs. Trimble, Louise, and that was because she lived next door. If she had a mobile home, who knew?

"Come on, let's go see Brooke. She's going to be flat-out thrilled to see you." He opened his door and swung a leg out.

"Dad?"

"What?" he said, looking at Peri hunched up in the corner of the seat.

"Oh, nothing. Let's go."

"Good girl." Carl reached out a hand and squeezed her softly, holding on until she pushed on the handle and opened the door.

Two doctors and Fran met them by the nurses' station. He hoped Peri didn't notice how the doctors eyed her, judgment in their expressions, but Fran moved toward her and took her hand.

"It's good you're here, Peri. I've told Brooke about your visit, and she is very excited."

"How is she?" Peri asked quietly, avoiding the doctors' faces.

The female doctor, whose name Carl had already forgotten, cleared her throat. "The pneumonia is completely out of her chest, but we've been using the ventilator at night. That will have to continue indefinitely. She has another five days or so of antibiotics. Her weight is up significantly."

Carl saw Peri flush and her eyes fill and then overflow. She brushed at her cheeks and nodded. The doctor went on.

"And the bedsores are all but healed. We were lucky we got to them in the early stages. She didn't need any additional discomfort."

"Okay, then," Carl said. "Can my daughter see her now?"

Dr. Murphy looked like he wanted to say something,

and not about Brooke's physical condition. Carl breathed
in and looked at him hard. Peri knew what she had done,
and she didn't need any more criticism.

"Fine," the doctor said, raising his eyebrows at Carl.

Fran took Peri's arm and led her away from the two
doctors, who stood like bowling pins by the desk. Carl
followed behind them. "I'm going to be in the room during the entire half hour visit," Fran was saying. "It's what
the judge decreed. But I'll be in the corner and hopefully you won't even remember that I'm there."

"Does she know what I did? Has anyone told her?"

"I think Carly initially told her you went somewhere,
but no one has said anything about your arrest. She's
asked for you every single day."

Peri turned back and pressed herself against Carl's
shoulder. "Oh, my God," she sobbed.

"Hush. It's okay. Hush." Carl smoothed her hair and
looked back at the doctors, but they were gone. "You'll
be okay."

Peri moved slowly away from him, and then wiped
her face. She dug in her pocket and pulled out a hair
elastic and quickly put her hair in a ponytail. She dusted
off imaginary lint from her shirt and then looked up at
him. In that instant, Carl's whole body grew still, blood,
air, bones. With that simple move, he was back in 1970,
and here was his girl, asking him for help with a math
quiz. How he'd been able to explain decimals and frac-
tions! How he'd been able to help her then.

"Let's go."

They rounded the corner and walked into Brooke's
room. By now, he recognized the shape of her small
body under the covers, not straight and smooth like any
other prone child, but bent at angles and restless.

"Brooke? Brookey?" Peri asked, moving slowly to the bed. "It's me. Mommy."

Brooke flung her head to them, kicking her way through the covers, and Carl held his hand to his chest when he saw her face break into what was for her an unnaturally huge smile. "Ma! Ma! Da u are! I mi u! Ma." Peri moved fast now, sitting on the bed and taking Brooke into her arms in a way Carl had never seen anybody do, cradling her like a baby, kissing her head and face.

"Oh, my baby. Oh, my baby. I'm so sorry. Mommy is so sorry." Peri pulled back, touching Brooke's face, pushing her red hair back from her eyes, and then Carl saw Brooke do something he'd never seen before. She bent her neck and smiled a deep, lips-together smile, her eyes slits. It was an exact copy of Peri's smile, the smile she'd had since childhood.

"Oh, baby. Oh, God." Peri brought her tight again to her body, rubbing her hands over her shoulders and arms.

"We ur u? Ma! Ka ted u ga!"

"I know, baby. Carly was right. I was gone. But I'm back. I won't ever leave again. I promise."

Brooke closed her eyes, humming with pleasure, and Peri began to softly sing a song he hadn't heard in a long time, not since Peri herself was a baby and Janice sang at her crib. He couldn't name it, but it brought him back years and years, and he sat down on a chair next to Fran, wondering how it would feel to let the memory crack him open, to let out the tears he knew were there. He swallowed, his gaze unfocused, willing the moment to pass, the scene to turn, a new thought to take him away.

*　　*　　*

Twenty minutes later, Carl was out in the hall, leaning against the nurses' desk. Peri had asked to change Brooke's diaper and clothes, and he'd left, letting the nurses and Fran observe. He hoped they didn't think Peri would do anything wrong now, after all this, and he wanted to tell them to leave her alone. But could he be sure of anything? He hadn't known what was going on in his girl's head the first time, would never have believed that she thought she was going to explode into a thousand vicious pieces, so he stood quietly, nodding at the nurses walking by, listening to the hospital noises, ripping plastic, machine beeps, murmuring voices.

"Mr. Randall, right?" The woman doctor was at his side, a file in her hands.

"That's me. Doctor?"

"Dr. Eady."

"Right."

"Your granddaughter is about to be released. She's done so well. Probably tomorrow. I've already talked with your son-in-law on the phone."

"Ex—ex-son-in-law."

"Oh. Well. Yes. I neglected to talk to him about the nursing home visit, but I see I should call him myself."

Carl stood straight and shook his head. "Brooke's going where? And who is visiting? What nurse?"

Dr. Eady looked flustered, the mask of all-knowing, I-could-live-your-life-better-than-you cracking for an instant. "Brooke is going to . . ." She looked at the file. "To your in-law's. Or your ex-in-law's. Mrs. Mackenzie's home. At least for the time being before she moves to . . . Well, until the court case is settled. In such cases as these, we have a nurse visit the home after discharge. Well, I'll call Mr. Mackenzie."

That little shit Preston couldn't have told me this? Carl thought. What was Garnet going to do with Brooke? How would Graham even begin to take care of her?

"Well," he said, trying to control himself. He was supposed to be on his best behavior with everyone. Who knew what would end up in court, moments of sorrow or rage or pain? He had to be good. This time. Now. "I guess you'd better talk with Graham about the nursing visit."

Dr. Eady nodded, relieved to be on her way, tucking the chart under her arm and *click, clacking* around the desk and down the hall. Carl walked back toward Brooke's room and peeked in. The group of women was circled around the bed making cooing noises, and he turned, moving down the hall to the lobby and the pay phone. He had to get on the horn to Preston and see what was going on. He had to call Noel.

"Carl. Carl!" He stopped and looked up, saw Rosie Candelero coming down the hall with a teddy bear in her arms.

"Hi there, Rosie," he said, suddenly lifted out of his panic. He could tell her what he wanted to say to Dr. Eady.

"What's going on?" She stood in front of him, and he breathed her in, some kind of perfume or soap floating around her.

"Come here." They walked into the small lobby and sat on the uncomfortable hardbacked chairs, Carl turning one slightly so he could look at her straight on. "I didn't know it until just now, but Brooke's going to be staying at Garnet's. With Graham. He hasn't even come to visit her yet, and the court is letting her go home to . . . that! I just don't get it. Preston keeps talking about the best interest of the child, and I don't see it at all. I guess I had this fantasy that they'd let Brooke come to my house."

"When did you find this out?"

"Just now. They're both being very slippery. Not a call, mind you. No heads up for Peri. And you should see her in there with Brooke right now. It about broke my heart."

Rosie set the teddy bear on the chair next to her. "Peri's out? I mean, released?"

"That's right. She came home Monday night."

"That's got to be a relief. Now she can get on with the business of getting well. It's going to take a while, but she's lucky to have you."

Carl held his chin in one hand, feeling the wiry stubble on the soft skin between thumb and index finger. He hadn't had time for a good close shave for what? A week? He hadn't played tennis or done a damn thing in his yard, and for a moment, he resented the hell out of Peri and her flipping problems. She should have called him, damn it, a long time ago. But then he remembered her face as she said, "Why did you leave?" And he shook his head. Peri was nowhere near lucky to have him. He was the lucky one, even if it pissed him off. He was getting a second chance.

"Thanks, Rosie. I mean, for everything. I keep saying it, but you've been great this whole time. I really don't know what we'd have done if you hadn't bailed us out."

She laughed, her teeth white against her olive skin. "Like I had something better to do than work? Or fix meals for my overgrown son? That little girl in there did something to me. I can't tell you how I felt when I

walked into her room at that apartment. And Carly. You
know how I feel about her."

"I'm going to have to pack up that apartment. Peri's
going to be with me during the trials—whatever is going
to happen."

"Well, you come over and pack, and I'll help. Then I'll
make you some dinner. Maybe some of my famous pork
chops. My son loves them."

Carl sighed. He'd never even asked her son's name or
occupation, imagining she was as involved with his
problems as he was. Who could have a son at a time like
this? "What's your son's name? I never asked."

"Ricky. He's twenty-four and a mama's boy—I'll tell
you that. I keep waiting for him to find a girl that sticks,
but no luck so far."

Carl smiled, patting her hand. "Maybe we'll have better luck with both our kids this year. Here's to hoping."

He stuck out his hand, and she took it, shaking with
him over this basic wish.

"He can't have her. He won't take care of her. He
hasn't even seen her. The nurses told me only Garnet's
been there, not Graham." Peri sat facing the highway,
repeating herself over and over again. Carl drove more
slowly than usual, as if the lower speed would calm her
down. Would shut her up. Would calm *him* down.

"It's just for now. Remember that. We haven't even
had a court decision." He used the voice he'd cultivated
for clients, soft, reassuring, seductive; a voice that promised a quick close, a smooth, clean escrow. It had always
worked before, but now Peri seemed on the verge of
something bad. He didn't know what he would do if she

flipped out again, and if she did, that would be it. No kids, a life of slow years at the funny farm.

"But now turns into forever," she said. "Haven't you of all people noticed? You make a decision in the moment and then live with it for the rest of your life. That's what could happen here. He could get them all because of this, *this* now."

Carl swallowed. "Peri, did you take your—your medicine today?"

She turned to him. "Am I acting weird?"

"A little obsessive, I think."

"I'm losing my daughter. The one I hurt. Don't you think that would upset me, Dad? Isn't that a normal feeling? I don't think I'm going to blow up and kill people. I just know—I'm sure I'm going to die if I can't be with her. If I can't make it up to her. Did you see her? Did you see her in that bed?"

Peri leaned against the dashboard and began sobbing. He reached over to pat her shoulder, and then scared by her ragged sobs, pulled over on the freeway shoulder, cars roaring past them. "Don't. I'm sorry. You're right. I just get nervous. I don't know how . . ."

"You don't, do you? And neither do I. I don't know how to do this at all," she said, her voice muffled in her arms.

"You will. So will I. Let's figure it out together," he said, grabbing her and sliding her across the seat to him. "I'm sorry. Let's go home. Let's work on today, Periwinkle." She nodded against his chest, her tears soaking his shirt. He wanted today to be the worst of all, each following day better with seconds that ticked into minutes and then hours. And he hoped that all the plans they made would turn into truths they could live with forever.

* * *

Noel was in the front yard talking to Mrs. Trimble over the rhododendron bushes when they arrived home. When he heard the Corvair rumble up the street, Noel waved to her, smiling as he walked toward the garage.

"She's a nice lady," Noel said. "Why haven't you ever told me about her?"

Carl shrugged and closed his door. "What are you doing here? I thought you had a long day at work."

"Don't worry about it. I thought you might want to go and play tennis or something. Maybe Peri and I will take a walk." He bent down and looked at Peri, who was combing her wind-messed hair.

"How did it go?" Noel whispered.

"Not good, not bad. She's okay now," Carl said. "Keep an eye on her. She's upset."

Peri stepped out and smiled at Noel, moving into his arms, and Carl felt something in his throat. He searched for a name for his feeling. Was he jealous? Was this a scene out of "Lousy father jealous that others are more important"? What could he expect? But no, it wasn't jealousy. It was pride. It was "Two damn good kids hang together despite all." Whatever he might have done in the past, at least their sibling relationship was still intact.

"Come on!" Ramon yelled. "That ball was completely in."

"I call 'em as I see 'em," Carl said, walking back to the base line. "If you want to make calls over here, you're on the wrong side."

"Ignore him," his partner, Bob, said, whispering to Carl as they plotted strategy for the next serve. "He's

trying to psych you out. He always says he gets hooked
on a call."

"Don't try to figure this one out," Ramon said. "No
amount of talking will prepare you for this."

Carl smiled, and then the ball was sailing to his fore-
hand—almost a sitter—and he whacked it back,
watched it skim past Ramon's partner Alex, a new guy.
Ramon stood slack-mouthed and then grimaced, ignoring Alex's feeble apology, obviously missing Ralph and
his killer backhand.

"That's how the game is played, boys," Carl said, giving Bob a high five. "That is how the game is played."

At the Big C an hour and two sets later, Carl sipped
his second martini and stared at the television, barely
listening to Bob tell Ramon about his ex-wife and her
new boyfriend, the dentist. With the conversation, the
noise, the everyday sound of the local news, the alcohol
in his blood—his first real drink in over a week—he
could almost imagine that the time since Peri had disappeared was a terrible dream he'd awakened from.
Bob nudged his arm, and Carl joined in the laughter,
not caring what he was laughing about, just glad to do it,
the sound rippling up his throat hard and gritty, like his
Corvair on a cold February morning.

"Damn straight," he added, not caring if it didn't
make sense, but it did, Bob nodding and moving his
hands, Ramon slapping his hand on the counter.

"Where the hell were you this week?" Bob said, the
topic spinning toward Carl like a can-opener serve. "We
needed to plan our trip down to the San Diego tourna-
ment in the summer. I called the house a couple, no
three, times."

"Me, too," said Ramon. "I left some damn funny messages, too."

Carl shook his head, vodka coating his teeth. He stuck the toothpick now empty of olives in his mouth, pretending to work an imaginary seed from between his back molars. "Yard work. That flipping sprinkler was killing me."

Ramon looked at him with dark eyes. "Yeah? That's it?"

"My neighbor," Carl continued, his lie stretching to the breaking point. "She's on my back about her rhododendrons. 'Prize bushes,' she tells me. 'Precious plants,' she says. So I had to dig up and replace one pipe and a head. Pain in the ass. But at least she's off mine."

Both of his friends were silent, staring at their drinks. *What?* Carl thought. *What do they want?* "So tell me about the San Diego trip."

Neither Ramon nor Bob said anything, the space between them filling with restaurant sounds, the clack of plates, the TV's endless whine. Outside, people rushed in and out of Arturo's Burritos Fabulosos and the new deli, carrying take-home in plastic bags; kids ran in karate uniforms to classes, parents racing behind them carrying duffel bags and water bottles.

"You know it was in the papers, Carl. Even on the news. You could have called us," Bob said, turning his beer glass in his hands.

"Yeah, man. It's not like you had to deal with this on your own," Ramon added. "We're your *compadres.*"

Carl nodded, thought of his car, the top down, the air all around him. *Go,* he thought. *Just go.* But where? Where could he go now? He'd run away from enough in his life, letting everything important play out around him. He hadn't gone to Janice's bedside once while she was sick, just showing up at the funeral and sitting in the back of the church, trying not to notice how Noel and Peri ignored him. His boy and girl had grown into adults without more than twice monthly visits; all their important life events going on as if on TV, things he could catch up on during summer reruns. But life had no reruns. He'd seen that this week, one inexorable moment moving into the next without time to take any of it back and make it right.

And now his tennis buddies wanted him to let them in. Something he'd never wanted himself. "It's—it's been awful," he said quietly, staring at the circles of water on the counter. "It's been terrible to watch."

"Are the kids okay, man?" Ramon asked.

"They are. Brooke—the one you probably read about the most—is great. She's getting out of the hospital tomorrow. I had the other two for a while, but now they're at their grandmother's—Peri's ex-husband's mom." It was exhausting, he realized, the permutations of family, the exes and the onces and the moves and changes, going all the way back to the day he had walked out Janice's door.

"Do you need anything? I've got a friend. A lawyer. A great guy." Bob waved off the bartender's offer of another beer.

"We've got it covered so far," Carl answered. "Not that he's doing squat. But it's early. What we're really concerned about is the custody case. The kids—" He stopped, jolted by the ghost of Carly's grip around his waist the day Graham took her and Ryan to Garnet's. "That's the hard part."

"And your daughter? Is she— Is she out of jail?"

"Has been for a couple of days. She's with me. My son is with her right now. That's why I could come play today."

"She's better?" Bob asked.

"Much. Still so . . . fragile," Carl said, remembering the tiny porcelain ballerina that had played inside Peri's music box, the one she'd left at his house that had irritated him to no end, the blasted *Nutcracker* song going and going and going.

"If you need anything, man. All the guys. We'll do whatever. Money, you name it." Ramon turned his dark eyes away from him, and Carl was thankful, feeling the pulse of tears behind his eyes.

He stood up and put a twenty on the counter. "Thanks, guys. I really appreciate it. I might not be at the courts as often, but I'll be back. Soon."

Carl put a hand on Bob's shoulder and then turned and left the Big C, walking up the street instead of toward the Corvair, needing air, needing exercise, needing anything to push the feeling back inside him where it belonged. If this kept up, he'd need to borrow some of Peri's drugs, filching them at night to tamp down everything.

Just over a week ago, Carl had imagined the past—years ago, months, even days—cauterized, sealed shut, red maybe, but not bleeding. Not life threatening. But it had opened up and was oozing. Time had bitten him in the ass after all.

Ignoring the kids hopping up and down on the pavement waiting for their classes, the woman walking her corgi, the man on a cell phone, Carl walked faster, his knee clicking slightly as he pushed up the street. He was sharing Peri's psychotic reaction, convinced he would burst at any moment, unable to contain the feeling that was turning his lungs into ovens. Later, he wondered what people must have thought, seeing an old, slightly drunk man in tennis shorts weeping his way up Mountain Boulevard.

Seventeen

"Can we get her now? If we're going to be here for good, can we have her back?" Carly stared at her breakfast, two slightly runny eggs looking back at her with yellow eyes.

Her father put down the front page of the Saturday *Chronicle*. "Who? Who can we have back?"

Carly looked at Ryan, who was pretending to ignore her and read the sports section, which he didn't even care about. She cared about Maxie, though, so she repeated herself. "Maxie. Can we go get her now at Sam's? If you're going to make— If we're going to be here at Grandma's, why can't we have her? There's a big enough yard. She can stay outside. I'll take care of everything."

Her father folded the paper and set it beside his own runny eggs. "Carly. I know you miss her, but there's too much going on here right now. I always told your mother that dog was dangerous around your sister, anyway, and we just got Brooke all set up here. Besides, I don't know if your grandmother could handle anything more."

"What can't I handle?" Garnet said, clipping into the kitchen and looking around, nodding at Maritza, who was wiping down the range.

Her dad seemed to flush, and Carly saw that he was almost scared of her, as if Grandma was going to spank him for being bad. Her grandmother scared her in the same way, and for a surprising instant, she wanted to protect her dad, make up some story to avoid this conversation. But he didn't deserve protection. He needed a spanking, a big one, with a leather belt like in the old days, and she sat back in her chair, waiting for his answer.

"The dog, Mom. Maxie. Peri gave her to a neighbor when they moved."

"We didn't give her to anyone," Ryan said loudly, looking up from the sports page. "We had to let Maxie stay with someone because where we were moving we couldn't have pets. We couldn't have anything there. We *didn't* have anything there."

Her father pushed a hand through his hair and then looked at Carly. The part of her that might have helped him died behind her gaze, and she stared without blinking, her eyeballs hot. He cleared his throat.

"Well. In any case, your grandmother has too much going on in this house to add Maxie to the pile."

"Do you think I can answer the question, Graham?" her grandmother said, taking a cup of tea from Maritza and sitting down at the table. "I think we can handle a dog. You and your sister had Pippin for years, and the yard was fine for her."

"But what about Eustace?" her father asked. Carly almost made a terrible sound with her lips, the kind that she used to make with Ashley and Kiana during recess when talking about Mrs. Blandi, their math teacher. A raspberry, her mother used to call the sound, a wet push of disgust through lips.

"The cat, like, lives under my bed," Carly said. "He'll be fine. I'll keep Maxie under control."

"Don't forget about Brooke," her father said quietly. Carly wanted to make the sound again. Her father had barely gone into Brooke's room since the ambulance brought her home. He'd considered nothing as far as Carly could see.

"What is your problem?" Ryan asked, standing up suddenly, the table rattling with dishes. "We had Maxie and Brooke. We had Maxie and a cat! Remember Olive? Before we had to give her away, they got along great. Have you, like, completely forgotten that we all used to live together just fine until you left us? Are you a total asshole or what?"

"Ryan, sit down immediately," Grandmother Mackenzie said, rising in her seat like a cartoon giant, her face looming over the kitchen table. "I won't have that kind of talk in my kitchen."

Ryan did as he was told and glared at their dad, who fiddled with a fork.

"It's also that you might be moving to Phoenix with me. And then we'd have to do something with Maxie again."

"We couldn't take her with us if we *had* to go with you?" Carly asked, surprised by his hurt look at her words. Did he really not know she'd rather die than live with him? Did he really not see that?

"Blair—your stepmother—is allergic to animals."

"Here is what I think could happen." Grandma Mackenzie put down her teacup and dabbed the corners of her mouth with her napkin. "I believe we could go and retrieve Maxie and let her live here for the duration. This case could go on for months, Graham. Why not let the children have their dog? We'll put her outside in the old kennel."

Her father nodded weakly, sighing. "Fine. Why not?"

Carly kicked Ryan gently under the table, and he looked up at her and smiled the biggest smile she'd seen since before they moved, since before the divorce.

Her father had made a very quick call to Sam's mom, and late that afternoon, Carly and Ryan sat in the backseat of Grandma Mackenzie's Lincoln Continental. Their grandmother had handed them a folded tarp before they left, saying, "Put this down on the backseat before you let the dog in." Grandma probably didn't want Maxie at all, and Carly was surprised that any of this was happening. She didn't care why it was happening, though, she was just glad. And as they drove through the Caldecott Tunnel and pushed out into the air of Monte Veda, she felt her blood tingle under her skin. She was home. She was going to have her dog back. Brooke was upstairs at Grandma's house. If their mom were all better and they could live in Monte Veda again, then maybe everything since her father left would pop open and blow away like a bad dream, one she felt she might be waking from. If they were getting Maxie, who knew what else good could happen?

Slowly pulling up to Sam's house, the last of the plum blossoms dotting the asphalt like tiny wings, her father braked and cut the engine, gripping the steering wheel and not saying a word.

"Dad?" she asked.

"What?"

"Let's go get her already," Ryan said.

"Why don't you two go? I don't even know— Maxie would be happier to see you."

"If she even remembers us," Carly said.

Her father turned and looked at them over the seat. For an instant, he was the dad she remembered, taking her to Saturday art classes, dropping her off at the first day of school. He was the dad in the second row at the dance recitals, videotaping everything, even the final bows. But he wasn't that dad anymore. He'd forgotten how to take care of her, and now he was too chicken even to go get the dog they'd had to get rid of because of him. "Just run to the door. It'll be fine."

Carly and Ryan slid out of the car, tugging the tarp over the seat before they walked up the driveway toward the house. They could hear Maxie barking behind the closed front door.

"He is such an asshole," Ryan muttered.

"Well, we're getting Maxie back at least."

"At least."

As they began walking up the steps, Sam opened the door and Maxie sprinted out, jumping up on Carly, exactly as dog school and Ryan had taught her not to do during all those weekly Tuesday evening classes. Wagging and bumping into Carly's shoulders, Maxie licked her wet red tongue up and down Carly's entire face, including her lips. She didn't care, leaning into the dog's long, soft fur, pressing her hands against Maxie until she almost felt the dog's quick breaths were her own. Carly closed her eyes, hearing the familiar jangle of collar and tags, and she imagined concentrating on the steel clack long enough to turn today into a year ago, Maxie's excitement an everyday occurrence, none of this—not one bit—out of the ordinary.

Maxie stilled, licked Carly once more, and then wagged over to Ryan, who knelt and held her in his arms, murmuring, "Hey, girl. Hey, girl. That's my girl." He avoided Carly's gaze and blinked fast, one-two, one-two, finally burying his face in Maxie's shoulder.

"Hi," said Sam, looking at her shyly, as if they hadn't played together for years. She thought about asking after her friends Kiana and Ashley, but then Sam's mom, Lara, came out to the front porch, smiling. Carly felt like turning, grabbing her mother's hand, walking into the house to the food she knew Lara would have laid out, smelling the coffee made just for her mother, who liked it. She and Sam would play for hours before turning on the television set to watch a movie— *Beethoven*, the one about the dogs. After a while, her mother would say "Let's go, squirt," and they would drive to the soccer field, where Ryan would run back and forth, his shin guards streaked with dirt, his face red, his hair blown wild.

For that instant, everything was like it had been, before Brooke.

"Now this is nice. Just what Maxie was waiting for," Lara said, putting her smooth hand on Carly's arm. "You've grown! My goodness, Carly. Your mother must be . . ." Lara brought a hand to her chin, as if she could whisk away the mistake. Carly's mother must be nothing in terms of Carly. She must be crazy. And that was all.

"Good girl. That's a good girl," Ryan said, petting Maxie's face and neck.

"Where's your dad?" Lara looked down the long driveway.

"He's in the car." Carly bit her lip, wondering if this was the time to ask for help again, like she had with Rosie. But how could Lara help them now? Everyone knew about what had happened—cops, doctors, social workers, her grandma and grandpa—and she was still stuck with her father. No one could change anything.

"I think I'll go say hello," Lara said.

"Good idea," Ryan said. He avoided Carly's surprised look and took the leash from Sam and clipped it on Maxie's collar. Carly picked up the bag of dog toys and peeked in, almost laughing as she remembered buying them with her mother at the Smart Pet. "She'll love this one!" her mother had said, holding it up and squeezing it so Carly could hear it squeak. "And look at this dog dish—Killer. That's Maxie all over!"

The four of them walked toward the car, and Carly paid attention to the shadow figure of her father, the way he shifted, sat straighter, and then stepped out of the car altogether. He might run down the street before daring to face Sam's mom or even Maxie, who didn't seem to smell him yet. Maybe even Maxie knew what he had done and had decided he wasn't worth the effort.

"Graham? Hi. How are you?" Sam's mother smiled one of those fake smiles Carly knew from years of going with her mother to mother/daughter cookie parties and holiday bazaars and mother-in-the-class days—a wide, toothy flash that said, "I'm really thinking something terrible about you," no flicker or secret in her eyes, dead set on her father, who shuffled and then put his hands in his pockets.

"Hi, Lara. Things could be better. Obviously. But really, thanks for keeping Maxie. The kids were desperate to get her back."

"Really. Of course. Too bad it had to happen in the first place." Lara smiled her fake smile again, and Carly began to like her more than ever. "So how is Brooke?"

Her father nodded and kicked at a magnolia petal that had floated next to his shoes, a pair Carly didn't recognize. Nothing he had on was familiar, his wedding ring a new, wider, bigger band. What had he done with the old one?

"A lot better than when they found her. Peri—" he started, and then stopped, looking up at Lara and then coughing. "Well, thanks again. Come on, kids. Let's take Maxie to Grandma's."

As her dad opened the rear door and made sure Maxie was settled on top of Grandma's tarp and not under it, Lara walked over to Carly and put her hand on her shoulder. "Don't blame your mom for all this," she said quietly. "I should have seen something. So should a lot of other people. Remember, she's sick, okay?"

Carly nodded and then opened the other door and sat down, holding Maxie over her shoulders, accidentally touching Ryan's hand as he did the same thing. Neither of them moved.

Her father didn't say another word to Lara, and as they drove down the street, Carly turned, watching Sam and Lara and Monte Veda disappear, just as they had before. But this time, there was nothing calling her home.

Back at their grandmother's, Carly and Ryan stood in the backyard with Maritza watching Maxie sprint around, stopping to sniff the base of a tree or plant, and then sprint some more.

"Su perro es muy loco," Maritza said.

"Sí," Ryan said.

"Huh?" Carly asked. "What did she say?"

"She's acting crazy. Look at her. It's like she's been locked up or something," Ryan said.

He and Maritza were right. Maybe Maxie imagined that this yard would also disappear, and she had to memorize it all right now before it was gone, a car dumping her off at another house with other people. But she seemed to be enjoying herself, looking back occasionally at them, wagging her tail, and then tearing off again.

"Si esa mujer espera que yo limpia la mierda, está loca," Maritza said, nodding at Ryan and walking back toward the kitchen.

"What was that all about?"

"I guess we're going to have to clean up after Maxie." Ryan smiled. "But I don't care."

"Me, either." They were both quiet for a second, the afternoon turning to that perfect gold light Carly had always loved, the way it slid liquid across the shiny backs of oak leaves and trailed across shingled rooftops. Piedmont was so much like Monte Veda that if she closed her eyes, she could imagine she was in her old backyard.

"What are you going to do tomorrow?" Ryan asked, sitting down on the thick wood chair and putting his feet up on the table.

Carly sat down, too, folding her hands between her knees. "What do you mean?"

"I mean about the visit. You know. With Mom?"

She shrugged, but she wanted to know if she really had any options. Could she not go? Her stomach felt empty from the last time, and simply thinking about her mother's sad, tired face made her stomach swirl as if she'd swallowed jungle bugs, creatures with long legs and prickly antenna. And then she remembered what Lara had whispered earlier in her ear. *Remember, she's sick.*

Maxie tore down the slope and then stopped at the patio, finding her water and lapping at it, her tags banging against the bowl. "Do you think Mom is sick? Is it, like, a disease that she's got?"

"That's what Grandpa said. Depression with some kind of reaction. He said it was as if her brain kind of made another universe that only she lived in and only she knew the rules to. And she thought she was acting fine because in her world, she was. To us on the outside, she was doing crazy shit."

"Like leaving Brooke in her bed. Like leaving me to take care of Brooke, who had a fever, who could have died."

"Yeah. That's the shit. That's the stuff that somehow made sense to her."

"What did she say to you after I had to . . ."

"What? Crap your guts out?"

Carly flushed. "Shut up."

"Just kidding," Ryan said, leaning back, his arms so long the armrests seemed like wood stumps. He closed his eyes and tilted his head up, the sun lighting the five long hairs on his chin, the vague red stubble above his lip. "Well, she said she was sorry. That she didn't mean to hurt us. That she loved us." He squeezed his eyes together, as if the sun were bothering him through his eyelids.

"Did you believe her?"

"Yeah. She wasn't always like this, Carly. You know that."

Shaking her head, Carly looked at her hands in her lap, the slick clear nail polish her grandmother had let her use flickering in the light. Ryan was right, but that old mother was as far away as her old father. Once upon a time there had been laughter and warmth and fun, like in a fairytale. Her mother took her shopping and braided her hair and came into her room at night and read *Pig William*, the story about the stubborn pig that wouldn't go to school. Somehow, though, that mother became the mother who was on the phone or in Brooke's room or meeting with therapists and nurses. And then that mother became the one who hid under her blankets, struggling to get up every morning just to feed Brooke. Now, there was yet another mom, one who was on drugs to make her normal, on drugs so she wouldn't bash in anyone else's front door.

"Are you going to visit?" Carly looked at her brother.

"Yeah."

"Even after what she did?"

"Because of what she did," Ryan said, sitting up, turning to Carly. "She's in trouble, Carly. If she didn't know what she was doing, I can't blame her. Fran told me she wasn't herself. And our being pissed at her probably won't be her only punishment. She might— She might go to jail. It's like we *have* to see her now."

Carly bit the side of her cheek. It was just like Ryan to be all wise now, after the hard part was over. Back when their mother was under the blankets and Brooke was falling out of her bed, he'd been like a dream she'd had once, something she could almost remember. Now that the adults were involved and Dad was back, everyone knowing exactly what was going on, it was easy to be big, act like he had the answers to the questions he couldn't even ask before. And while he was running around cutting class and smoking Lucky Strikes, there she'd been, pushing formula through a syringe into her sister's stomach.

Maxie was barking at the end of the property, and Ryan stood up, ran up the slope and then over past the oak trees on the crest, and then the barking stopped, but he didn't come down. For a few minutes, Carly sat still, closed her eyes, let the air wrap around her face like a friend who'd been gone and was now back in town, so happy to see her. After a while, she sat up and followed Ryan's path up the slope, past the fancy landscaping her grandmother's gardener tended, bushes with fuzzy purple flowers, plants that seemed to wave at her with yellow hands.

At the top of the slope, she looked past the oak trees, but Ryan and Maxie were gone, both probably slipping through the hidey-hole in Grandma Mackenzie's fence, the spot Grandma would never know about because she didn't venture past the first tier of plants. The gardener probably left it there so he could run away from her if he had to, Carly thought, starting to walk toward it. But then she stopped, turning back to the house. The sun was a golden eye hovering over San Francisco, and she squinted and then looked down at the roof of the house, the shingles like gleaming teeth.

High above the house, high above Piedmont, and even Oakland, she felt made of half air, half earth, something in the middle. Maybe she was like her mother, two people at once. The good Carly did what she was told, took care of whoever needed her help, worried about everyone. The bad Carly, the one inside her skin now, hated everyone: her mom, dad, Ryan,

Grandma, maybe even Grandpa Carl for letting them come here. Back in her old life, the bad Carly only came out at times. Once when Kiana teased her about a new haircut and Bret Watson tormented her about Brooke, calling out on the bus, "Crooked little sister, bent in two." A feeling had spread like black ink in Carly's body, and she had told Kiana, "You're stupid and fat," and with Bret, she had stood up while the bus was moving and yanked his hair so hard, his head hit the back of his seat. When she thought about her actions days and months later—even now—she was filled with shame, wishing she could go through the events in reverse and pull them all back into nothingness.

Closing her eyes against the orange sun, she took one last deep breath as if it were a wish she could hold in her body. She and Ryan used to play a game as their mother drove past the Lafayette Cemetery. Ryan would say, "Ready? Okay! Go!" and they would hold their breaths as their mother laughed and joked that she was going to take her foot off the accelerator. When Carly asked what the game was for, Ryan said they were saving themselves from evil ghosts, but really, it was the deep breath at the very edge of the green lawn that they wanted. That amazing rush of air that meant they were still alive.

Walking down the slope toward the patio, feeling the crush of new grass under her feet, Carly took in a breath as she had all those times with Ryan. She'd lived through the long days and scary nights with Brooke, and she'd never breathed in, never felt like it was over, the cemetery going on and on and on forever. Now, she didn't have to hold her breath; she didn't have to turn away from her mother as if she were an evil ghost. Here was her chance not to regret what she was doing. Already, Carly cringed when she thought of running down the hall at the jail, knowing she preferred sitting on the toilet to talking to her own mother. Maybe Ryan with all his fake new wisdom was right. Here was her chance not to want to erase her life. Here was her chance to move forward. Here was her chance to breathe.

That night, Carly got up to go to the bathroom, and on her way down the long hall, she heard a sound in Brooke's room, and she moved soundlessly toward the door, her feet sliding bare and smooth on the wood floor. She held on to the door trim and pushed slowly, stilling herself against any squeak. The doors at the apartment had cried like animals every time they moved, but this door swished open smoothly, and there, right by Brooke's bed, was her father. He sat toward the head and was gently stroking Brooke's hair. The nurse her grandmother had hired for nighttime was in a corner of the room reading a *Time* magazine, the pages *flick, flick, flicking* as her father touched her sister.

Without thinking, Carly walked in, looking at her father. The nurse glanced up and then went back to her reading, but her father almost started, pulling his hand away from Brooke.

"Don't stop," Carly said. "She likes that. Even if she's asleep."

"I know," he said, putting his hand back. "I know what she likes."

"Then why don't you do it more? Why didn't you?" She pulled a chair close to the bed and sat down, reaching out to touch Brooke's knee.

Her father didn't say anything for a while, and she

watched him. He looked different. Older? Or was it sadder? Or did she just not recognize him anymore, already forgetting his face in the time since she'd seen him?

"This could have been avoided. She didn't have to be like this," he said quietly. "I knew it right away, the minute your mother went into labor."

"What do you mean?"

He shook his head like he was trying to bang something out of it. Did he blame Mom for what had happened to Brooke? It wouldn't have been her fault. Brooke was born like this, everyone said so.

She was just about to tell him that when he said, "It's nothing. Never mind. She's just so hurt. I can't stand to see her like this."

Carly was confused. Her sister had always been like this, and she wasn't hurt. She just was. "She's usually happy. She's not hurt."

Her father sighed. "I know. I guess I look at you and Ryan and think about what Brooke could have been like if things had gone—gone differently when she was born."

"So . . . so did you leave us because you didn't like to look at us? Is that why?" Her father gazed at her and then stood up. For an instant, she thought, *Don't touch me, don't touch me*, but she knew she didn't mean it. Before, back in her old life, she liked the feel of her father, his warm body as she hugged him around the waist, the way he would let her walk on his shoes, the tipping, monster walk across the living room floor as he sang "Monster Mash," a song from forever ago. She was ready for his embrace, but right as he neared her, just as he was close enough to pick her up and bring her up to his face, he stopped, reaching a hand out instead, his fingers so light on her head she could barely feel them.

"No. It was never about you. Or Ryan. It was always— It was between your mother and me," he said, and then his fingers were gone and the door swooshed open and then closed. Slapping her magazine between her palms, the nurse pushed to her feet and followed her father, going to the bathroom while someone was still in the room. The door closed once more, and Carly was alone again with Brooke.

"It's all decided," her grandmother was saying Tuesday morning as she sipped tea and ate dry toast. She was waiting for Maritza to fry her an egg, but Maritza stood still at the stove, listening to Grandma. "We are going to enroll you in Piedmont schools. They are the best, after all, and you can both walk every day. I'll go down with your father today when you are having your little visit."

Carly looked at Ryan and then at her father. "Grandpa wanted to get us into the school by his house."

"Nonsense, Carly." Her grandmother sat down with her tea. "Oakland and Piedmont are worlds apart educationally. There's no comparison. Your father and Aunt Marcia received a wonderful education here."

"But if we end up having to move, you know, to, like, Phoenix," Ryan said, keeping his eyes on his plate, "then we have to start all over again."

Maritza rattled her skillet and brought the egg to Grandma Mackenzie. No one said anything for a while, and Carly tried to chew quietly, as if she wasn't really eating at all.

"I have to go home," her father said quietly. "I have to get some things."

Carly looked at her grandmother who was saying

things, not with her mouth, but with her eyebrows and chin, her fingers thrumming on the table, her teacup clicking on its saucer.

"Do they know? Does everyone know you're leaving?" Carly asked.

"Of course." Grandma stood up, her eggs untouched. "It's just for three or four days, maybe a week. Your father did have to come here straight from a long business trip after all."

"Can we stay with Grandpa Carl while you're gone?" Her grandmother's body quieted, the room suddenly empty of air and motion, even Maritza still behind her stove. Carly wondered if it was possible to hurt her grandmother's feelings, make her stop telling everyone what to do. If she'd upset her, Carly didn't want to care. Maybe Grandma had let them go get Maxie, but it wasn't because she really felt sorry for them or the dog; it was because she was stacking up good things like stones in the wall that would keep them away from their mother. She only wanted what was good for her son.

"No. You can't live with your grandfather." Her father put down his napkin. "Not yet. There's too much going on legally. Your mother isn't fit— She isn't ready to have you there."

"Can you imagine her trying to take care of Brooke at this . . ." Grandma trailed off. "Well, enough of this. You two need to get ready for your visit, and Maritza needs us out of here. So go to it. Right now."

Carly and Ryan stood up and walked toward the sink together, their shoulders rubbing. "Bitch," Ryan muttered, only loud enough for Carly to hear. As their plates clattered together in the sink, the woman on the other side of the rhododendrons, the one Grandpa Carl thought was a witch, bloomed in Carly's mind. If she had to decide who was worse right now, the biggest witch of all, her grandmother or the woman with the pruning shears, she'd pick her grandmother despite everything she was doing for Brooke. Carly would pick her because she never listened, didn't care, only wanted things neat, clean, and smooth, like the long dark wood of the living room floor.

Eighteen

"Do you think it was a conscious decision to stop tending to Brooke as much?" Dr. Kolakowski asked during Peri's Monday afternoon appointment.

Peri closed her eyes and nodded. "Conscious in a different way. It felt like there were directions I was following, like I always had. I did what they told me, all of them. Get her into swim therapy. Work on her speech. Call Baltimore and find out about the new treatment. Whatever they—"

"They?"

"The doctors," she said, shrugging. "The nurses. The social workers. The school. The therapists. My husband."

"What did you want to do with her?"

She shifted in her chair, crossing and then uncrossing her legs, finally sitting with them straight together. She hated the thump of her knobby knees banging together, the hard press of her long thigh bones. "I don't know. Keep her alive. Make her better. Make it all go away. Make her like Carly."

"Did you think you were doing her a favor by keeping her in bed?"

"I don't think I knew what I was doing or why," she said, closing her eyes against the image of Brooke, the way she turned to her, so happy, so grateful for every touch. "I guess— I guess maybe I thought she'd be better off. . . ."

"Dead?" Dr. Kolakowski asked, not sucking down the sound of the word as most people did.

"Maybe. But not so clearly. It was like I was underwater looking up into my old life. I didn't really know what I'd done until later when I woke up. When I heard about how thin she was and how much her muscles had atrophied. God . . ." She leaned her head against the chair, wishing she were anywhere but this office, anywhere but in her own body, this body that could have actually done that to Brooke.

"In that plan, she'd have been happier."

"You know what happens to kids like Brooke. Ever since she was diagnosed, I've learned too much about what her life will be like. It could be her heart that goes in twenty years or it could be a bad case of pneumonia. But not just that. Maybe she'll get better. Maybe she'll learn to articulate every letter in the alphabet or there will be some way to improve her muscle tone, but she's not going to have any kind of life. No one will fall in love with her. She won't have children. She'll never be able to work."

"And she'll have to live with you for her whole life," Dr. Kolakowski said.

"Yes."

"Or she'll have to live in some kind of institution. Maybe you were imagining something out of *One Flew over the Cuckoo's Nest*, bars and terrible staff and the like."

"Yes."

"So maybe you thought, What's the point of her living at all? Maybe you thought, I'll never have a life while I have Brooke."

"No! Oh, no!"

"Do you think Graham ever thought anything like this? Do you think that's maybe why he left?"

"He couldn't handle it. He just couldn't stay with her."

"Could you?"

For an instant, Peri was back in her bed at the apartment, hiding under the blankets, the sound of Brooke's thrashing in the bed across the room as close in her ears as whispers. "No. Not by myself."

"So somehow you got the idea that you were making her life better. That her life was pointless."

"Sometimes I wonder, what's the point? I don't want to eat. I don't want to keep living like this, each day as bad as the one before it. No miracle, no cure. Just my poor baby girl the same, and it's because of me. Because of my body." Peri shook her head, looking out at the waterfall between the doctors' offices, a gurgle and rush of water over stone, forever recycling.

Dr. Kolakowski looked at her and continued to write on her pad. Peri wished she could look at those notes, not because of the terrible truths written about her in permanent ink, but because she wanted to see if the words were legible. She wondered if the doctor just pretended to write to make Peri feel that what she was saying was important.

"You think it's all your fault?"

Peri pressed her hands against her thighs, staring at her pale skin. "I didn't go to the hospital when Graham

wanted me to. I kept telling him that everything would
be fine. And it wasn't. And the mother carries the MD
gene. I gave it to her."

"So you need to be punished? Is that what you
think?" Dr. Kolakowski crossed her legs, leaning forward a little.

"I . . . I don't know. Yes. Yes." Peri leaned her head in
her hand, hearing Sophia from the Martinez jail say,
"You aren't ever going to get those kids back."

Dr. Kolakowski sat still, not writing anymore. "Well,
so what is the point of you going on? Why should you
eat? Why should you stay alive?"

Her face opened, her mouth slack, her eyes heavy and
wide open. Someone agreed with her—it would be easier if Peri didn't eat, was gone, disappeared so everyone
could go on. But then she knew she was angry, wanting
her own doctor to defend her life, tell her she had to eat,
must eat, for herself and for her children.

"I—I need to stay alive."

"Why?"

"Because I'm better now. Because I want to try again.
I want to be alive . . . for my kids."

"So they need you? You think they count on you?"

"Yes!" Peri said, her face flushed and hot, the room
closing down on her. She crossed her arms over her
chest and took shallow breaths, as if the oxygen in the
room was reserved for good people. "Well, they will.
When they come back."

"Does anyone else need you?"

"My dad does, I think. Lately."

"Who else?"

Peri flashed to Noel in the hotel room, his hair standing on end, his eyes full of their entire childhood as they

lay side by side in the twin beds, just as they had forever, as long as either could remember. "My brother. Always."

"That's it?"

"My mother used to. I took care of her when she was dying."

"But of the living, that's it?"

Peri let her hands fall to her lap, her palms slapping on her knees. In a way, three children and two adults didn't seem like enough at all, her old life full of friends and acquaintances Peri had been sure needed her beyond a doubt. Without her, the Brownie meeting would fold, the bake sale would flop, her friend's marriage would dissolve. She'd been the stable center that had kept the neighborhood-watch meetings in order. Without her carefully gridded schedule, Brooke's physical, occupational, and speech therapists, teachers, and social workers would converge in a swarm of confused people in the entryway. But all along, Peri hadn't been stable, just pretending, everything inside her wavering. So none of that—and none of those people—were real to her now as she sat in front of this doctor, here because she'd been arrested and was soon to face charges that she'd hurt her own children. The only thing that had made any sense since she awakened in Phoenix was family— her brother, her father, the children. They'd saved her even if they hadn't forgiven her. She didn't need Graham and she didn't need her old friends. "Isn't that enough?" Peri said finally.

"Well, yes. Yes, isn't it enough?" Dr. Kolakowski smiled and sat back, writing even as Peri nodded and listened to the water's pure smooth sounds, thinking, *It has to be enough.*

* * *

Two weeks ago, a shower hurt, the water falling sharp on her skin like tiny knives. Sudsing her hair had been unbearable. But today—the day of her visit with Ryan and Carly at Montclair Park—she took extra time, wanting to make sure she looked as much as she could like her old mother self, the one from before Brooke, clean and put-together. After her psychiatrist appointment yesterday, her father had taken her to a salon up at Lincoln Plaza, a place that still had a barber pole out front, even though the women inside cut to all the latest style books. "Honey, we are going to heighten and lighten," Leticia had said.

As Peri blew her hair dry in the bathroom, she did feel lighter, and not because of the blond streaks. It was as if her longer hair had held the poison from the years before and now it was gone, leaving her with another chance, a chance not to make mistakes.

Leaning close to the mirror, she stroked on mascara, feeling clumsy, her hands shaky from the medication. Standing up straight, she tucked her T-shirt into her new jeans, which were a full two sizes smaller than the last ones she'd bought—what was it—over a year ago? With her hands on her hips, her elbows bent, her arms looked like chicken wings, the kind no one wanted to eat, not an ounce of flesh on them. She hadn't had much of an appetite before her talk with Dr. Kolakowski, but now she somehow felt she wanted to grow, fill up, become part of the earth so she wouldn't float away and miss any more of her life. After the hair appointment, her dad had taken her to Mel's Diner in Berkeley—always his favorite hamburger place—and she had eaten an entire tuna melt and half a serving of fries. This morning as she almost passed up some oatmeal, she thought, *It's enough reason to eat.* And so she did.

Her father knocked on the bathroom door. "Peri. We need to meet them. Come on."

"Coming." She put away the makeup her father had brought her from the apartment and wound the cord around the hair dryer. Since the last visit with the kids at the jail, she'd tried not to think of Carly and her pale, nervous face. *What if she runs away again?* she thought. This time, they would be at a park, where Carly could run forever. "It might happen again," Dr. Kolakowski had warned, "but that's okay. You just have to keep showing up."

Closing the drawers and turning off the light, Peri stood for a moment in front of the mirror, her reflection muted just enough that for a second, she could almost see who she was supposed to be. A mother. A real mother.

Peri hadn't been to Montclair Park for years, not since she'd brought Ryan and Carly out to play after visits with her father. Someone with an eye for potential lawsuits had taken down the fast, slick, steel curly slide with the two-foot drop to a sandless hole, the metal swing set, back-and-forth plastic animals that rocked on corkscrew metal stands. Everything had been replaced with a smooth, rubber-coated steel and sanded-redwood play structure, all oiled and new and safe. As she and her father sat on the stone wall watching children run across the bridge and duck into tunnels, she had a clear image of Carly in the baby swing—the kind with a web for a seat—laughing as Peri stood in front of her, pushing and making noises, "Whoop! Whoo-op!"

each time Carly swung toward her. Ryan pumped his legs on the bigger-boy swing next to Carly, trying to stay in the same rhythm with his sister, his skinny little legs trying to push himself into motion, saying, "No! I can do it myself" when Peri tried to give him a boost.

Her father spun on his seat, craning back to look at the tennis courts. Peri followed a particular toddler, a dark curly-haired girl, as she waddled to a swing and held her arms up to her mother, who swooped her up and carefully put her in a swing. Brooke had never done that, not like the toddler, not like her siblings.

None of the past year would have happened if Peri had only had the two children, happy with her amazing luck. Two healthy children. But as she'd moved closer to thirty-five, her womb had seemed to ask the question each month, "Well, is that it?" She'd convinced Graham that one more child would make them a complete family, though the convincing wasn't difficult, that part of their life so natural, his body in hers, the feel of his shoulders in her hands. Was it simply Brooke and her illness and the daily demands of her poor body that had broken them up? Or had something changed in her brain after Brooke's birth, as Dr. Kolakowski had suggested, her serotonin levels dropping to a point where she felt no pleasure in anything, where life seemed to be the tragic story she'd invented on her way to Phoenix. As the toddler in the swing screamed in joy, Peri knew it didn't matter how any of it had started. She was here, sitting with her father, waiting for her children to visit her.

"Mom," Ryan said, breathing a little heavily as if he'd run all the way to them. "We're here."

"Hey, champ," her dad said, standing up and hugging

Ryan, something she couldn't remember Ryan allowing, not for years and years. She stood up, waiting her turn, and then gently put her arms around Ryan, tentatively, as if he might fling her off, like his sister would.

"Hi, honey," she said. He moved into her, pressing back, harder, and she felt how much he had grown, his shoulders coming up to her neck. He smelled like something she remembered—maybe it was her freshman-year boyfriend, Brad, his Clearasil and Dial soap and Old Spice deodorant—and she breathed in more deeply and almost started. Ryan smelled like Noel, she realized. How he used to smell, the boy smell, a skein of sweat, hormones juicing to the surface.

"Where're Carly and Fran?" her dad asked, but Ryan didn't answer because they rounded the corner, Carly's eyes down, Fran McDermott efficient in matching cotton pants and top, ready for a park picnic.

"Hey, you," her dad said. "How's my girl?"

Carly smiled, avoiding Peri, smoothing an imaginary wrinkle in her pants. New pants, new top, things Garnet must have bought her. Peri looked at Ryan and realized he had on a completely new outfit as well, a huge short-sleeved button-down shirt and baggy pants, inches of fabric lined up like incoming waves over his shoes, as usual. Even Garnet hadn't been able to change that.

"Hi, Carly," she said. Her daughter was so close, Peri imagined she could smell her too, the floral whiff of clear green soap, Keri lotion smoothed on her thin arms, fresh, clean cotton clothes. Someone—Garnet, Peri supposed—must have bought Carly some eye shadow because there was a whisk of gold flecks on both lids. "I'm so glad to see you."

Carly nodded but still didn't look at her, nervously

pulling on her shirt hem. In only two weeks, it seemed Carly had indeed grown breasts, something to fill out the baby bra. *What else has changed?* she wondered. *What else have I missed?*

"How are you, Peri?" Fran asked. "You look great. I just love your new hairstyle."

Peri brought a hand up to her neck, feeling the blunt ends of her hair, the air on her nape. "Thanks. I had it done yesterday."

"We've got some great food," her dad said, picking up the basket and thermos. "And don't worry, I didn't make any of it myself. I got everything at A. G. Ferrari's."

"Awesome," Ryan said. "I'm starving."

"You, like, just ate breakfast," Carly said sullenly.

"Hours ago," Ryan said. "And it was Maritza's eggs, fried in that fat-free shi— crap Grandma makes her use."

"Well, we can set up and talk for a while. Maybe we can walk around the lake after lunch," Fran said.

"Remember that time we fished for crawdads with string and hot dogs?" Ryan asked, taking the thermos from Carl and turning to follow him toward the picnic tables.

"I remember that a duckling swallowed one of the strings and the hot dog got stuck in his throat. Mom had to yank it out," Carly said in a flush of words, walking faster and then ahead of the group, her words caught between them.

Peri remembered that day, Ryan maybe six, Carly four, the duckling foundering, flapping, trying to squawk out the hot dog. She'd leaned over, more than half her body over the dirty, bread-crust infested waters, and grabbed the string, pulling it out, feeling the tension in the poor thing's neck. Everyone who'd been watching clapped, telling her "What a great save," but she didn't have the courage to explain that if she hadn't allowed her children to fish for crawdads in the first place, none of it would have happened.

At the picnic table, Fran helped her dad unpack. "What a lovely spread," she said, encouraging Peri with the same smile her mother once used. "Go on," her mother would say at ice-skating lessons or the first day of school or at her first junior-high dance. Peri would look back over her shoulder and Janice would smile and pat her on the rear end. "You can do it, honey."

But Peri stood at the end of the table, unsure what to do, forgetting what she might have done before. Everything back then had been automatic, as if her actions were hardwired, and she never gave anything a second thought—arrange dishes, pass out plates, tell stories, laugh. Now it seemed to her she was like an alien brought to a strange earth ritual, and she didn't know the customs or the very body she was in.

"Peri? Do you want a turkey or ham sandwich?" Fran asked, holding out two paper-wrapped sandwiches.

"I want . . . I want to talk to Carly."

"Oh." Fran turned to Carly. "Do you want to talk with your mom?"

Carly shrugged, but she didn't run away as Peri had earlier imagined.

"Could we go over to that bench?"

"Sure," Fran said, putting down the sandwiches. "We'll eat while you two talk."

Peri thought to reach out for Carly, but the Carly who would have accepted her hand, squeezing back, her skin so warm, was no longer there. Peri would have to make friends with this new Carly, the child who'd been abandoned and forced to take care of her sister. They walked side by side to the table and sat down, the air warm on their shoulders, the sounds of cars whizzing by on Highway 13 filling the space of their silence.

"So how is it at Grandma Mackenzie's?" Peri asked finally, looking back to see her dad, Fran, and Ryan eating and talking, napkins blowing onto the dirt below the table.

"Fine."

"Are you in your same room? Daddy's old one?"

"Yeah."

"Do you talk to the cowboys still?" she asked. Carly tried not to smile, turning to the lake so Peri couldn't see her. "Who was there? Buster? I remember Buster. Isn't he the one asleep on his horse? And the other one? Jed? He has the lasso."

"No. Jed's asleep, and Buster's riding," Carly said. "It's stupid anyway. It's from when I was little."

"You used to tell me stories about them. You said they rode all night."

"I was little then!" Carly turned to her with a face only the new Carly would have, older, full of pain that only experience brings, the experience Peri had sworn to herself to shield her kids from. "I'm not little anymore. I've done a lot of things I didn't know how to do then."

Peri nodded. "You have. Things you shouldn't have had to do. I'm so sorry about it. I wasn't thinking right."

"You were crazy," Carly said. "Maybe you still are. That's why you can't have us back. That's why we'll have to go to live in, like, Phoenix with Dad and that wife."

Peri hugged herself. Carly sounded the way she herself had felt all during her childhood, the rage at her father flaring through her body at birthdays and holidays and Mother's Days, times when her own mother would cry, missing the life she thought she was going to have. How would Peri's life have been different if she'd actually said what she'd been feeling, letting her father and mother know how angry she was instead of saving it all for nighttime talks with Noel? Maybe there was hope for Carly and Ryan, despite her mistakes.

"That's right. I did go crazy," she said quietly, kicking at the gravel under the table. "And I'm going to be seeing a doctor for a long time. And I'm on drugs, too, to help me get well. And it's because I was sick that I left. And it's because I was sick that you aren't with me. You're right. And it's not fair for you and Ryan and Brooke. Not at all."

Carly looked at her, her eyes wide. "I don't want to live in Phoenix."

"Oh, baby, I know." Peri moved toward her and then stopped, not wanting to be pushed away, not now.

"I'd rather live with Grandma Mackenzie than go to Phoenix."

"I know."

"I hate him more than I hate you," she said and then gasped, a short whistling sound coming from between her teeth, as if she were trying to suck the words back in. But it was too late. There they were between them.

"We didn't do a good job. But I love you. And I'm going to try really hard to make it right."

Carly shook her head. "It's too late. Look what's happening already. Dad says after they find you guilty, the custody case is going to be a piece of cake."

"He said that to you?"

"I heard him talking on the phone. To his wife, what's-her-name. Blair."

Peri heard Ryan laughing. She turned to the table to see her dad smiling and patting Ryan's shoulder, Fran wiping her eyes with her napkin. She wished she had that kind of feeling in her body, but she hadn't warmed up to that yet. So much of herself was still submerged in the drugs and the fear that she'd never snap out of it. She didn't want her daughter to be like her and she knew she had to try harder, work harder with Dr. Kolakowski, try to push up into the light. "Listen. I'm doing all I can. I want to get better. It will never be like it was but—"

"I hated how it was," Carly said.

"I mean, it will be better. But it might take a while, and in the meantime, you have Uncle Noel and Grandpa and even Grandma Mackenzie. All of them want you to be happy."

Carly swung herself to the other edge of the bench and stood up, looking down at her mother. "But will I have you? Will I have Brooke?"

The sun beat jewels on Carly's lids, her cheeks red and smooth like a Botticelli cherub, her neck and arms exactly what Peri wanted to kiss and touch. But she couldn't move toward her daughter yet, even though she was desperate for her child's skin next to hers. Her need reminded her of the times when she was pregnant with each of them, the months before birth a waiting game until each was finally in her arms, their flesh directly under her hands, not separated by womb and muscle and skin any longer.

"You will have me," she said. "I'm going to be right here. I promise."

"Okay," Carly said, putting an index finger against her mother's arm, the heat of her fingertip moving immediately to Peri's heart. "Don't do it again. Don't ever do it again." Carly ran back to the table and sat down, and Peri looked out toward the lake. For the first time in weeks, she believed she would rise, surface, float like a duckling across murky waters, its throat and voice sore but whole.

"Here's how it's panning out," Kieran Preston said, sitting behind his desk, surrounded by stacks of folders, each neatly labeled. "They don't want to prosecute. They want to cut a deal. But it means pleading guilty to a lesser charge of neglect. Very common, very common."

"They want her to plead guilty?" Noel asked. "Why should she plead guilty? She was sick. You know we don't want that."

"Yes, yes. We know she was sick. They know it, too. Peri's a credible witness. The story is sad. People aren't behaving like monsters. There's the state system that failed. That's why they don't want to go to trial on this. But if we plead to the misdemeanor, we avoid one, a trial, two, jail time if the jury finds her guilty—"

"Guilty?" Noel said again.

"Yes, Noel. It's possible. You know how people think mental illness is just a sign of a bad character or a personality flaw. Most people would think Peri should have pulled herself up by her own bootstraps and figured another way out. And they'll point to all the *normal* things she did. They'll suggest she was sane enough to move, sign a lease, hook up the cable, register the older kids for school. It looks thought through. Premeditated."

Noel squeezed the space between his eyebrows with his thumb and forefinger. He was scared, and Peri began to feel a nervous lightness in her stomach.

"And then there's three, the publicity." Preston went on. "I think the story has died out in the papers now, and a trial would only bring it back. You have to think of the kids on that one."

Peri focused on her nails, pushing back the cuticles that she hadn't tended in well over a year. Before, back in her other life, she'd gone to Alysse at the Village Circle Beauty Spot for once-a-week manicures, twice-a-month pedicures. Now she wasn't sure what her toenails even looked like.

"Peri?" Noel stared at her. "Well? What do you think?"

"I don't know. What does it mean?"

Preston pushed back and crossed his legs. "It means we go straight to sentencing."

"I know that. But what does it mean for the custody case?" she asked.

"Well, it can mean a couple of things. One . . ." Peri grimaced. Preston seemed to be talking to her from an outline he'd written and memorized. "One, it helps your case because you weren't convicted of a felony, and two, you pleaded guilty to a misdemeanor count of neglect. However, if you, three, throw in the mental illness and the reports from Phoenix and your new doctor, there's hope."

"It's on her record though," Noel said. "It will always be there."

"That's true."

"What about the sentencing? What will the judge do to her?" Noel asked.

"That's up to him. He's one of those judges we can't pin down, lenient one minute, a hard-ass the next. But it's possible. . . ." Preston turned to her and she tried to look at him, her eyes starting to water. "It's very possible that you might serve some time."

"Shit," Noel muttered.

"Or—and this is a big or, Noel—the judge might go with time served and commute the rest, opting for parenting classes and therapy and visits from social services. Or maybe probation. There are a number of options he could pick from."

"I was only in jail for three days. How would that count?" Those three days had been forever, Sophia's scabby legs, the nighttime din of sobs and horrible dreams, the harsh closing clack of heavy doors keeping her from her children. But to a judge? Or a jury? Three days wouldn't seem like enough punishment. They would want her to do more and more and more.

"You don't know what I've seen," Preston said. "I've seen a man who beat another man to death get off with a two-year probation and five hundred hours of community service. This man wanted to kill the other guy and did, with a bat. All sorts of people who meant to do what they did don't serve even three days, so think about your case. You were ill; you didn't mean to do it. You are sorry. Those are things a lot of guilty people can't claim." Preston looked at the clock, and Peri knew their hour was up, an hour Noel and her father were paying for.

"I'll call you later," Noel said. "We need to talk about this."

"So, Peri, the kids? How are they?" Peri looked at him, this man, her lawyer, and saw for a moment he'd dropped what drove him, the case, the puzzle of the legal system, the desire to patch up another person's life and claim victory.

"Good. Brooke is doing really well. My mother-in-law. Ex . . . well, Garnet called and found the private physical therapist we used to use. Brooke's already stronger." She knew that how much better Brooke was reflected on her wrong mothering. "And I had a good visit with Ryan and Carly yesterday. They're . . . they're okay."

"And you?"

"Better." Her body was adjusting to the Zoloft and her new drug, Zyprexa, her mind righting itself back to a time even before Graham left. With Dr. Kolakowski's daily help, she'd begun peeling apart the last year, one layer at a time, and managed not to die while facing her mistakes.

"Great. Look," Preston said. "They are pressing me for an answer, but I can wait a day. Go home. Talk with your dad. But my advice is to take this offer. Custody can be reevaluated. A felony can't as easily. Trust me on this."

That afternoon while Noel and her father sat in the house drinking beer and talking about her case, Peri went to the garage and found a garden trowel, work gloves, and the twenty foxglove seedlings her father had bought for her on his way home from clearing out her apartment. Dr. Kolakowski had suggested she get outside, walk, garden, or just sit in the sun, so her father had cleared a corner of the yard for her to plant. Dirt and plants seemed so much more manageable than obsessing about the varied ways she might spend the next months or even years of her life—jail, probation, a halfway house for the mentally ill, or home, with her dad, or even better, home with her kids.

Outside, a fog pressing in from the Bay had finally cleared just in time for evening, and the ground was wet under her gloved fingers. Kneeling on the lawn, she bent over the patch of earth her father had cleared for her, digging the exact four inch holes the containers suggested and smoothing the dirt over the exposed roots, pressing down gently to keep them in the soil. After planting almost half the seedlings, Peri stood up and stretched, taking off her gloves and pushing the hair away from her eyes. In the moment of lifting her newly shorn bangs, she saw that the person in the SUV across the road—the Suburban she hadn't paid more than a split second of attention to—was Graham.

The last time she'd seen her husband had been the night he packed and left the house without waking the children. She'd followed him to the door as if in a dream, everything slightly hazy and slowed down, as if she would wake up and find his absence part of a nightmare. What she remembered was his back, his white shirt reflecting in the outside lights, a drizzle illuminated and dancing in swaths, the neat click of his shoes on the wet asphalt. Then the car started, the lights beaming into her face, and he pulled out of the driveway. She stayed by the door for a long time, maybe even an hour, the rain soaking the hem of her nightgown. She blinked, waiting for the moment when she would wake up, one, two, three . . . but she never did. She still hadn't.

The Suburban's door opened, and Graham stepped out, looking at her without saying a word. Preston would say, "Don't talk to him. Don't say a word." Her father would want her to tell him off, saying all the things she'd kept inside since the night he'd driven off, leaving her with three children. Maybe her father would want to take a swing at him. And that would feel good.

Even from across the street, he was still so handsome, still the man she'd fallen in love with in college, amazed that he sat down next to her in the cafeteria. He was still the man he'd been before Brooke. She would like to transform his face so it matched hers, the pain under her skin transmitted to his. She'd thought about this moment for a long time, many of her afternoons under the blankets a prolonged fantasy of this very minute. But now, she had no idea what to do, so she stood there, moving her feet back a couple steps, and then stopped and stared at him, this man, her husband. Her ex-husband.

As if taking her stillness for opportunity, Graham walked across the street, his hands in his pockets, his eyes on his shoes. Noticing he wasn't paying attention to traffic, she looked down the street to see if a car was coming. If a truck or an armored car or a special education bus was barreling toward him, would she scream out? Or would she let him get hit, spin to the concrete, die in front of her, die as she had felt she would a hundred times? But he made it to the sidewalk, and Peri swallowed down the drug dryness in her mouth so she could say what she had to.

"Peri," he said, putting his hand on a white picket, looking down at her work. "Planting?"

"Yes," she said, looking down at this work, the first she'd done in so long that showed, the plants spaced exactly twelve inches apart, the soil rich, sprinkled with the blue fertilizer her father had told her to use.

"How are you?" he asked, leaning against the fence now, his arms folded across his chest. Why was he so comfortable when he clearly was in danger? After all, wasn't she the same woman who had battered down his door just weeks before? Wasn't she the one who had injured their children? She was clutching a trowel, and it was deadly, the tip sharp, the dirt stuck to it rife with bacteria, tetanus, chemicals. In half a second, this happy discussion could be over, Graham bleeding as she had bled, needing stitches as she had needed them, her arm still red and puckered from the stitches' kiss.

"Better—good," she said. "I have to go in now."

"Wait. Don't go in. I need— I need to talk."

Peri dropped the trowel and stepped on it, as if that would keep her from using it on his forehead. "About what? And why now?"

He rubbed his mouth and chin, sighing. He wasn't really as handsome as always, his eyes red, his skin blotched and puffy as if he'd been drinking. But her old self, the one who had fallen in love with him so long ago, was still inside her, waving from the dried-up pool of her heart, saying, "It's him."

"I want to know why."

"Why what?"

"Why you did it."

"I can't talk about that. You know that. Whatever I said to you now, you'd use it against me. I have to go in— I don't want to talk about it with you."

Peri turned to go, and he grabbed her arm, exactly where her stitches were. "Ow! Let go!"

Graham let go and pulled back. "I'm so sorry. I forgot what happened."

"You're lucky. I can't."

"You didn't mean it, did you? You didn't want it to happen."

Peri brought a hand to her heart and imagined squeezing silent her old self, squishing her in her fist until she was gone, nothing left but a last cry and then nothing but the air around her. She looked at Graham and finally saw him as someone who had left, someone who had walked away from her and their children, someone who was almost able to pretend that years of his life had never happened. "No. I didn't want you to leave. I didn't want to take care of them all by myself without money. I didn't want Brooke to fall back by years because I couldn't afford Leon and then had to drive her to the clinic. I didn't want to sell our house and move to an apartment. I didn't want any of it, but I was too tired and too sad to care. Everything seemed so hard, so dark, so all up to me. And then I woke up strapped to a bed in a strange city, knowing that all I wanted was for you to fix it."

Graham stared at her, his face pale, the freckles on his cheeks dark constellations.

"But you can't fix it. Even if all the courts and lawyers and social workers say that you can, you can't. You can never come back to the past and be the man you were supposed to be, see that there was something wrong with me, take care of us all. It's too late. The kids had to see me depressed, and I can't take that back. And now look what's happened. Look at our children, Graham. Look what we've done."

She was still clenching her fist, and when she stopped talking, she felt her hand throb and opened it, almost expecting to see the lifeless corpse of her marriage flat in her palm.

"You're right," he said.

"Now maybe."

"Peri. Oh, Peri," he said, and she closed her eyes. "I'm—I'm sorry. I don't know how to explain . . . Brooke. She's so hurt. She'll never be . . ."

"Normal. Is that the word?" Peri asked.

Graham almost nodded, and she remembered the way he'd looked when the doctors gave them Brooke's diagnosis. Graham had almost waved away their words, wanting them to start over and change the script, make it so his girl could be fixed. But she would never be fixed and would probably get worse, and that's what he'd run away from.

"I want to make it up to . . . her." Graham moved closer to her, almost leaning over the fence.

"You can't. It's too late now. I've got to go back in the house," she said, turning without looking at him again, rounding the house and leaning against the wall in the side yard where he couldn't see her. Pressing her body against the stucco, she listened to him walk across the street and then slam his door, the engine starting after a couple of minutes and then idling for a while before he drove away.

"You were strong out there," a voice said, and Peri nearly jumped, feeling the sharp edges of stucco scratch her neck and arms. She looked up, and her father's neighbor was peering at her over the fence, her straw hat hiding her eyes. "I shouldn't have listened, but I did."

"Oh."

"I bet you wanted him to take care of you again. To make it all right." Mrs. Trimble nodded as she spoke.

"Maybe. But he left."

"That's right. And you let him go this time."

She nodded, and Mrs. Trimble handed her a rhododendron bloom, a deep purple flower, the petals floating even as Peri held it in her hand. "You get better and then take care of those children. Like he couldn't."

Mrs. Trimble moved back, swallowed into the bushes. Peri rubbed the flower on her cheek and lips, closing her eyes to its softness, wishing the next weeks and months could be as easy and painless as Mrs. Trimble made them sound, everything as smooth as the flower against her face.

Nineteen

They'd started in Ryan's room, cigarette butts, roaches, and girlie magazines easier than Brooke's sad bed, the evidence of the final night of their hard year scattered about the room. Carl had already come once to get all their clothes and bathroom articles, staring for a few seconds at a pink razor, knowing it was Carly's, amazed she was already old enough to shave. Shave what? Thin blond hair like the kind that sparkled on top of her arms?

He'd loaded all their personal effects into his car, and now he and Rosie were working mostly with bedding and furniture and kitchen items, much of which hadn't even been unpacked. As he worked, he tried to forget that Noel and Peri were at Preston's Walnut Creek office, focusing instead on each item, a folded blanket, a sheet that needed washing, a pan crusted with something cooked weeks ago and pushed into a kitchen corner. He also expected at any moment to come across checks from Graham, uncashed, hidden in a jar or a glass, but he'd found nothing, not even a dime in the carpet.

"It's amazing they lasted here as long as they did," he said into the living room, where Rosie was bagging magazines to put downstairs in the recycling bin.

"It was sad, Carl. Honestly, I would watch Carly and Ryan in the mornings going to school, and I could tell something was happening. Peri barely came out, and I saw Brooke maybe twice. It's really a damn good thing it all unfolded this way."

Carl looked up, shaking his head. "A good thing?"

"Well, yeah. Think about it. If Peri hadn't taken off, this life for them could have gone on for weeks, maybe months. Who knows what condition Brooke would have been in by then. In a way, Peri saved her by leaving."

Rosie stood up and carried the full bag to the door, then sat on the couch to pack up books she'd piled there earlier. Carl stood still over the sink. Was she right? Ramon often talked about things that were "meant to be," even though he was usually referring to lost or won tennis matches. Maybe this was something that was meant to be, Peri back with him, he with a chance to make things right with her, Brooke with all the care she needed, Graham forced to make the payments he should have been making all along. *But why this way?* he wondered, stuffing sponges, Comet, and Formula 409 spray in a grocery bag. *Why so dramatically?*

By one in the afternoon, they'd packed up everything they could and arranged the furniture so that the movers who were coming the next day could get in and out, mattresses and box springs leaning against walls, the bed frames folded on the floor, the hospital bed ready for the company that owned it to carry it away. Carl had half a thought to tell them to take it to his house, but that would jinx the whole thing. If Brooke were ever able to stay with him, he'd just order up a new one. A better one, dammit, with all the bells and whistles.

The backseat and trunk of his Corvair were piled to bursting, and he had at least another hour of work once he got home, arranging everything in his garage. Someday soon, Peri would want her photo albums and scrapbooks, every family year except the last photographed down to the dog's birthday party. She'd want her books and the china pigs Janice had given her on each birthday. She wouldn't want them with her furniture at the storage place with the bigger things from the apartment and the Monte Veda house.

"You've done good for them," Rosie said, leaning against the car, wiping her hands on her jeans. "It's all going to work out."

Carl shrugged, leaning a hip against the car and crossing his arms. "Who knows? But it feels good to clean up the mess. At least something's getting done."

"It's been a real experience for me, I'll tell you. I'll sure know what to do the next time a thirteen-year-old girl comes knocking on my door."

"I'm just glad it was your door. Thanks. Thanks so much."

Rosie smiled, and then bit her lip, her teeth white and perfect against her dusky lips. Rose-colored lips. She'd been named perfectly. "Well, I'm going to say it. I was hoping that maybe it wouldn't have to end here."

The part of him that had been asleep for too long flushed awake, his whole body alive with nerves. Weeks ago, he'd been looking pretty intently at the woman at the bridge club, wondering when he would ask her out and how long it would take before she said yes. And Rosie—well, she was warm, the scent of her even from here something he wanted to dip his head into and find himself stuck in for a good long time. Lately, while driving Peri to Dr. Kolakowski's office and to Fran's, he'd filled the rides with fantasy, wondering if the rest of Rosie was as smooth as her arms. As he looked at her now, he couldn't put a cap on his smile. In less than ten minutes, they could be in her bedroom, skin against skin, all the courtship carried on these past weeks, Rosie knowing everything about him and his family and his past, nothing for him to hide. And he'd gotten to know more about her and her son, her job, her ex-husband, José, the jerk from San Diego.

He was seconds from moving closer, taking her hand, saying, "I was hoping the exact same thing," when he remembered Peri sitting behind the table at the jail, her face so thin that he thought he would hurt her by kissing her cheek. He saw Carly, felt her arms tight around his neck; he heard Ryan's cries against his shoulder, tears hard for a teenaged boy to part with. And then, as Rosie's fingers touched him, warm and soft from constant nurse washings, he saw Janice, the way she'd looked over thirty years ago when he said, "I don't love you." She had looked so surprised, and no wonder. He'd never lost the flare of blood and skin when he looked at Janice, the same pulse that he had now felt radiating up his body from Rosie's touch. Even as he had left, he wanted Janice, loved her fine, lovely hair, her smile, the way she could hold both children on her lap and read them a bedtime story. But he wanted everything, more, all, and so he walked away to a long life of nothing.

"I would like that, too," he began.

"But."

"But . . . but I have Peri. I finally have her back, and I've got to take care of her."

Rosie nodded, smiling. "Good."

"It's not that I don't want to."

"Okay. Maybe later." Rosie held out her hand, and he took it, closing his eyes briefly to the warm feel of her, the exact way he thought she'd be.

"Yeah. Later. When this is over."

"It won't be over."

Carl opened the car door. "No. It won't be over. But it will be better."

She took a few steps away from the car, and he sat down and started the engine. "Thanks for—for being there, for all of us."

"You have my number," she said, lifting a hand, and he put the car in drive and pulled out of the parking place, looking at her in his rearview mirror. For maybe the first time in his life, he was leaving something he could actually come back to.

"My God! Preston wants her to do what?" Carl asked, leaning forward in his chair, his elbows on his knees. Noel sat across from him drinking a St. Pauli Girl pale ale.

"Plead guilty. I felt the same way, too, Dad. When he first brought it up, I was ready to walk right out of the office. But—I've been thinking. It might be the best thing. Probably no jail time. Probably, and I mean probably, she'll be able to stay here with you. And Preston really wants the best for Peri." Noel took a sip.

Pushing himself back in his chair, Carl grabbed his beer, staring at the girl on the label, peeling the edge with a fingernail. *Guilty*. It would exist forever, and not just in her mind. She'd know that somewhere, someone had typed it on a record, that infamous permanent one, and there it would be, tailing her like a shadow. But in a way, then this part would be over, and she could focus on her kids. "What does Peri think?" Carl asked.

"I don't know really. We didn't talk much on the way home."

"What about the kids? What does this mean for her getting custody?"

His son shrugged. "That's the custody battle. That's for the court to decide. But if she's found guilty and made to do what—more therapy? A parenting class? Probation? She won't get custody. Not now. Not right away. Graham at least doesn't have a criminal record. He might be a complete asshole, but he hasn't been convicted of anything."

"He should have been. Thrown in for being a shitty father." Carl paused, taking a swig, hearing Noel's pause echo in the room. He flushed, realizing he deserved to be in the same jail with Graham, hobbled and linked by chains, like father-in-law, like son-in-law.

"Yeah." Noel looked over his shoulder. "What's Peri doing?"

"Her therapist wants her to get outside more, so I bought some plants. It's good exercise." He almost laughed. Now the father he should have been, making sure Peri was fed and healthy and on time for appointments. While he was keeping her active, he hadn't a clue about what she was feeling inside, each day about making a pattern she could live by, a focused, thoughtful pattern a jury would see as healthy and improved and sane. But inside her? Carl might never be granted a permit. The same was true of Noel. Oh, he knew about Noel's job and his apartment and his new mountain bike, but had he heard much about these girlfriends who were a part of his life and then not? Did Carl know anything about what Noel wanted?

"So," Carl began slowly, "what's next?"

"We make a decision. Or Peri does. I've got to call Preston by six. If she says okay, we get ready for the sentencing. If not, we get ready for the hearing."

"No. I mean, yes. But I really meant about you."

Noel almost missed the coffee table as he put his beer down. "What *do* you mean?"

"Well, now that Peri is here, and some plan or another will be put in motion, you don't have to be so focused on her. For a long time, it seems to me, you've been maybe too involved."

"Someone had to be. Mom died. Someone had to care."

Carl nodded. "Yeah. That's true. And I care now. I know it's too little too late. But I'm in for the long haul. The kids—they can stay here too if the court allows."

"Even Brooke?"

"Even Brooke. But like you said, it's kind of a wait-and-see thing. I'll take care of it though, so what about you?"

Noel looked around the room, putting an arm on the top of the couch. "Work. More work. The usual. I want to be around for her though."

"Of course. Do you have a lady friend or somebody?"

"Not now."

"Who was your last one? You never mentioned anyone special."

"Listen, Dad, I don't know what you're doing." Noel stood up, putting his hands in his pockets and facing the large picture window. Outside, house finches chattered and fought in the sycamores, flying away in a flash of brown and orangey-red as a girl with a yip-yapping dog walked down the sidewalk. "We've never talked much about this stuff."

"I'm just curious, that's all. I'd like to see you—see you happy. I never said anything before. I know that. I never asked. You're so good with Peri's kids. I wondered if you wanted a family of your own some day."

"You're going to extol the virtues of family? You?"

"Stupid, huh? But right now, even with all this, I'm glad I have you both."

Noel turned to look at him, and in a space of seconds, Carl could see him as a boy, reading on his stomach in the living room, his legs crossed and swinging, his chin in his palm. So serious, always so serious. His boy. His only boy.

"Dad."

"What, son?"

"I think . . . I don't know how to be with a woman for more than six months. I always think I'll end up being . . ."

"Being me?" Carl asked.

Noel shook his head and turned away. Carl could see his pulse beating in his son's neck, his blood full of the words he'd almost said. Noel was scared of being like his old man.

All the things that had never been said coiled in Carl's throat, the "I love you's," the "I'm unhappy's," the "I need help's." No one in this family had ever practiced the simple art of the truth, wanting to shield others from the terrible fire inside. In the last weeks, he'd heard more from Peri and Carly and the hospital staff and even Rosie Candelero than he'd heard in his whole adult life. Even his tennis buddies wanted him to articulate his sadness. Why hadn't he ever learned to say the things that helped? Why hadn't he ever listened to what his family needed to say?

"I did screw up. Royally. But you aren't me. You aren't, son. You've stuck by everyone in this family: your mom, your sister, the kids, me. You're the only one. You know how to do family more than any of us."

Noel put his head in one hand, his shoulders shaking. Carl stood up and walked to him, pulling him close. He hadn't hugged him since he was a boy and Noel's head used to reach only to his chest. Now Noel's quick breaths were in his ear. "What is it, Noel?"

After a minute, Noel pushed away and wiped his eyes with his shirtsleeve. "God. I haven't done that in a while."

"I saw someone on *Oprah* who said we should cry every day." Carl tried to find a place for his arms, not knowing if the moment had passed or he might need to hold his son again.

"Since when do you watch *Oprah*?"

"When I don't make it up to tennis. Don't tell Ralph," Carl said, finding the right laugh, one that lightened but didn't suggest he was ready to stop talking. "Noel?"

"We can talk later. We will. There is someone, maybe, but I just can't think of anything except Peri right now."

Carl shrugged. Part of him didn't want to let this go, needing to expose every truth and buff it clear with Lemon Pledge. But a son—a man—wasn't a table or a counter, and he knew, at least, that one day Noel would come to him. "That's fine. You know I'm always here."

The front door opened and Peri walked inside hold-

ing one of Mrs. Trimble's prized rhododendron blooms.
That woman, thought Carl. *I bet she talked Peri's ear off*.
His daughter closed the door and put the flower carefully on the entry table, its long droopy petals hanging
over the edge.

"He was here."

"Who?" Noel asked, all traces of his tears gone.

"Graham."

"That son of a bitch." Carl walked toward the door,
but Peri moved in front of him, holding his arm.

"He's gone."

"What did he want?"

She shook her head, gripping him tighter, more holding on to him for support than holding him back. "I
don't know. He asked about me and how I felt. He
asked me about what I did. He talked about Brooke."

"Shit!" Noel slapped his thighs. "I hope you didn't say
anything."

"Maybe I did. I think . . . I got angry."

"Shit!" Noel said again. "He's probably on his way now
to his lawyers. Maybe he was even taping the whole thing."

Peri was silent, still, pale, dropping her hand from
Carl's arm and backing against the wall. There was a different look in her eyes, fear freezing her flat and empty.
Is that what she'd looked like that last month in her
apartment, the shell of a mother Carly found every
morning under the covers? He wouldn't let her go back
to that, not ever. "Hold on, Noel. Just wait a minute.
Peri, come sit down."

He led her to a chair and she sat, curling her legs up
under her, leaning her head against the back. He sat on
the coffee table and patted her knee. "So do you think
he had a motive?"

She shook her head, the new haircut making her look more like the girl he remembered. "No. He—he seemed like he wanted me to tell him something. To tell him what to do. Like he was the one who needed direction. He said he was sorry."

Noel paced back and forth in front of the window. Carl shook his head at him as Peri rubbed her eyes, not wanting to scare her any further. "So that doesn't sound like the kind of thing he'd want on tape. If he wanted to frame you, it would be oilier, sneakier, snake-in-the-grass questions, I think."

Sighing, Noel sat down next to Carl. "That's right. He'd lead you into saying the worst kind of thing. I'm sorry. I just don't trust him."

"He seemed sad." Peri looked up at them. "And he was trying to tell me something. But I remembered what you told me, and I left. I didn't say all the things I wanted to."

Carl and Noel looked at each other, and then Noel said, "I better let Preston know about this." He stood up but turned back to Peri. "Have you thought about what you want to do? I mean, with the case? How do you want to plead? You know what I think."

Nodding, Peri exhaled. "I want to plead guilty." She glanced at them both, her eyes watering. "I am guilty."

That evening just after dinnertime, Carl drove up to Garnet's to take Ryan and Carly out for an ice cream at Fenton's. After phone calls with Fran and Dr. Kolakowski, Noel had called Preston to tell him to accept the deal. Preston had promised to get back to them in the morning with the sentencing date. Noel and Peri went to a movie, that romantic one about the time-traveling man, and once they left, Carl decided to visit the kids and tell them what was going to happen. Maybe he'd also get a chance to check out Graham, he thought. *See what the SOB was up to.*

Garnet was actually sitting in the living room as Brooke's physical therapist, that guy, what's-his-name, rolled Brooke around on a large rubber ball.

"Leon had some free time and decided to come visit Brooke," Garnet said, standing up stiffly, smoothing her pants, and then walking briskly with Carl into the entryway.

Leon raised a hand, and Brooke said, "Gapa," her consonants already more pronounced after only a few visits with the speech therapist.

"That's right, honey. Have a good time."

Garnet led him into the dining room, motioning to a chair. "Let me get the children."

"Where's Graham?"

"Oh. I . . . I . . ."

"He came to the house today. He talked to Peri." Peri. His girl, out in the yard because it was good for her, so thin, so alone, forced to talk with Graham, who had let this happen.

Garnet turned back, confused, her eyes dark. "What?"

"That's right. Graham came up to her while she was gardening and started asking her questions. Scared her to death. Made her think he was trying to get her to say something bad. What's going on, Garnet?"

Garnet bit her lip, flecks of red lipstick sticking to her teeth. "Well, I don't know. I didn't know he was going to do that."

"Where is he?"

"This is inappropriate, Carl. You are here to take the children for an ice cream. We can't talk about this. It might come up in court."

"Peri's pleading guilty to a lesser charge. She's going to be sentenced soon." The words were out before he had a chance to think, the truth a new habit to which he was becoming addicted.

"Oh. My."

"It probably means she won't get custody right away."

Garnet quelled a smile using her lipsticked teeth. "Oh."

"So I was wondering what he was doing at the house."

Garnet grabbed a chair back and leaned toward it, looking down at him. "He went home for a few days. He needs to get some things in order, and now it seems doubly important."

"Maybe. But what did he want with Peri?"

She shook her head. "I don't know."

"He needs to leave her alone. She's doing so much better, but she was real shook up afterward."

"Maybe she needs to . . . well, fine. You're right. I'll tell him. He shouldn't have done that."

"Exactly," he said, turning to avoid Garnet's raised chin, narrowed eyes, puckered lips that always said, "Cast no stones here." In the frame of the kitchen door, Maritza's dark form flickered past.

"Well."

"Good." He looked up, as prepared for Garnet as for one of Bob's big serves. "The kids ready?"

Ryan ordered the largest sundae on the menu, a concoction with eight scoops of ice cream, bananas, whipped cream, and three sauces that spilled over the dish and pooled on the table. Carly had eyed it as well, but chose the hot fudge sundae instead. Carl ordered two scoops of peppermint stick in a dish. After the waitress set the ice cream on the table and walked away, he remembered the flavor had been Janice's favorite, not his.

"So I wanted to tell you two about what's going on with your mother's case." He licked his spoon and placed it in his dish. Both kids' lips were covered with chocolate they wiped away as soon as they saw him notice.

"What?" Ryan asked.

"Her lawyer decided that it might be better for her to plead guilty to a charge that's not as bad as the one she was arrested for."

"Guilty? Does that mean jail? Will she have to go back to that place?" Carly dropped her spoon, the metal clattering on the table.

"No. Well, probably not. If she does, we'll have to visit her there instead of at the park or at Fran's office."

Carly looked down at her lap. Carl reached over to pat her shoulder. "I'll go with you. So will Uncle Noel."

"But she might not go, right?" Ryan kept eating as he talked, almost all eight scoops gone.

"That's right. Jail time is really not that likely. Your mom has done great since she came home. The medicine is working, and she goes to her doctor every day. And she gets to visit you and Brooke once a week. She's feeling really good."

"But will she get us? If she's guilty, how can we live with her?" Carly bit her lip in the same way Garnet did, shocking Carl into remembering his grandchildren were actually related to that woman.

"That's what I wanted to talk with you about. Your mom might not get custody, but those arrangements can be reevaluated. Whatever a judge decides now doesn't have to be forever."

"I don't want to go to Phoenix. I hate Phoenix," Carly said, crying now.

"Dad left for Phoenix today," Ryan said, sliding his spoon into the melted ice cream at the bottom of his dish.

"I know. When exactly did he leave?"

"In the afternoon or something. He said he had to go home to do some stuff but that he'd be back in a couple days. He packed everything."

"Maybe he thinks he won't have to come back. Maybe he thinks we'll have to go down there and live." Carly's voice was rising, and Carl shushed her under his breath, patting her shoulder and leaving his hand there to calm her.

"It wouldn't be that fast. He'll have to come back to court. Don't think that," Carl said. Graham was up to something, though. His wife surely could have flown up with whatever he needed. Or if there were bills to pay or matters to organize, couldn't she have done that for him at least? And Graham must have this much or more vacation time at whatever job he had. Hell, he could claim it as personal leave. These were his kids, for Christ's sake!

"I'm not going down there," Ryan said flatly. "I'm staying here. I'm going to tell the judge that. I'll even stay at Grandma's before I move in with him."

"You okay with Grandma Mackenzie?" Carl tried to keep the answer he wanted out of his question.

"Yeah. It's cool," Ryan said. "We start our new school

tomorrow. She went down and signed me up for a skate-boarding class at the new skate park."

"What about you, Carly? Is it going okay?"

She looked down at her half-eaten sundae. "It's okay."

Carly was holding back something, maybe words she imagined would hurt him. What? That she liked it? Or that she didn't? Ryan shifted, kicking the table pedestal, and then shrugged. "Are we, like, done yet?"

Outside, Carl took Carly's hand, and she let him keep it, her skin cool against his. Peri used to walk beside him waiting for him to hold out his hand, grabbing on to it, not wanting to let go until the last minute. If he closed his eyes right now, he could be back in 1968, his two children walking with him down this same sidewalk, Peri chatting about school, Noel quiet, one step behind them but watching everything.

"Listen. You know I don't want you two to live any-where but here. But whatever happens, I'm here for you. Do you understand?"

Both of them nodded; Carly almost smiling.

"I'm serious. Don't think I won't know what's happening with you for one second." And he closed his eyes, wishing it was 1968, and he was saying this to Peri and Noel, and they were nodding and smiling like Carly and Ryan. Like these children, they would actually believe him. Like he did now, he would mean every word.

Twenty

A lready, even though she pretended not to sigh, to sink into her sturdy desk chair, to breathe in the smell of a newly carpeted, clean classroom, Carly felt better. Back when she started school in Walnut Creek, she refused to look in the corners of the room at the stacks of old tests, rolled up maps, and broken overhead projectors piled on the dusty linoleum. She'd tried not to compare Walnut Farms Middle School with her old school in Monte Veda with its brand new Macintosh computers and HP printers and Sony televisions in every classroom, not to mention the computer lab, the performing arts building, the auditorium that even the high school kids sometimes borrowed. If she'd thought of all those things plus what was going on with her mother and Brooke, Carly wouldn't go to school at all.

Even though she didn't know one single person at Piedmont Pines Intermediate and tried to smile as the first period English teacher announced her name and the students all turned at once to stare at her, she was happier. She'd be lonely and whispered about, but this school was clean and ordered like the one in Monte

Veda, full of computers, moms working in every classroom. And the best parts were that Brooke was with a speech teacher right now, and Ryan walked Carly to school and even talked to her on the way, and her mom was just down the street and not crazy anymore. Who cared about the rest?

But at lunchtime, some of her relief vanished, and she sat by herself at a table with the bag lunch Maritza had packed her. "Don't look inside until lunch, *Mí'ja*. It's good." And it was. A *torta*, as Maritza called it when Grandma wasn't listening, a thick ham sandwich in a soft roll, a bag of crisp potato chips, and a huge brownie. She didn't want to go stand in line for a milk, drawing more whispers and stares to herself. Carly could hear them even now, the "Her mom was in jail," and "Her sister is, like, a cripple," the story changing like a sentence in the telephone game. By the time school was over, her mom would be on *America's Most Wanted,* and Brooke locked up behind brick walls in a dark mental hospital in England or Bulgaria or somewhere.

"Hi. I know about you." A girl sat down next to Carly, sliding so close, Carly felt her thigh against hers. "I read it in the paper. Mom says your grandma lives up the street from us."

Carly froze, holding her sandwich in her hands, looking at the girl's black hair, short and wild and gelled in stiff pointy spikes. Ryan would want to know her in a couple of years, a girl who hung out with skateboarders and smoked Lucky Strikes in the culverts under the overpass after school. Carly put her sandwich down. She would just pack up and go outside and sit on the lawn. Then the girl moved even closer.

"But I won't say anything to anyone."

"You won't?" Carly had said this too loudly, her voice froggy, two girls from the next table turning to look at her.

"No. No one else around here reads the paper anyway. They're all into boys and shit. I don't think they know anything. I've read all of George Eliot's books."

"Oh." Carly raised her eyebrows, pretending to know who George Eliot was, saying with her expression, Like, everyone knows *him*. She'd have to go into Grandma's library and look when she got home; the name sounded as old as the shelves and shelves of ancient books Grandma warned her to be very careful with.

"Are you here forever? Or do you have to, like, go to some different house with a whole new mother and shit? I've read about that. Maybe someone really famous will adopt you, and you'll live in like Beverly Hills or Zimbabwe or some amazing place."

Carly shook her head. "I don't think so. I think I'm going to be here for a while. There's a case and stuff."

"I've read about that. Oh! My name's Simone. That's not my real name. I took it from Simone de Beauvoir. You know."

Carly raised her eyebrows again, thinking, *How will I remember that name?*

"My real name's Brittany. Can you believe that? Like I'm going to go around with that kind of name? So I changed it last year. Well, like in December. No one calls me it though."

"I'll call you Simone." Carly understood the need to change, knowing that if she really wanted to, she'd have to start with the past two years or even more, imagining a new life to fill in her story. But you couldn't just change a life like you could change a name. All that had happened and was happening would be with her like the color of her eyes and hair, different from the rest of her families', all her own.

"You will? That is, like, so cool. And I mean it. I won't say a thing about, you know, your sister and mom and all that. It's, like, our secret."

"Our secret," Carly repeated. Simone grabbed a chip from the bag, and Carly smiled and picked up the sandwich that Maritza had made for her, glad to have someone to share her secret with at last.

That night, Carly turned sleeplessly on her sheet, listening to the sounds of a late spring storm against her window, the push of new leaves hitting the glass, twirling and twisting before falling to the ground. Carly tried not to think about Maxie, continuously curling and uncurling in the dog house, trying to find a warm spot. Sighing, she silently promised Maxie that she'd wake up early and let her out of the pen, sneak her into the laundry room, and give her some of Maritza's fluffy scrambled eggs.

Brooke's nurse walked up and down the hall every twenty minutes or so, stretching her legs, and someone was on the phone, probably Grandma, the constant lull of her voice rising through the floorboards. Finally, around twelve, Jed and Buster still on their last roundup, Carly got out of bed and put on the soft slippers her grandmother had bought her, not wanting her to "run around like a savage in bare feet."

Quietly opening her door, she peeked out into the hall. Ryan's door was shut, no radio or computer games seeping into the hall. Carly walked to the stairway, and held on to the banister, sliding down the slick wood, her slippers *shif, shiffing* as she moved. On the second floor, she followed the sound of her grandmother's voice, and then stood next to the bedroom door, her ear against the cool wallpapered wall.

"But, Graham," her grandmother said. "But, Graham."

In the pause, Eustace, who had followed Carly down, twisted and twirled around her ankles, purring and licking her bare skin.

"You can't just do that. This is not about you, Graham. . . . Well, I know. But the children? Brooke? . . . I am not the one to call them. . . . No. No. Someone has to face this with some rigor. . . . Fine. You do that, and let me know immediately what they say. You can't let this go on one more second. . . . Of course I will! What did I tell you? What have I always told you?"

Carly felt an ache in her lungs and breathed in deeply. Maybe her heart had stopped as well, her whole body trying to decipher the mystery of her grandmother's conversation. What was her father doing? Who did he have to call? Eustace purred, his orange fur muted, his two long front teeth slick and gleaming with moonlight.

"I know what is happening." Maritza glided past Carly and leaned against the wall, smoothing her plain cotton robe against her sides. "I have seen everything, *todas cosas*."

"What? What are you talking about?" Carly's heart was pounding now, Maritza having appeared like a ghost in the long dark hallway.

"He will not come back. He is staying away from now on."

Carly looked down at the cat. Even though she had seen her father at breakfast and dinner every day for going on two weeks, his shirts ironed and hanging in the laundry room, he hadn't really been there. He had been on the phone with the lawyers or his wife, Blair, talking and talking about his plans for them in Phoenix, but he'd never really looked at her. Sometimes, she would stare at him and blink, trying to bring him into focus, wondering if the next time she opened her eyes, he would have disappeared altogether. Her mother, whom she saw only once a week and who was miles away, was more home than he had been.

"How do you know that?" Carly asked.

"*Ay*, well, I listen. I hear him one night in Brooke's room, talking to her while the nurse, she downstairs. He say, 'I can't do this to you,' and 'You will be better off, *Mí'ja.*' *Verdad*, he not say *Mí'ja*, but he mean it. He want her to be happy, I could tell, and that mean he will not be here. It mean he will not drag her to that desert he lives in."

"What will happen to us?" Carly whispered. They moved down the hall toward the stairs, and then her grandmother's light flickered off, and the hall was a tunnel with no end, Maritza's eyes the only light.

"That one," Maritza said, nodding toward Grandma's door. "She's a *meticona*. How you say? A pain in the ass. But she take care of you. *Verdad, Mí'ja.* She drive me crazy every day, but inside, she a strong woman. And she love you all. Maybe not like your grandfather. That Carl, I like him, but she take good care of you. Look at your sister already! Now you sleep. Go to bed."

Maritza touched her arm and then swished away, the air around Carly full of lavender. She walked up the stairs, her feet cold on the wood through her slippers, Maritza's words still in her ear.

The day back at the Monte Veda house when she first woke up to find her father gone, his shirts and razor and aftershave packed up and resting in some other room, in some other house, far away from her and her family, she'd searched the house for clues, not wanting to upset her mother, even then. All morning, she'd pulled back pillows and dug through sweaters, needing a note, a receipt, a phone number, but by afternoon, she still had nothing. As she'd sat on the back deck, the wood wet from a nighttime rain, she finally found what she was looking for—a huge empty spot in the middle of her chest that pulsed and burned, the true sign of his absence.

Now, reaching her room, she went in and closed her bedroom door after Eustace slinked by, turning to see the cowboys of her father's childhood ride on without him. She didn't have to search for anything this time. He was gone, and nothing inside her hurt one single bit. Maybe he'd never been there at all.

Twenty-one

"Peri? Peri? It's me."

Peri sat up in bed, her heart pounding, the phone pressed hard against her face. *The kids?* she thought. *What's wrong with the kids?* figuring in her half-awake mind that Graham knew something, had to have bad news, just like he always did. *Brooke*, she thought. *Oh, my God. Brooke.*

"What is it? What now?"

"I need to talk. I wanted to talk with you the other day at your dad's."

She turned on the light and looked at the clock. Twelve thirty. "I pleaded guilty, if that's what you wanted to know. I can't have the kids for a year, so you won. You got it all. You get them, and I don't."

He didn't say a thing, the silence behind him like a sad ghost. Her dad had told her Graham had gone home, back to that great stucco house, the door that must be fixed by now, the gate keeping everyone out, the wife who screamed and called the police. *She saved my life*, Peri thought now, touching the smoothed-out but still-red scar on her arm. *Graham's wife saved my life.*

"I don't want them."

"You don't want them?"

"I can't have them. I . . . don't know how to live with them anymore. I only knew how to live with them when you were there."

Peri felt the old balloon of rage in her chest grow, and this time it found voice. "You don't want the children? How could you not want them?" she said before willing the words back, the ones that might convince him she was right. Why did she care so much about his words, when it meant that the children would stay here, in Piedmont or Oakland, near her? How could he not want the best thing they'd ever done together? Breathing sadness out into her room, she knew she was hearing Graham's words as Carly and Ryan would hear them, words from a father they'd loved for years before things went wrong. She saw their eyes, blue and brown, their hurt during these weeks when she'd not been able to be the mother she knew they needed, and she wanted to find the trowel and do what she'd held back from doing that day in the garden. "They are beautiful!"

"I know. I know they are. But it's too late. I waited too long to remember how to be their father. And Brooke."

"Too much work, right? Like always. You couldn't hire someone like your mother does? I saw that house of yours. You could give them everything."

"Not everything."

"What do you mean?"

"I couldn't give them you."

She stopped talking, staring at the wall, the yellow reading light casting her shadow against it, a shape she was used to seeing, the lump of her body under the covers. But now she felt charged, her anger at Graham, her sorrow for her children, beating all her nerves alive, even those the drugs tried to tamp down. And when his words repeated in her head, his acknowledgment that she was good for her kids, the tears came.

"I know you didn't mean it. You were sick, Peri. And I can't . . . I can't live near you and see what I did. I know I did it. I tried to pretend, and it was easy to for a long time. But when I saw the kids and they kept telling me they didn't want to be with me, I realized how I screwed up. And it started years ago. I let you be the main parent, especially with Brooke. And you were a good mom, Peri. All those years. I'm sorry. I really am. I know it doesn't mean anything now, but I am so sorry."

The silence behind him filled with the echo of his sorrow, his tears against her ear. He'd cried in her arms in joy at a baby, with anger at his mother's harsh criticism, in frustration at yet another diagnosis for Brooke. There were times in their marriage when he'd turned to her. These were moments that she'd mentally put in snow domes, shaking them now and again to relive the moments when he'd needed her. And now, even though they were no longer married, this was one of them, a time she'd think about over and over again, shaking her mind to remember his apology, his gift of their children, watching the snow fall over the moment when he gave them back to her.

"I've withdrawn my petition. My mother is filing for custody on Monday. I made her promise that she won't fight you when you're able to petition for custody again. And I won't let her change her mind."

Peri's father quietly opened her door, and she waved, letting him know everything was all right, and he closed it softly. "What about support?" she asked Graham.

"Everything is fixed. I've made the payment to make up for everything from before, when I didn't pay. You're getting the wheelchair and the van. I have to special order both and Brooke will have to be fitted for her chair. There's a great place in Berkeley. But it won't be long."

Peri felt her body relax and shift, her pulse slow and rest. There were so many words lined up on her tongue, but did they matter now? Even if she kept pounding him with sentences, she would still be here, at her father's house, her brain chemistry righting itself, her arm healing, her children safe and sleeping at Garnet's. If she told him again and again what a terrible father he'd been, they would still be divorced. He'd still be living in the stucco house in the desert with another woman. He still wouldn't love her anymore.

"Okay," she said finally. "I'll tell my lawyer tomorrow. You know there is a chance the guardian ad litem might not think Garnet's is the best place for them."

"I know. But that's not likely. They are all together. Near you. Near your dad and Noel. With my mom, their grandmother. At least in this I think we'll be okay. They like being there, Peri. It's safe. It's solid. It's known."

She nodded, hearing Ryan skating off to his lesson at the park, Carly telling her about a friend at school, Brooke giggling with Leon. "You're right."

"So, I'll—" he began.

"Do you love them?" she blurted out, remembering their tiny bodies, the swaddled infants the nurses had passed to Graham, who had cooed and held them to his chest. If she searched through all the photos in storage, she'd find him, his arms on Ryan's and Carly's accepting shoulders, his laughter at birthday parties, his serious Christmas-card face, all their bodies pressed together.

There were only a few photos of him with Brooke, and then none at all, as if he'd been trying to erase himself from their lives, as if those other photos had never been taken at all.

"Of course. Oh, God, Peri. I do."

"But not enough to keep them."

"Maybe I love them too much to keep them. Maybe I know I'm not good enough," he said, and then they were silent together, holding each other in space, listening to what wasn't said as they had done so many nights in the last years of their marriage.

"Noel. It's me. Nothing's wrong." Peri heard fumbling in the background, a clock falling to the floor? A book? The scratch of Noel's whiskers against the receiver, the rustle of blankets.

"What's wrong? Is it the kids?"

"Nothing's wrong. I think things are right. I'm sorry to call this late, but I had to tell you."

Noel covered the receiver with his hand, and Peri listened to the scratch of his voice, the intense whisper of someone hoping not to be heard. He wasn't alone. Peri closed her eyes, swallowed down the joy in her throat, trying to take in the possibility that at this minute, both she and her brother were happy.

"Sorry. What's going on?"

"Graham called. Now wait! It's not bad, at least not for me. He's withdrawing his petition for custody. Garnet's filing. They're going to be able to stay here."

"He what?"

"He changed his mind. He's going to let Garnet have them for the year, and then—they'll probably come back to me."

"Oh, Periwinkle."

To be honest, Peri hadn't known for years what an actual periwinkle looked like. Without asking her father, who knew the regular and fancy name for every plant, she decided it was a purple flower, purple for the *p* that began the word, purple for the royalty in a special name, the one her brother and mother and sometimes her father called her, their hearts tender for her, the name making her tender for them, her family. Later, she discovered that the flower she'd picked in the backyard as a child, the blue-and-white star-shaped flowers tucked deep inside green leaf clusters, weren't simply the "sweet" flower, the name she and Noel had given them after learning there was nectar at the base of the flower. Careful of the poisonous petals, they would press the flowers with greedy lips, waiting for the sweet nectar to hit their tongues. Those flowers were periwinkles. *"Vinca,"* her dad had said. "Periwinkle, too. Why didn't you ask?"

Back when they were little, she and Noel would sit in the shade of the yard and pick the flowers, sucking out all their juice, throwing the flowers behind them when they were finished. That's how she'd felt for years, sucked out and discarded. But now, she was the undiscovered flower, the one hiding in her leaves, full of nectar no one had touched, a happy future she could almost believe in.

"I know. I can't believe it."

"That coward. He's such a coward, Peri. Why would he do that?"

She was about to agree, but then prickled defensively. There it was, her old habit of covering up for everyone and making everything look all right. Maybe now, though, Graham was actually being brave by admitting he wasn't good enough for his children. "I don't know. I just know it might be fine. It might turn out okay."

There was more rustling, and Noel paused, the shape of his silence round and full of expectation.

"Who's there?" she asked.

He sighed. "How could you tell?"

"You weren't as organized as usual. Things were falling. There's noise. I'm not used to hearing *that*."

"This probably isn't the best time to talk about it."

"You deserve somebody, Noel. You deserve everything you want, and I want to know. I want to be a part of your life."

"You have so much on your plate, Peri."

She brushed back her bangs and sighed. "I know, I know. But I need to be there for you, too. Like you've always been there for me, Noel. Even when we were kids. Even before anything happened. Before Brooke. So tell me."

"It's someone I started seeing recently."

"What's her name?" she said.

"You know her."

"I do?"

"You remember—Susan."

Peri bit her lip, thinking back through the first names of Noel's girlfriends, the ones she'd chanced to meet. Yes, Susan was a couple of summers ago, dark and tall, smiles for the kids. For Brooke. There was a picnic, a visit in Susan's car, a convertible Volvo, the story of a swift breakup. "Oh. From that summer. How did you reconnect?"

"I don't know. I was sitting in that courtroom, and I kept wishing for someone to look at. Someone to turn to when the lawyers started in. And I guess I was wishing for Susan. So I called her."

Peri smiled. "So did you have to promise you were a changed man?"

He was silent, and Peri realized that of course he had to tell her he changed because he had. They all had, these last weeks stripping off the past to find some luster beneath.

"Yeah, and I hope she believes me."

"Where is she now?"

"In the bathroom."

"So . . . this time? Is it going to work?"

"Maybe. She knows about me, you, us. Everything. All of it."

"I'm sorry. I'm so sorry," she said, not wanting to think he'd never had a committed relationship because of their family, the way they all left when they were needed the most.

"Don't be. It's not your fault. Look. I'll come over after work. We can talk about it—about everything—later."

"All right. Noel?"

"What?"

"I love you."

"I love you too, Peri."

She hung up, and she sat in her bed. She didn't really know Noel or Graham, two men she'd loved and needed so deeply.

Putting the phone down, she got out of bed and walked into the living room, the streetlight sending yellow streaks through the blinds. Peri sat on the couch, looking out toward the bottlebrush tree and then the street, the night a distant unknown planet, no one moving, no cars, the air still and light. This is what her life would be then, a moving into what she didn't know, everything a mystery, her own body different, changed, made whole by chemicals and talking and love. She'd never again live her life the way she had—not only because it was impossible, but because she didn't want it anymore. At last. She didn't want the Monte Veda house or Graham or the old patterns of doing everything and feeling nothing. She'd be a mom again, her children a couple miles away, and she'd move into it slowly, as if adapting to a new atmosphere. She'd live with her father and learn to love him in another way, not like she had before, desperate and clinging and full of despair. Closing her eyes against the night, Peri breathed in, holding the night scene in her mind. From this point on, anything might happen.

Carly and her mother were on their knees reading a page from the old copy of the *Sunset Western Garden* book her grandfather had left in the garage for emergency information, flipping through pages for directions on how far apart to space Mexican sage. Grandpa Carl had dug up another spot, ripping sod away from the fence, and the mean old witch from next door, Mrs. Trimble (who supposedly was really a nice lady), had given them twelve sage seedlings. "Plant them in the sun and won't you have a surprise! The purple blossoms are just wonderful!" she'd said, handing them over the fence. "I see Mr. Randall even changed the sprinkler head for you. That's something in itself."

After a few minutes without finding the exact directions, her mother closed the book and smiled. "We'll just have to guess. Not too close together. But not too far apart, either."

Carly nodded and they set the plants in the soft dirt, not saying much, the air clean from the rain two days ago. They'd come to Grandpa's after her mother had gone to Grandma Mackenzie's to visit Brooke. Fran McDermott was now in the living room with her grandfather drinking coffee. Ryan was playing a computer game, the muffled sound of guns and blasts and helicopter battles slipping out his window.

"So how is your new school?" her mother asked.

"It's okay. I have a friend."

"You do? That's wonderful." Carly looked at her mother, hearing something in her voice, a lurch over tears. She wondered why a friend would make her mother sad. Did she think that meant Carly didn't need her?

"I just met her. I mean, I barely know her. Her name is Simone. Not really Simone. Brittany. But she wants everyone to call her Simone."

Her mother laughed and looked at her. If she had been crying, they weren't sad tears. Not at all. "She sounds interesting."

"She is. I had to look up all these, like, totally old writers that she's read. Grandma had the books in her library. Simone's really smart."

Her mother took off her gloves and sat back, crossing her legs at her ankles, closing her eyes and looking up at the sun. For a second, with her new haircut and pale skin, she looked like a teenager, not a mom at all. Carly sat back in the same way, her mother's shoulder against hers, her skin sun-warm and soft.

"So I went to court."

"I know." She didn't want to tell her mother she'd been waiting all yesterday morning, her stomach full of pins. Finally, her grandmother had come in to tell Carly and Ryan what had happened, her face full of too many emotions for Carly to know if the verdict was good.

"Did she tell you what happened?"

"Sort of. She said she'd let you tell us the whole thing."

Her mother widened her eyes. "She did?"

Carly nodded. "Yeah."

"Well, listen." Her mother sat up and took Carly's hand. "I pleaded guilty to a charge of neglect. And the judge said that I didn't have to go back to jail for now."

Carly nodded. She'd asked her grandmother the first thing, made her tell the most important parts because she didn't want to think of that terrible place again, her mother's stringy hair and empty eyes, the long corridor she had to run down. "That's good. I hate that place."

"But I have to do other things. I have to stay with Grandpa like I'm doing now. And I have to go to my doctor and take classes and meet with Fran."

"Oh."

"And I can't live with you. Not for a year at least. Then the judge will decide. He'll look at all my records, and talk to my doctor and Fran, and make sure I went to all my classes. He'll also want to talk to you and Ryan. Maybe Brooke if she keeps doing as well. Did you see her sitting up today?"

Carly nodded, feeling her leg bones against the lawn, everything in her so heavy. A year. A year with her grandma in the big house and the new school. A year in the same place, no more moving, no more being by herself. A year she wouldn't have to take care of Brooke. "Yeah. I saw her. Leon comes over all the time."

Her mother hadn't met face-to-face with Leon, but

Carly had heard him talking about her with Maritza, saying, "I don't know if I can forgive the woman. Look what's happened to Brooke!" He didn't even know the worst, the way it had been in the apartment, the smell, the red patches on Brooke's skin—bedsores—the terrible way she'd looked at Carly in the morning. If he'd seen that, he'd think this Brooke was a miracle, rounder, happier, saying, "Car-e, Car-e" instead of "Ka." He didn't know anything.

"So you're okay not going to live with your dad?"

Carly pressed a finger into the soft soil. Her dad. He'd been gone so long, she didn't know who he was. The dad she'd known from so long ago had disappeared into the desert.

"Yeah."

"Are you . . . how do you feel about that?"

She didn't want to go to live with her dad; everything she knew was here, even if it made her mad, like her grandmother keeping Maxie out at night when all the dog wanted was to sleep on the rug in the laundry room. But that wasn't anything. She knew that now. "I want to stay here."

"With Grandma?"

"Yeah."

Her mother breathed in deeply, pushing her short hair off her forehead. "Good. I'm going to talk to Ryan later, but I think we'll be okay. I mean, I know . . . I know I left you, but I promise I'm going to do my best. From now on."

All along, that's what her mother had been doing, even when she was in the bed, silent, unmoving. She hadn't died or hurt herself or them. She'd even run away because she was scared something worse was going to happen. And because her brain was sick, she couldn't imagine what that would mean for Carly or Ryan or Brooke. The last thing she'd thought of was not hurting her children. Carly looked at her mother, nodded and then closed her eyes again, her whole body alive in the spring air, feeling summer and the rest of her life just on the edge of the sky.

Twenty-two

Carl hadn't been able to stand it, his legs twitching, his face full of imaginary welts that he couldn't stop scratching. He and Noel sat next to each other at Peri's sentencing hearing, and from the moment he'd sat down, Carl shifted and jerked as if he'd been attacked by fire ants that traveled his whole body, biting and stinging, his heart racing at his imagined demise. Noel nudged him once, twice, and then Carl patted Noel's leg and slid out the aisle, almost running to the courtroom door, pushing out into the hallway. Air. He leaned over, his hands on his thighs, and took in breaths as if he'd just had a long rally, the tennis ball going back and forth and back and forth, Ralph finally hitting it into the net.

"Carl? Carl? Are you okay?"

Wiping his forehead, he stood up and saw Rosie Candelero in front of him. He nodded and breathed out, taking in a smaller breath and then a smaller one, trying to stop the room from spinning. As he took in air, she jabbed a hand in her purse and pulled out a crumpled paper bag, smoothed it a couple of times, and then shook it open. "Here. Breathe into this."

Grabbing the bag by its neck, he pulled it to his face, breathing in slowly, his head beginning to clear, the pin sticks all over his face disappearing under Rosie's calm gaze.

"What's going on in there?" she asked finally, leading him to a bench. He breathed once more from the stale bag, and then handed it back to her. She balled it up and tossed it into the trash, laughing. "At least I've cleared one thing out of this messy purse. So . . . what's happening?"

"Absolutely flipping nothing. We are just waiting and waiting." He gave her a half smile and then ran his hand over his head, smoothing down his hair. People in leather shoes *clop, clopped* across the floor, and for an instant, Carl found himself waiting in another hallway, with another nurse thirty-eight years ago as Janice labored with Peri. He'd had the same light feeling, the same stupefied amazement that other people could be walking down the hall, going on with their lives, while his seemed to pivot on the edge of tragedy and disaster and joy, all at the same time.

"Sit here for a minute. Let me go look." Leaving her purse on the bench, Rosie stood up and walked to the door, cracking it slightly and peering in. Carl watched her, again impressed by the way she could take in what no one else wanted to, a disabled child, a crazy daughter, a courtroom drama. It couldn't have been simply her nurse's training that taught her to keep her eyes open and move toward the people who needed her. That was who she was, all the time, always Rosie.

"I've got to say, Carl, things look good in there. There's an awful lot of nodding going on." Rosie sat back down and patted his knee, just as he had patted Noel's.

"Good. I can't take one more thing, I think. If Peri has to go back to jail, I think it will kill the kids. Carly barely handled going there the once. And if there's more? I don't know what we'll do."

"Oh, Carl. You'll do what you've always done. Be the dad, pull your kids out of trouble."

"But I haven't always done that. For a long time, I was out of the picture. They couldn't have cared less about me, and I let it stay that way because . . . well, because it was easier. Hell, I could go on with my fine life, say I had two great kids, and then play tennis the entire weekend."

Rosie sighed. "We screw up. No doubt. But then if we're lucky, we get a chance to make it up. Instant karma. It's like a gift, even though it looks like crap. With me and my boy? I tell you, I'm making up for first marrying my husband and giving him to my son as a father, and then divorcing him and taking him away. It's a catch-22. But you do your best."

Carl nodded, relaxing, leaning against the wall, his breath steady. "You're right. I know I shouldn't wish for things, but she needs a break. This lawyer Preston seems okay to me now. So maybe it'll work out."

"How's Brooke?" Rosie asked after a pause.

"You wouldn't believe it. She's like a lawn gone brown finally watered and fertilized. Even her speech is better. For all her holier-than-thou, queen-of-the-universe act, Garnet has been great for Brooke. For all the kids. And believe you me, I never thought I'd say those words aloud."

And as he smiled at Rosie and she smiled back, the comfort between them spreading into the warm air, the courtroom doors opened, and there were Peri and Noel and that Preston fellow, arm in arm, all smiling, and Rosie reached out her hand and squeezed his. Later, as he was hugging his children and shaking Preston's hand, he turned back to wave Rosie over, but she was gone. The only thing she'd left behind was the warm spot she'd pressed on his hand.

After the hearing, Noel and Preston went back to Preston's office to hammer out the details of Peri's next year, and Carl took Peri to her appointment with Dr. Kolakowski, dropping her off at the front of the College Avenue building, watching her walk down the slated hallway. For a few minutes, he stared at his watch and then the steering wheel, and then found himself driving the Corvair down College Avenue, turning onto Broadway, and then taking a left on Pleasant Valley Boulevard before he realized where he was going. Actually, he was surprised he even knew where to go, because he'd not gone to the interment, barely staying for the reception in the church hall after the service. He'd told the kids he had a meeting to get to, but truthfully, he'd been scared to stay in a room full of Janice's friends, the women who knew the stories of his life, the way he'd been as a husband and a father and a man. And probably, he would have ended up seeing one or two of the women he'd slept with during his marriage, and on the day of Janice's funeral, that didn't seem kind. *After all this time,* he'd thought that day, *I'm developing a conscience.*

So it was by feel and memory and partial description from the man inside the visitor's building that he made it to Janice's grave, the tombstone a simple JANICE LYNN RANDALL, 1937–1997, BELOVED MOTHER AND GRANDMOTHER. He'd never said good-bye, and he didn't mean at her deathbed. Carl had never explained himself to her, not one bit, leaving without the courtesy of telling her it wasn't her fault. All those years, he'd let her think what she wanted, blaming him or herself or the world. But he'd never been brave enough to face her until now, when it was too late.

He leaned against a crypt and then backed away from it, realizing what he was doing. It was so weird to build yourself a little fortress after death. Like anything could protect you in the ground, your bones turning to powder. He looked around at the fields of stones and markers and family crypts, seeing for the first time as he stood almost on top of his dead wife, that this was another way people could stay together. Maybe his desire to be cremated and thrown into the ocean was another way for him to separate, to leave nothing behind for anyone.

Carl crossed his arms and shifted on his feet, finally sitting on the ground just beside Janice's plot, smoothing the grass—a thick Bermuda—with his hand, the one Rosie had touched.

"Our girl . . ." he began. "Our girl is going to be okay. Like she used to be. Or not like she used to be. What she might have been if things had been different. If I hadn't messed up royally, Janice. I know you'd never have let it get this bad, but I'm really trying now. She's going to be with me for a year, while she gets better. And Garnet has Carly, Ryan, and Brooke. All of them. I know. Unbelievable. But she's been great. Not at first, but now."

Folding his knees and circling them with his arms, he looked around the cemetery, the plot on top of a hill, the view of Oakland and San Francisco before him. The sun hung over south San Francisco, beginning its fall into the Pacific Ocean. By the time it rose again, Carl and Peri would be one day into their new lives, a year of starting over. Like Rosie said, instant karma.

"I'm sorry, Janice. That's what I came to say. I'm sorry about what I did. I'm sorry I wasn't a good husband. And that it's too late for us. For you. But I promise I'm going to make it okay for Peri. And Noel."

He stood up slowly, his knee clicking as he rose. "I'm going now. I probably won't be back. But I thought I'd tell you what was happening. I thought I'd tell you about the kids. If something happens, I'll let you know. And this time, you can trust me."

He wished he'd brought a flower or a plant or something, looking briefly over at other graves carefully adorned with potted azaleas and chrysanthemums, but he shrugged and turned away, walking down the cemetery slope, careful to notice the time, not wanting to make Peri wait one minute.

"*How was your appointment today?*" her father asked, his eyes on the road.

"*Good.*"

"*Oh? How so?*"

Peri felt the words she would use to explain form in her throat, words like understanding and sorrow and forgiveness, but then she stopped. He cared again, or maybe he cared for the first time. Not since she was small and listened to him do crossword puzzles had she felt his . . . attention, his concern, his one hundred percent awareness of her. Like she was a person. Not his child. Not his crazy child. His daughter, a woman, part of his life. Had he ever asked these kinds of questions of her mother? Did he come home from work and say, "Honey, how was your day? What happened?" Peri didn't know. She couldn't remember those hours at the kitchen counter except in her myopic way. Her need for him had blotted out everything else.

But that was over, too, just like her life with Graham, her life with her children in the apartment, her fear that she was rotten, poisonous, explosive. There was nothing

*more than this for the next year, her father and her, her
children, her health. People were helping her now, they
cared, even Graham in his own way. Her family had
saved her, after all. She turned to Carl, wishing her
mother could see him now, a hero despite everything.*

*"We talk about the whole thing," she said finally. "Dr.
Kolakowski helps me with it all."*

*"That's great, honey. I'm—I'm so happy." He adjusted
his hat and wiped his nose, and Peri sat back deep in the
Corvair's old leather seat, the wind all around and in her.
For this second, she was not scared, even though the future was unclear, like the view of San Francisco from her
father's house on a foggy day, nothing but the tops of
buildings and bridges visible in the swirls of white air,
everything else only shapes she could imagine.*

Acknowledgments

If Ellen Edwards hadn't beaten metaphorically about my novelist's feet and head, this story would have remained relegated to my pile of short stories. So I thank you, Ellen, for pushing me to dig it up and bring it to larger life. Mel Berger, my new agent, said the honest things and helped me leave another project to commit to this one. Thanks, Pam, for your continued support. Thanks to Lexi Adams and Julia Fleischaker at New American Library. My writing group—Keri Mitchell, Joan Kresich, Marcia Goodman, Julie Roemer, and Gail Offen-Brown—urged me on, discussed at length, kept me from disappearing too often into flashback. Susan Browne, Lisa Wingate, and Carole Barksdale all read chunks sent by e-mail and deserve praise for that accomplishment alone. Sue Graziano Adams, Mara McGrath, and Pat Mejia helped me understand the body and life of a child so disabled, and I thank them for their expertise and encouragement. The true story of a mother who neglected her children inspired me to tell the story of this mother and this family, and I can only hope she and her children are doing better. And finally, great thanks to my boys and husband for letting me sit alone in my room making up lives while my real one goes on without me.

When You Go Away

Jessica Barksdale Inclán

This Conversation Guide is intended to enrich the
individual reading experience, as well as encourage us
to explore these topics together—because books,
and life, are meant for sharing.

A CONVERSATION WITH JESSICA BARKSDALE INCLÁN

Q. A mother's abandonment of her children is such a tough subject to tackle. What inspired you to write this novel and what questions did you ask yourself while you were working on it?

A. I have a habit of cutting newspaper clippings when a story interests me. More often than not, they stay stuffed in my drawer, but in this case, a clipping about a woman who abandoned her severely disabled twin girls provoked questions in me that demanded answers. First, I wrote a short story told from the point of view of the older sister, who has to pick up the pieces. Later, I realized I had more to say, and the story began to grow and evolve into its current, longer shape. The true story was much different from my fictional one and had a tragic ending. When the girls were found after having been abandoned by their mother, they were very ill and malnourished, and the mother spent time in jail. But I suspect that like Peri, the real mother was scared and depressed and frustrated beyond measure.

While I was writing the novel, the questions I asked myself every single day were: "How could this happen? How could a mother leave her kids? How could their father, their grandparents, and the people in their community allow it to happen? Where were they while this family was falling apart?" I also asked myself how a family could put itself back together again afterward, and I don't mean just Peri and her kids, but Carl, Noel, Garnet, and Graham too. I didn't know how after such extreme betrayals these folks could forgive each other and forge new relationships. And yet I've known countless families who forgave family members and readmitted them into the fold. I knew it was possible, but I wasn't sure how my characters would get to that point—or if they ever could.

Q. Not every writer would choose to portray Peri as sympathetically as you do. What about her—both her character and her situation—inspired your understanding and compassion?

A. Most mothers have days when they say, "That's it. I've had it." One of my favorite phrases when things get weird at my house, when my family is angry or loud or unkind, is: "I'm moving out." I'm kidding, but obviously imbedded in that joke is a truth—that sometimes leaving seems easier than staying. Also, when creating Peri, I was thinking about how depression—and especially depression combined with a psychotic reaction— might fuel the desire to leave. Although Peri is trapped in mental illness, I understand what she's going through. I think that the pressure of a special-needs child would add immeasurable difficulty for a family that was already beset by marital and financial strife. I feel sorry for Peri. I love her for all her weaknesses. I don't condone what she does, but I understand it. Deep inside her is a woman who needs to protect her children, even from herself.

Q. As a mother of two boys, do you think any woman could potentially have a breakdown like Peri's? Did writing this novel make child abandonment seem dangerously possible?

A. I don't think just any woman could have this kind of breakdown. I seriously believe that one is genetically predisposed to certain mental illnesses, especially depression. Other women might react completely differently—remarry, go back to school, fight for money from their ex-husbands, return to work. When I feel beset by problems, I plunge into activity. Others retreat, bury themselves, and perhaps they are more likely to develop clinical depression, which can also have psychotic components. I did a lot of research on the subject of depression with a psychotic reaction. It is not a common combination, but left untreated, it can be very dangerous to the sufferer, as well as to those around him or her. Sadly, about the same time I was writing the novel, Andrea Yates, the woman who murdered her five children, was constantly in the news. During the trial it was revealed that she suffered for years before she hurt her children. Peri leaves her situation before she reaches such a severe breaking point—and luckily, she has people around her who are willing to help.

Q. Brooke is one of the most vivid characters in this novel, though she doesn't appear in many scenes. Did she guide you through the writing?

A. Brooke is like an angel to me, the innocent, the person for whom this abandonment is the most potentially dangerous. Yet she is the one character in the novel who doesn't really know what is going on, as her siblings and then the rest of her family and her doctors shield her from the truth. I thought of her always in her room, waiting for her mother. Her connection with Peri is what keeps her healthy, so I did feel an investment in getting the two back together. But I can't imagine how hard it must be to care for a child like Brooke. I have a friend who has a special-needs child, and when I am with them both, I always think: I could never take care of this child, day after day. I don't have the patience or the kindness that my friend and her husband have. I know I would never, ever choose to parent a special-needs child. But many mothers do every day, and they do it remarkably well. I admire them so much!

Q. How do you think the themes of When You Go Away *compare to those of your first novel,* Her Daughter's Eyes, *in which a seventeen-year-old mother secretly hides her newborn infant in a closet so that she can go to school and try to continue her normal life?*

A. The idea of parental betrayal lies at the heart of both novels. In both, the parents have left, either willingly through divorce or unwillingly through death. Both Kate, the teenage mother in *Her Daughter's Eyes,* and Carly, Peri's teenage daughter in *When You Go Away,* attempt to live out the normal routine of their lives despite their parents' abandonment and the tremendous responsibility they feel to care for the innocent children involved— in Kate's case, her baby daughter, and in Carly's case, her sister, Brooke. Most of us have a strong inner drive to live, to survive, to continue even under extreme circumstances. We still try to carry out the "normal" routines of our days. Both Kate and Carly represent for me something inside of me that wants to move forward, even when everything seems to be falling back. To me, Kate and Carly's strength and resilience represent the best part of me, the best part of each of us.

The idea of parental betrayal also runs through my second novel, *The Matter of Grace.* In that story, Grace's mother, Doris, does not protect her as a child, allowing some kind of abuse to happen, and

Grace is twisted into the person she becomes—a person who betrays her own daughter, her friends, and her family.

Q. The issues of family, crisis, and redemption are central to all of your novels. Why are you so drawn to these topics?

A. Without our families, we would be nowhere. Every part of us—our personalities, our values, our likes and dislikes—is forged in our earliest homes. Nothing interests me more than what happened in my own family of origin, and in various ways, I explore aspects of my own past through my novels. Directly and indirectly, I am still struggling to understand events in my life that happened long ago. For instance, I have a sister from whom I am estranged. Even though this estrangement is years old, I still haven't figured out why or how it happened. In fiction, I am able to explore the tensions and dramas within the relationships that define who we are. And in my fiction—unlike my real life—I am able to make sense of those relationships.

QUESTIONS FOR DISCUSSION

1. Parenthood is perhaps the most important topic in *When You Go Away*. What characteristics make a good parent? How is Peri both a good and a bad mother? How are Graham, Carl, and Garnet both effective and ineffective parents?

2. Carl and Graham both abandon their families in different ways and also make amends. In the end, are they similar in their approach to fatherhood? Do you think that Graham can hope to some day be truly redeemed, as Carl is, through his children?

3. How does the novel portray the changing nature of divorce in our society? How does Carl and Janice's divorce, thirty years ago, compare to Peri and Graham's recent divorce? Have the roles of wives and husbands or those of mothers and fathers after divorce changed? Do you think that adult children of divorce are more likely to follow in their parents' footsteps?

4. Peri's mother died several years before the novel opens, yet one senses that if Janice had lived, Peri would have gotten the help she needed and perhaps never have abandoned her children. Similarly, in *Her Daughter's Eyes*, the death of the

mother, Deirdre, is the "abandonment" that sets the events of the novel into motion. And in *The Matter of Grace,* both Grace and her own mother essentially abandon their daughters. Discuss how mothers often act to hold families together, and what sometimes happens when through neglect, ignorance, fear, illness, or death they are no longer able to do so.

5. This is the story of a woman who betrays her children, yet survives and fights for the right to reclaim them. What does Peri learn by the end of the novel? Are her children, and the other members of her family, really able to forgive her? Where do you see this family in five years? Discuss the different ways in which the lives of these characters might progress.

Read on for an excerpt
from Jessica Barksdale Inclán's
new novel

WALKING WITH HER DAUGHTER

Available in trade paperback
from NAL Accent in April 2005

In the first moments of waking, Jenna could feel the soft arms of the mattress around her shoulders, cradling her hips, the fine cotton sheet on her ankles, stomach, cheek. She hung between her dream and the sunrise on the sound of the waves just outside her cabaña, the soft touch of the air, the absence of memory.

And she slipped back to her inner eye, floating above the island, seeing the rice terraces of the interior, the mud built up in agricultural temples. Then she moved up and out, past dense foliage, to the tall, drooping green trees she couldn't name with their large red flowers and long fuzzy stamens, the waving palms, the red canna flowers, the wetness everywhere. Past the Shiva statues and the stone Buddhas, through the soft air, to the white Balinese beaches dotted with yellow and white umbrellas, thin wooden boats floating on calm seas. Away to the horizon, a sunrise flared gold, peach, fanning into blue. Up to the mountains that peaked over the water, green and brilliant against the aqua, and back down to her cabaña.

"No," she said, or thought, as the scene began to tear,

what had happened a week ago ripping a ragged edge on this peace, this floating, this pure, white light. *No,* she thought again, sinking into soft cotton as if it were a lover. Weren't she and Mark going to come here, before, earlier, Jenna walking into the house with brochures, ideas, plans?

"Look," she'd said, pointing to a photo of a cabaña nestled in fronds, the aqua sea lapping at its door, palm fronds frozen in perfect sway, people stuck forever in unnatural, happy poses. "There's a glass bottom in the bar. You can watch the fish swim under you. Those manta ray creatures, too."

Her husband, Mark, had adjusted his glasses and nodded. "Some day," he'd said. "Maybe later."

"When, Mark?" she'd asked, leafing through the glossy brochure the woman at the travel agency had given her. "We should make reservations."

"Soon." He waved his hand as if to make her stop talking, and she did, sitting down next to him on the couch as he read another medical article or chart, making notes as he did. "One day."

But one day, some day soon had never come, and then later he'd left her and Sofie for another woman. An older, smarter woman, with whom he would never have children.

Blinking against the filtered morning light, Jenna felt her dash two days ago through the airport to the pay phone, the terrible message she'd left with Mark's service during her one hour layover in Los Angeles. And then hours and hours of flying, the sky too soft, too smooth, the phone bringing her too soon to the island full of fire.

Turning on her side, pressing her eyes closed, she listened to her skin slip against the linen, the bed made daily by silent workers who were frightened to meet her eye. When would Mark be here? When would he find her? Would he know how to look for her in this place he had never taken her to? Eventually, he would show up, but it might be after it was over, like usual. As he had for Sofie's graduations from eighth grade and high school, for her dance recitals, for her moving-in day at the dorms at Cal. Why didn't he see what Sofie meant to him? Why did he leave them both in the first place since he'd never really left, coming back to her bed after a day trip with Sofie or a back-to-school night or a visit to his sister's house?

So many nights in the past years, he'd knocked on her bedroom door after tucking in Sofie and then come in, sitting on the edge of her bed, slowly moving his hand to her covered shin, knee, thigh.

"Jenna?" he'd whisper, his breath at her neck, his mouth on her cheek, his glasses on the bedside table.

In her laziness, Jenna opened up, pulled him down, let the memory of their marriage take over for a half hour, hour. And then he'd be gone again.

Mark was neither here nor there, but both, like she was now, asleep—her mind filled with the past—and awake, the sun on her arm, the sounds pressing closer, words she could almost hear.

She turned under the sheet, holding her ears. *No. No. Why?* Why all this? What were the reasons? Why did he leave in the first place? Was it space for thought? Peace and quiet? Why did he marry her at all? Why was she here without him? *Oh, yes. No. No.* Her body stilled as the daylight through the bamboo shutters shook her, filled her with memory.

"No," she said again, but of course it was too late. She was awake. She was conscious in a world where her daughter no longer existed. Where Sofie was no longer a college girl on a vacation in Bali, having flown here to meet the Australian boyfriend she'd met when he'd come to Cal for a two-week conference on international water rights.

Covering her eyes against the light with both hands, Jenna felt her daughter's absence on her face and chest like death's night dog. Her daughter was dead. She was no longer all the Sofies she'd ever been. No longer a kindergartner with a large orange chrysanthemum pinned behind her ear, insisting that it was beautiful. Sofie was beautiful, even as it began to slide down her hair, which was the same color as the flower.

She was no longer the seventh grade girl in her baggy jeans and striped t-shirts listening to rap music on her Sony Walkman during dinner. "Why do I have to turn it off?" Sofie had asked. "You're reading a magazine! Just admit you're not paying attention to me, either."

She was no longer a high school girl crashing her car into the trash cans at the bottom of the driveway, laughing so hard that Jenna smiled, laughed, hugged her daughter to her because she was all right. Safe. The only thing damaged was the can pressed up against the retaining wall, spewing forth white Hefty bags and a broken mop handle.

"I'm fine," Sofie said, holding her sides, her pale face flushed. "I'm going to hecka fail the driving test, though. Unless there's a trash can part. I'll ace that."

And then, finally, there was the last Sofie, the college Sofie, turning away from Jenna and going inside, up the dorm stairs into her new life.

All Jenna's daughters were gone now, all the Sofies Jenna had ever had. Jenna had seen each of them when looking at her daughter, as if Sofie stood in front of a three-way dressing room mirror, each refracting a girl from the year before and before that and even before that. Jenna knew that there would have been more Sofies in the years to come, working Sofie, married Sofie, mother Sofie. Sofie at Christmas and birthdays; Sofie when Jenna was old; Sofie when Jenna wasn't even around anymore, becoming Sofies to other people, her own children and grandchildren. All those Sofies had been murdered, and Jenna knew that, again, as she lay wide-eyed on her bed in her Bali hotel, remembering why she was here. To find her daughter's body. To take her home.

National Bestselling Author
JESSICA BARKSDALE INCLÁN

One Small Thing
0-451-21119-7

Avery Tacconi has everything she ever wanted: a husband, a
career, and a beautiful home. The only thing missing is a baby.
But when her husband finds out he is the father of a son he
didn't know about, Avery must learn to see her unexpected
family for what it is—a perfect blessing.

Also available from NAL Accent:
Her Daughter's Eyes

0-451-20564-2

The Matter of Grace
0-451-21185-5

And look for
Walking with Her Daughter
Coming April 2005

Available wherever books are sold or at www.penguin.com